Candy King

Also by Christine d'Abo

Candy King

Christine d'Abo

LYRICAL CARESS
Kensington Publishing Corp.
www.kensingtonbooks.com

LYRICAL CARESS BOOKS are published by

Kensington Publishing Corp.
119 West 40th Street
New York, NY 10018

Copyright © 2020 by Christine d'Abo

All Kensington titles, imprints, and distributed lines are available at special quantity discounts for bulk purchases for sales promotion, premiums, fund-raising, educational, or institutional use.

Special book excerpts or customized printings can also be created to fit specific needs. For details, write or phone the office of the Kensington Sales Manager: Kensington Publishing Corp., 119 West 40th Street, New York, NY 10018. Attn. Sales Department. Phone: 1-800-221-2647.

Lyrical Shine and Lyrical Shine logo Reg. U.S. Pat. & TM Off.

First Electronic Edition: December 2019
ISBN-13: 978-1-5161-0668-4 (ebook)
ISBN-10: 1-5161-0668-7 (ebook)

First Print Edition: December 2019
ISBN-13: 978-1-5161-0669-1
ISBN-10: 1-5161-0669-5

Printed in the United States of America

Chapter 1

With great effort, Simone Leblanc managed to not smooth down the front of her skirt, play with her hair, or push against the bridge of her glasses while she waited for her boss to finish reading whatever the hell he was pretending to read and finally look at her. Carl liked to make her squirm, and he knew that she knew, which made the entire game all the more annoying.

Simone hated being the low girl in the pecking order of the newspaper, but with any luck, she was about to move up a notch. Maybe two, if Carl was finally willing to acknowledge that she'd earned her stripes.

Because, really, how many fluff pieces on sushi restaurants and community association events did a girl have to do before she got her shot? Ten? Twenty? Fighting the urge to let out a huff, she kept her lips sealed and her gaze locked onto Carl's face.

Any minute now.

He was going to look up.

Instead of doing what she was silently willing him to do, Carl licked his thumb and flipped to the next page. Simone internally screamed.

The clock on the wall continued to tick, each snick of the second hand moving Simone closer and closer to simply quitting. *You have two minutes, Carl. That's it, and I'm—*

"Interesting piece." Carl flipped the paper over and finally looked up at her.

Okay, things were about to get interesting. She straightened ever so slightly, took a breath, and made sure she was smiling. "What were you reading?"

"A piece on the by-election that Mark wrote. He might have uncovered a data breach by the candidate, which could turn the tide for this election." Carl was smirking by the end of his sentence. "Did you get your piece finished?"

He knew she had. This was the same song and dance he made her do every single time she walked into his office. Simone was tired of being on the receiving end of his lack of faith and confidence in her journalistic abilities. But he'd given her a job when no one else had—an opportunity to publish articles both online and in the paper. Each one was a success, a feather in her cap that served to increase her reputation and give her valuable experience.

If he wasn't such an asshole, she might even express her thanks.

"I did. You should have received it in your in-box yesterday morning." Her cheeks were sore from maintaining her smile. "I'd assumed you'd read it and had some comments."

"Not yet." He leaned back in his chair and gave her a once-over. There was nothing sexual in his gaze, and not for the first time, she couldn't help but feel he didn't quite know what to make of her. "I'm sure it's fine."

Ugh. She hated the word fine. That was the fucking kiss of death when it came to Carl. He might as well have said *passable* or *adequate*. She'd worked too hard over the years, put far too much into each and every story that was assigned to her, for her boss to see the end result as anything less than stellar.

Simone took a deep breath and brightened her smile. "Thank you. Your faith in my abilities to produce excellent articles is greatly appreciated." *Suck on that, asshat.*

Carl grunted.

Okay, here was her chance to push things to the next level. "In fact, I'd like to do something more than looking at the top food trucks in the city or interviewing kindergarten students about the weather." She lowered her chin and inched closer to his desk. "I'd like to do a story on the growing sugar daddy phenomenon here in Toronto."

The look of pure, dumbfounded confusion on Carl's face was worth the chance that he'd shoot her down. He knew she'd wanted more from her career, wanted to take risks to see how far she could push things, but he never seemed willing to let her run with an idea. Simone never knew why.

When he opened his mouth, only to close it and frown, she braced herself for the worst. But when he finally spoke, it was her turn to be surprised. "Why?"

She cocked her head as she narrowed her gaze. "What do you mean, why? I want an opportunity to prove myself as a journalist."

"Why this particular story? Why involve yourself in a world that you clearly know nothing about?"

For a heartbeat, she almost told him that she *did* know something about this world. That her best friend, Kayla, had found the love of her life through a sugar daddy site and they were now engaged and getting married in a few months.

Almost.

"Remember I did that interview with Marissa Roy and Vince Taylor last year?"

"I do." Carl leaned forward. "You're not telling me that Vince Taylor signed up for a sugar daddy site."

"I'm not. Because that's not something on the record, and I would never, *ever* pass along information that hasn't been fact-checked and verified. Or that was said to me in confidence." She gave him a look, knowing there was no way he'd interpret it as anything other than *There's a story here if you just let me chase it.*

"No, you like to play things far too safe to ever do that." He tapped his finger on his desk blotter for a moment, before finally nodded. "Too safe. What makes you think that you can handle this type of story? Men buying women for sex isn't exactly something that you'll be able to get easy interviews for. You'll need to insert yourself into that world to make any real headway."

Simone blinked. Then she leaned in and tilted her ear toward him. "And you don't think I could pass as a sugar baby?"

"You absolutely would." His gaze never once left her eyes. "I just don't think you could handle it emotionally."

Simone was many things: smart, hyper, really enjoyed a good food truck, but being emotionally resilient was something she'd had to work on since she was a child. She was quick to laugh, love, and cry, and her anger could come to a head faster than she cared to admit. Every situation that she found herself in, Simone took to heart. Which meant that, for once, Carl's assessment of her was closer to the truth than she would like.

Clearing her throat, she looked away for a moment before pulling her shoulders back and nodding. "I'm the first to admit that I'm a bit of a marshmallow. But I think that's exactly what this story needs. The men and women who sign up to be sugar babies aren't doing it for sex. They need cash because of impossible situations, such as to help pay for school so they can make their lives better. They need to be treated with respect, not denigrated for their life choices. The men and women who have money and are looking for sugar babies also need respect. Despite what the public thinks, they're not all after sex with people society has deemed too young. Some are lonely, awkward, have no way of finding companionship without their bank account being front and center. They too need someone who isn't going to pre-judge them."

Carl didn't make a sound throughout her speech. His gaze never wavered, and Simone couldn't help but think he was looking into her soul. Maybe he was. Carl was a bit different from everyone else. Maybe he was psychic or something.

After a minute that stretched on for a day, he nodded. "Run with it."

"Really?" Simone blinked, terrified she'd misheard him.

"Don't make me regret this. I expect you to come back with something good that I can run as a feature. I don't want excuses. And I don't want us to get fucking sued. Make sure that you have everything backed up, verified, and sources wrapped up tight."

Excitement and fear coursed through her like a powerful wave of angry butterflies. "You won't regret this. I'm…I have an angle that I know is going to be amazing."

"Dare I ask?"

"I'm going after the Candy King."

Carl cocked an eyebrow. "Who the what?"

"That's the pseudonym of the site owner. I'm not going to expose him or anything, but I want to interview him, find out what started him on this venture."

"Fine. But if there's even a hint that this is above your capability, I'm going to have Mark step in and take over."

Fuck you, Mark. "That won't be necessary."

"I hope not." Carl turned back toward his computer monitor. "Get out of my office and go work."

"Yes, sir." Simone didn't wait to be told again, spun on her heel, and marched out of his office.

Finally, this was it! Her heart pounded as she marched past Carl's secretary, giving her a little smile and a super quick thumbs-up as she walked past. Not only was her interview with the Candy King a surefire way to make a name for herself in investigative journalism, Simone couldn't help but hope this story would help her gain the respect of Carl, Mark, and every other journalist at the paper.

She was the youngest by several years, and she'd grown tired of being looked down as the kid, the one who hadn't lived enough life to really know what the real world was like. Sure, her life growing up had been pretty easy. That didn't mean she hadn't had her fair share of problems, that she didn't know that life wasn't all sunshine and roses.

Well, maybe things had sailed a bit more smoothly for her compared to others. Even her best friend, Kayla—who, granted, was now a multimillionaire—had had to fight her way through tough financial times to get where she was today. But that didn't mean that Simone's experience was any less valid. If anything, she was as representative of a twentysomething, middle-class, white Canadian girl as anyone could be.

Jesus, no wonder people roll their eyes at me.

Well, she couldn't do anything about where she'd come from, but at the very least she was ready to use her privilege for the forces of good—as soon as she could make her big break so people would *listen* to her.

The elevator was packed, but she managed to slide into the throng before the doors slid shut. The smells of perfume, cologne, and Tim Hortons coffee pressed down on her, making the short ride to the lobby nearly unbearable. This was why she didn't come into the office very often—the overwhelming world of scent could give her a migraine at a moment's notice. It was as frustrating as it was painful, especially when she was ready to dive into her first real story.

Simone bolted from the elevator the moment the doors opened wide enough for her to slide out. Sucking in a deep breath of fresh air, she pulled her cell phone from her pocket and hit the speed dial for Kayla.

"So, how'd it go?" Kayla always sounded slightly amused when Simone called her. Probably because nine times out of ten, Simone would go off on some crazy tangent of an idea.

But not this time. "It was awesome."

"He's going to let you go after the story?"

"Yes! So if you're trying to get in touch with me, chances are I'll be unavailable. Well, I mean, I'll be around, but depending on what's going on, I might be in the middle of an interview or chasing this guy around or something."

Kayla chuckled, and Simone stopped walking. "You never did tell me what you were planning."

"I didn't?" That was, unfortunately, not as surprising as it should be. "I'm doing an exposé."

"On?" Kayla suddenly sounded far more interested. "And is it dangerous?"

"Are you kidding me? I'll never be one of those war zone journalists. Too much of a chicken." She took a breath and looked around, just in case one of her colleagues was hovering nearby. "You know that site I showed you. The one where you and Devin—"

"I'm aware." The fact that Kayla and her fiancé had met on a sugar daddy site was still something that Kayla didn't like publicized. "What about it?"

"I'm going to do a story on the owner. He goes by the pseudonym the Candy King."

"Is that a good idea?"

"Hell yes, it is! It's going to be the story that puts me on the map. With a story like this, I'll finally have a byline with some meat. And if the paper closes up or switches to fully online content, then I'll have something substantial on my résumé to help move me into a higher-profile website or paper." Excitement surged through her so strongly that she was able to ignore the small voice in the back of her head that was talking to her.

Kayla chuckled again. "Well, good luck. It sounds like you're going to knock them dead."

"That's the plan. I just need to figure one thing out before I can get started."

"What's that?"

Simone squeezed her cell phone a bit tighter. "Who the Candy King really is."

* * * *

Simone sat down in front of her computer and stared at her Word document, which was filled with all of the information she'd gotten so far on the mysterious Candy King. The sole proprietor of millionairesugardaddies.com, he was Canadian and lived in Toronto.

And that was all she had.

Leaning back, she held her now-warm can of hard cider to her chest and sighed. She wasn't going to get very far if she couldn't get more information on him than this. The website itself didn't reveal anything, and the URL was set to private, so there wasn't any information to be had that way. She clicked on the icon that took her to his profile once more.

At the very least, he could have put a picture up, something mysterious that had a hidden clue that she'd find in a moment of clarity, like they always show on television shows. But she wasn't going to get much out of this blank icon nor the mostly empty profile.

"How am I going to get to you?"

If this was going to work, she would need to play ball. It only took her a few minutes to set up an account on the site, though she too didn't add a picture and left as much information blank as she could. The bits that she needed to fill in she faked, not wanting her real name and vital statistics out there someplace she couldn't control.

She set her cider down, went back to Candy King's profile, and clicked on the e-mail me button.

She typed out a quick message about her being a reporter and wanting to do a story on him and the website. It was quirky and rambled as much as she did in her daily conversations. She was about to hit send when she stopped, tipped her head back, and sighed.

There was no way someone like the Candy King would be willing to reveal his true self to someone for no reason. If he'd wanted to be interviewed by reporters, he would have put his name on the site to begin with. No, she was going to have to take a different approach if she wanted to make this work.

Deleting what she'd written, Simone tried to think of what might entice a man like the Candy King into talking with her. She wouldn't trick him into revealing his identity or anything like that. But she suspected it would be far easier to convince him to sit down for an interview with her if he she could intrigue him.

And that's what she'd have to do.

Cracking her knuckles, she started again.

Hail to the King.

I've been on your site looking for the right kind of man and haven't found him. Are all your subjects the same? Maybe I should be looking for royalty? Or perhaps I should resign myself to my mundane existence?

Poor me.

Sugar Tart

Wow, that was the corniest thing she'd ever typed. She was embarrassed to have a degree in journalism and to have those words come from her fingertips. Simone grinned and pressed send. While he might not respond to her, at the very least, she'd now laid down her first bread crumb. Maybe he'd notice.

Or maybe not.

Simone waited for all of ten minutes before getting up from her computer to get another cider. When she'd returned to her laptop, she was surprised when there was an e-mail in her in-box.

Hello, little Tart.

Now, aren't you sweet? But your Candy King isn't playing with his toys right now. Maybe you can find a minion in my playground who will help you out. If you put your picture online, I have no doubt someone will reach out.
Your Candy King

Simone chuckled as a bolt of excitement rushed through her. It was him! While he didn't give her an open invitation to come over to his place, it was a start. Because now that she had him, Simone wasn't going to let go until she got exactly what she wanted.

She lifted her cider in the air. "Hail to the King."

Chapter 2

It had been two weeks since Simone first contacted the Candy King, and while she'd learned more details about him—he was over six feet tall, had brown hair and brown eyes, and was filthy rich—she really was no closer to determining his identity than she was when she'd started. That wasn't exactly surprising—really, she hadn't given him a great reason to expose himself at this point—but what had surprised her was how much she was enjoying the flirting.

Dear God, did he know how to flirt.

Hello Sugar Tart. I was out at a club dancing with a woman and wanted her to be you. Was it you? I don't think so. She didn't smell as sweet as I know you will.

Hello sweet thing. I just got out of the shower after working out. Still wet and naked but will dry off as I walk around my condo. Too bad I don't have anyone to show off for.

Hello little Tart. I keep picturing you sitting there, your fingers caressing the tops of your breasts. I'd like for that to be my hand one day.

Simone had installed the website app to her phone and was thoroughly enjoying their sexy back-and-forth banter all day. There was something wonderfully freeing about engaging anonymously with someone online. She could pretend, or not, as she wanted. There was no pressure to dress a certain way or worry about being bloated. Every time she read one of his texts, the lonely part of her that she did her best to ignore relaxed a tiny bit more.

It was proving to be a bit too much of a distraction, especially when she was trying to focus on writing up an article for the paper's online site on the upcoming summer activities around Toronto for the next long weekend, but for once she could legitimately chalk it up to research.

Real, honest-to-God research.

And if she happened to get a bit horny and had to take a little extra personal time in the morning before getting ready for work, then what harm could come from that? Even if her arousal was the least interesting part of their conversations.

Her phone was currently facedown on her desk with notifications set to vibrate. The Candy King had been quiet this morning, and as much as Simone wanted to poke him again, she also knew that playing coy was sometimes a good thing. Still, it had been a few hours since he'd last talked to her, and things were getting to the point where she was getting twitchy.

Not that he owed her a conversation.

Not that she really wanted one.

This was all for research.

As she slowly typed out the next sentence in her article, her gaze drifted from her computer monitor to her phone, where it eventually stopped. *Come on, my dude, don't keep me waiting.*

"You having a hard time over there?"

Simone sat up, her heart pounding, and stared at Elena, her co-worker and partner in crime when it came to the city beat. "I guess I'm a bit distracted."

"More so than normal. You waiting on hearing from a hot guy or something?" She spun side to side in her chair, grinning at Simone. "Because you don't normally stare at that thing like you are today."

While she didn't want to lie to Elena, Simone didn't know exactly what to tell her about the details of her new project. Because as much as she liked her, Elena wasn't exactly known for keeping secrets to herself.

Simone shrugged, turning her attention back to the computer monitor. "I'm actually waiting to hear from a source for a new story I'm working on. He promised to get back to me today, but so far it's been radio silence."

"Source? Did you find out about a new restaurant or something?" Elena gasped and leaned closer. "Can you get us into the Cork and Pig? I will love you forever if you say yes."

"God, I wish. No, it's nothing that exciting." *Just the chance to learn the truth behind a secret identity and write a story that will push my career to the next tier. That's it, that's all.*

"That sucks." Elena groaned. "I've had my name on the list to get a table for a month now, but they keep pushing me off. I think they're scared that I'm going to give them a bad review or something."

"You're not exactly known to be the easiest to please when it comes to food reviews."

"And you're not exactly known as a good liar." Elena smiled at Simone and spun all the way around in her chair. "But keep your secrets for now. I know you'll spill sooner or later."

"Never!" Simone said with a laugh, knowing she would have to be extra careful, especially if Elena's curiosity was piqued. "You haven't told me the best restaurant to check out this month. I need to know how many pennies to save up."

"There hasn't been anything exciting recently. But as soon as I find a spot, you can be my plus one." Elena leaned closer. "We get to expense it that way."

"God, I love food." Simone leaned back and made a happy sigh.

"That's one of the things I love about you."

Her mom was a baker for a downtown bakery. Growing up, Simone was constantly smelling freshly baking bread, cookies, muffins, whatever new recipe her mom wanted to try out before introducing it at work. That was the upside to her mom's job. The downside was her never being home in the mornings, leaving Simone home alone with her dad.

Simone nearly jumped out of her chair when her phone buzzed. She snatched it from her desk and was on her feet before Elena could even move to intercept. "Sorry, I need to take this."

She took a quick peek to confirm that, yes, that was the icon from the sugar daddy app at the top of her notifications bar, before racing to the private bathroom and locking the door. She went to the toilet and sat down, taking a moment to catch her breath before reading his message.

Hello Sugar Tart.

Or maybe I should start calling you a curious kitty? You seem to want to know a whole lot about me. I don't know if you're just curious, wanting to make friends, or trying to find out something else.

To answer your question, yes, I went to university. And no, not all of my wealth comes from the website. My family is also well off, though I don't take anything from them. I earn my own way in life.

You must really want to be my sugar baby if you want to know how much I make.

Even though I'm not looking for a playmate right now, you've certainly caught my attention. I can imagine what you look like with your blond hair loose around your shoulders as you lie naked on my bed. I bet your skin is pale. You'd look sweet against my dark sheets.

Maybe someday we'll have to try that out.

Your Candy King

Simone took a calming breath and read the message a second time. It took effort to ignore the idea of being naked with a man she'd never met before and focus on the facts she'd learned about him.

He went to university and came from a wealthy family.

"Who the hell are you?" She was still looking at the screen when another message popped up.

I dreamed about you last night.

Unlike every other message he'd written her, this one lacked the fake formality. There was an intimacy to his words that she hadn't anticipated that hit her with a wallop. This wasn't the Candy King, mysterious website owner. This was the man behind the mask talking to her, and the thought of what that might mean had her chest tightening with excitement. Somehow with all the (quite frankly) terrible flirting, they'd formed a bit of a connection. And if she'd met him online as an attempt to find love and not because she was chasing a story, she wouldn't have thought twice about pursing things with him.

Because he'd turned her on without even trying.

Her nipples hardened, and her pussy pulsed as a wave of desire washed through her. She could respond back with her coy persona, teasing him the same way she had over the past two weeks to keep up appearances. But there was something about the unexpected honesty in this single sentence that shook her.

With her thumbs hovering over the keys, she took a breath and typed a response. Then she deleted it and tried again, this time pressing send before she changed her mind.

What were we doing?

Holding her breath, she didn't have to wait long for his answer.

I'd taken you out for dinner. Then we fucked in the back seat of my car.

Whoa.

Simone swallowed hard, her fingers shaking as she tried to type out a semi-coherent response. It wasn't the sex in his car that had her revved up, but rather the thought that he'd fantasized about taking her out to dinner. She hadn't anticipated that, and it told her something far more unexpected about him than she'd anticipated—he'd dreamed about wooing her. In her opinion, there was nothing sexier than a man who wooed a woman. *Focus on the sex. That's easier.*

She'd attempted three answers before finally settling on the basics.

Did I come hard?

Because really, if she didn't at least get off in someone's dreams, then the world was a sad and depressing place. More importantly, if she didn't get off soon, then she wasn't going to be able to focus at work. For the first time in her adult life, Simone considered doing something she'd never even thought of before—masturbating in the office bathroom.

Shit, what the hell was this guy doing to her?

She continued to think that even as she undid the buttons of her pants and slid her hand down the front. Simone waited to press her clit until she heard back from him.

Oh yes. You screamed, called out my name as I ate you out. Then I fucked you doggy style and made you come again.

"Jesus, dude." She pressed her clit and sucked in a breath. There was no easy way to text and masturbate, not without making a ton of typos.

Tell me more.

The phone buzzed, and she furiously tried to get herself off as quickly as possible. The last thing she wanted was to have someone knock on the door and interrupt her. Or worse, guess what she was doing.

Are you a naughty girl? Are you doing something now?

Yes. More.

With her orgasm hovering on the periphery of her awareness, she kept her gaze locked onto the screen as she rubbed small circles on her clit.

You're getting yourself off. God, that's making my cock so fucking hard right now. If I weren't at work, I'd jerk off picturing you doing that.

Simone burst out laughing, even as she increased the pressure on herself.

At work 2

The next message took a bit longer to come, and for a moment, Simone thought that this would be over before she heard back from him. But when her phone finally buzzed again, the message he sent left her breathless.

I'm in the bathroom.

Shit, they were going to get off together. At work.

Simone pulled her hand out so she could quickly type. *I'm so close. I have my hand down my pants in the bathroom. I can picture you at work in a similar place. You're picturing my mouth on your cock, aren't you?*

Yes.

Simone typed one final message before resuming her pleasure.

Tell me when you come. I'm so close.

She let her imagination take over. While she couldn't put a face to her mysterious Candy King, she had enough to go on that she was able to picture someone tall, strong, his face between her thighs as he licked her pussy. She pressed harder, tried to hold off as much as she could, but the first wave of her orgasm washed over her. She had to bite down hard on her bottom lip to keep from crying out as pleasure washed through her body. She was doubled over, and she was left panting as the waves of pleasure finally stopped.

Only a few minutes later did her phone buzz one final time.

I have cum all over my hand.

"God, you're going to kill me." Standing up, Simone went over to the sink and washed her hands before typing a quick response.

Well, I don't know about you, but now I need to find a way to focus on work. Thanks for the "break."

Anytime, little Tart

Simone slipped her phone into her pocket and left the bathroom.

Of course, someone was waiting there, and of course, they gave her an odd look.

"Sorry." Simone ducked her head and went back to her desk.

Sitting down in her seat, she felt more than a little shell-shocked. She'd just gotten herself off in the bathroom, while a complete stranger somewhere else in the city did the same. If that didn't underscore the weird and incredible power of the Internet, she didn't know what did.

Placing her hands on her keyboard, Simone took a breath.

Right.

Research.

The idea of doing anything but replaying this little adventure over and over in her head was probably ambitious. But the alternative was pondering how she'd react if she ever came face-to-face with her Candy King. There was little chance that reality could possibly live up to the fantasy man she was creating in her head. It wasn't fair to him or herself to build him up in this way, nor would it make doing her job any easier.

Focus on the facts. They won't lead you astray.

She didn't need to look back at their earlier conversation to remember what he'd said. Her mystery man had gone to university and was from a wealthy family, though he had his own personal wealth as well. The Candy King name seemed to be far too specific a handle to use online, and perhaps it was a nickname of sorts.

Or it could merely be a name he randomly picked to run a sugar daddy site. Either way, Simone would need to do some digging to, at the very least, rule people out.

She typed in a few words, only to stop and stare at her screen. Was she doing the right thing here? She'd just had cybersex with him after doing her best to pull information from him. If she managed to track him down, what the hell would he think of her? Would he accuse her of using sex to get what she wanted from him? Or would he be so angry that she'd dug into his past that their online sexual relationship would be the least of her worries.

If she wanted this story, was she going to have to compromise her ethics, or would she let things go too far and get her heart broken? She closed her eyes and gave her racing mind a chance to slow down. Everything would be okay if she didn't cross any lines. Flirting was fine, but she couldn't let there be a repeat of what happened this afternoon ever again.

Adjusting in her seat, her body still humming from her orgasm, she took a breath and started typing again. "I'll find you yet."

And when she did, boy did she have some questions for him.

Chapter 3

Simone had a plan. It might not be a very good one, but it was a place for her to start. Armed with her bare-bones description of who her Candy King might be, she headed out to do some in-person digging. If he was a local living in Toronto—and she had no reason to believe he wasn't telling the truth about that—then there were only so many universities he could have attended. He was rich and from an affluent family; no doubt he went to a prestigious school rather than a local college.

She wasn't even going to consider the possibility that he might have gone to school in another province. Because no fucking way was she willing to take on that particular challenge quite yet. No, she would start her search with the Toronto schools; then only after she'd exhausted every other possibility would she begin to look elsewhere.

Walking into the student alumni office of the University of Toronto, Simone realized immediately that while she might only be twenty-six, she was closer to thirty than she was to a university student. She didn't see herself as old, not at all, but being out in the workforce for a few years had undoubtedly added a few bumps to her optimistic outlook on life. She certainly looked older than the young woman who was currently in the office typing something on her computer.

Simone waited until the woman looked up and smiled. "Hey. Can I help you?"

"I hope so. My name is Simone Leblanc, and I'm with the *Toronto Record*. I was trying to find some information on a U of T alumni and thought I might check here."

The girl blinked before standing up and coming around to meet Simone. "Ah, I don't think I can share anything that we might have on file. There's the privacy law stuff that we have to consider."

"I completely understand." Damn, she'd been worried about that. "Do you have anything that would be considered public domain? Something that I could take a look at? Old school newspapers, or even yearbooks?"

The woman looked around the office and shrugged, as though she were answering some silent question she'd posed to herself. "Sure. We've been moving everything to digital records for the papers, but there are files with old ones. Yearbooks might be an easier place to start. We have bookshelves of them. Do you know what year?"

Simone had tried to do some mental math on when her mystery man might have gone to school. "Can I see what you have from the mid to late nineties? If I don't see what I'm looking for, I might ask for a few more."

"Sure. If you want to go across the hall, there's an empty office you can use. But I have to leave in about an hour, so you'll have to be done by then."

Simone wasn't about to look a gift horse in the mouth. "You're amazing. Thank you."

It didn't take long for the woman to bring her several piles of yearbooks, and for Simone to start searching through. She didn't know why, but she couldn't let go of the idea that the name Candy King had personal meaning to him. Something about the way he'd use it in conversation, his teasing nature, gave her the impression that it had been a moniker he'd had for a while.

But after nearly forty-five minutes of looking through pictures and reading blurbs, Simone was beginning to doubt her premise. Maybe he hadn't gone to university here and this was all a complete waste of time. Perhaps this entire enterprise of hers was a waste.

Her phone had been buzzing off and on while she'd been here. Needing the break, she pulled it out and quickly scanned her e-mails. Nothing that couldn't wait until tomorrow. Then she saw that there was a message waiting for her from the sugar daddy app. Quickly looking around to make sure that someone wasn't about to come into the office, she snuck a peek.

Hey Sugar Tart.

I haven't been able to stop thinking about you and what we did yesterday. You might not believe me, but I haven't done that before. I can't get you out of my mind.

I might have to jerk off again just thinking about you.

CK

Shit, she'd completely fucked this up with him. Here he thought that she was after him for a relationship, and all she'd wanted was to get a story from him. Well, if she were being honest with herself, she wasn't averse to engaging in their mutual online sexy fun times, but there was no way she had the time for their relationship to go much beyond that.

If she did ever track him down, she didn't have a clue how she'd explain all this weirdness to him.

Simone closed her eyes and placed her forehead on top of the open page of the 1997 yearbook. God, she was a complete idiot for thinking she'd be able to pull off a story like this. There was next to no information for her to go on, and the man apparently wasn't interested in revealing his name to her on his own. What right did she have to dig up his identity? Even if she promised not to disclose it to the public, how could she possibly reassure him of that? He'd say that she'd led him on just to get the story, and she couldn't exactly deny that.

This was pointless.

"Are you okay?"

Simone lifted her head to come face-to-face with a man who looked to be in his mid-forties. "Hi. I was doing some research on someone who I think might be an alumnus. But I don't have a whole hell of a lot to go on."

The man, somewhat handsome and relaxed, smiled at her as he crossed his arms. "I did my graduate degree and have worked there for years. Maybe I can help?"

"Unless you know someone who went by the nickname Candy King, I doubt it."

The man straightened. "Ah, actually I might be able to help with that."

Simone was on her feet, all the pain instantly gone from her muscles. "I would love you forever if you could even point me in the right direction."

"It might not be who you're looking for, but when I was doing my master's degree, I played rugby for the Varsity Blues. There was an undergrad I knew who went by a similar nickname. Something about him being sweet and slick with his moves. I don't really remember much as he was a few years behind me."

Simone's mind was screaming for more information, but she did her very best to maintain the illusion of being a calm and collected professional. "Would there be any publicly available information on who the team members were? And what year was this?"

"Are those yearbooks?"

She moved away from the desk, motioning for him to come closer. "Everything from the nineties."

He came entirely into the office and flipped open the top one when the girl from the alumni office came in. "I'm sorry, but I have to head out."

Simone practically flew across the office to take her by the hands. "Can I borrow some of these? I promise I'll bring them back."

"Sorry, no. They're school property."

"I'd only need them for a night. I'd be more than happy to leave my work information, or even give you some cash for them. I really just need to do a bit more reading—"

"There he is. I remembered the nickname because everyone said his moves were sweet like candy."

Simone abandoned the girl and joined her mystery man at the desk. "Dylan Williams?"

The picture in the yearbook was of Dylan at a rugby game, running hard with the ball under his arm. His body was lean, the muscles in his thighs firm, suspended in time for her to ogle. She didn't know the first thing about rugby, but there was something sexy about the look on his face. His brown hair was pushed back, the muscles in his jaw clenched as his focus was squarely on his goal—whatever that had been. She couldn't imagine having that intensity fixed on her for any reason, even as her body responded to it.

The caption read: Dylan "Candy King" Williams, making his move.

"I didn't know him well, but I do remember he was quite well off. I'm still paying off my student loans." He nodded. "I'll let you get out of here."

"Thank you, Professor McKenna." The girl moved to the desk and began to collect the yearbooks.

Simone took a picture of the page with her phone before holding out her hand for Professor McKenna. "Yes, thank you. This is incredibly helpful."

"My pleasure. Good luck."

Simone turned to the girl. "Thank you as well. You've just saved my ass."

"Sure." Clearly, she wasn't at all interested. "Can you find your way out?"

"No problem."

Simone's mind kept saying his name over and over—Dylan Williams—trying to see if it felt right. Was this the same guy who'd jerked off with her in the bathroom two days ago? She wanted nothing more than to find out.

The minute she got into her car, Simone opened the picture and stared down at him. "Who are you, Dylan Williams?"

It was time to find out if he was indeed her mystery man.

Then she needed to figure out what exactly she was going to do if he was.

* * * *

Kayla was in her pajamas when Simone showed up at her house later that night. Kayla's hair was loose around her shoulders, and she didn't have any makeup on. "Do you know what time it is?"

"Ah, no." She didn't wait to be invited in before pushing past Kayla to make a beeline for her coffee maker. "I think I found him."

"Devin is sleeping in the living room." Kayla poked her head around the corner, no doubt looking to see if her fiancé was still snoring. "And found who?"

"The Candy King. The owner of the sugar daddy website." She'd been buzzing from excitement for hours and knew there was no way she'd be able to sleep for a while. As per usual, Kayla would be on the receiving end of her boundless energy.

Simone helped herself to a coffee, drinking down half of the hot liquid without really thinking about it. The burn was good to refocus her mind and to calm her down enough that she'd be able to speak in full, non-run-on sentences. "At least I think it's him. I was able to miraculously track his nickname down to an entry in a university yearbook. I need to reach out and see if he'll bite on my questions. But I'm close."

She would need to reach out to Williams tomorrow, but the question was should she do it through the sugar daddy app and see what his reaction was, or should she reach out to him at work? Would he see that as a threat or an attack? She really didn't want him to think of her contacting him as either of those things. Maybe she'd do the app first. "I could really use your advice on what you think is the best way to approach this. I mean, I know you're not a reporter, but I think I need a sanity check or something."

When she turned around to face Kayla once again, she'd been expecting to see the same facial expression her best friend wore whenever Simone showed up late at night or unexpectedly. Kayla always looked amused with a side dish of exasperated, generally because Simone didn't let her get a word in edgewise.

Tonight, she merely looked tired.

"Are you okay?" Simone put her mug down and practically flew across the kitchen to her friend. "Did something bad happen? Do I need to kick Devin's ass for something?"

Kayla took a deep breath and closed her eyes for a moment, before pulling Simone into a hug. "It's late, and I'm just a little tired."

"But if there's a problem, I'm here to help you." Simone always hated the expression *take a bullet for someone*, but Kayla was that person for her.

"I know you are. And I love that about you."

"Whatever you need, I'm here for you. Well, as long as it doesn't interfere with the research that I'm doing."

Kayla smiled, looking more than a little exasperated. "Darling, I don't want this to sound harsh, because I don't mean it that way. But in this particular instance, you're the problem."

Simone stopped moving and stared, wide-eyed, at her friend. "What?"

"You're clearly really excited about your break, and I want to be excited too. But it's nearly midnight." Kayla pushed a piece of her dark loose hair behind her ear.

Simone turned and looked at the close. "Oh shit. I had no idea."

"I know you didn't. I was about to throw a blanket on Devin and go to bed. He's been studying up and getting ready for his school semester on top of volunteering at the soup kitchen. And I've been going all week on a special project at work. I really want nothing more than to go to bed and sleep."

Simone knew her face was flushed. "I'm so sorry."

"It's okay, and I love you. Maybe next time give me a bit of warning if you're coming by this late at night? I'll drink a coffee."

She'd always come over to talk things out with Kayla in the past. No matter the time. Had her friend always put up with that? Simone's chest tightened, and it suddenly became hard to breathe. "I didn't know you hated when I'd come over like this."

"I don't hate it. And don't think for a second that I hate you." Kayla pulled her into a quick hug. "I just wish that sometimes you'd look at a clock."

And just like that, Simone felt like the biggest asshole on the planet. "I'm sorry."

"Don't be sorry." Kayla sighed. "Honestly, it's just tonight. I'm wiped out, and I have a big meeting again tomorrow."

"Hey." They both turned around to see Devin standing, sleepy-eyed, in the doorway. "Everything okay?"

"Simone was just heading out. Go to bed, and I'll be up shortly."

"Okay. Night, Simone." He turned as though someone else was piloting his body and disappeared up the stairs.

"Shit, I'm sorry." Despite how long Kayla and Devin had been together, Simone still wasn't used to sharing her best friend with someone else.

"It's fine. He'll be back asleep before his head hits the pillow." Kayla rubbed her eyes and bit back a yawn.

"Sorry. I'll go."

"I'm not mad." Kayla's smile eased the tension in Simone's chest.

"Okay."

"Give me a call in the morning, and you can tell me all about who you found. If you have time, we'll do lunch."

Simone gave Kayla a little wave before trudging back to her car and getting inside. All the joy, the excitement she'd felt since finding Dylan Williams's picture in the yearbook finally faded away. She'd never considered herself a selfish person, never had thought she'd taken advantage of Kayla, but, clearly, she'd grown too accustomed to having her friend at her beck and call. While their friendship was solid, Kayla had changed since she'd gotten engaged to Devin. Simone was happy for her friend and wanted her to have all the joy that was coming her way.

And yet, there was a part of her that wished everything had stayed the same. That Simone, not Devin, was the center of Kayla's world.

What kind of person did that make her?

A lonely one.

Simone turned her car on and pulled onto the road. Well, if she couldn't fall back on her relationship with Kayla as a sounding board for what she'd found, then this was an excellent opportunity for her to fly on her own. Not only would she prove to Carl that she was an excellent reporter, she'd prove to herself that she didn't need to rely on anyone for anything.

She could do this. She *would* do this.

Dylan Williams wouldn't know what hit him.

Chapter 4

Dylan Williams stood nursing his second whiskey and listening to his brother extol the virtues of doing yoga while people he didn't know mulled around them. This was the third engagement party he'd been invited to by his brother in the last ten years, and there was a small, cynical part of him that suspected that it might not be the last. Though if anyone could keep his brother in line, Sarah was it. While she was seven years younger than Jonathan, Sarah had a calm wisdom to her that his older brother had yet to possess.

"Seriously, within a month Sarah and I were doing headstands against the wall." Jonathan drained his glass and winked. "I mean, I fell on my ass within about five seconds, but it makes her happy when I try."

"Happy wife, happy life." Not that Dylan knew the first thing about matrimony. Unlike his brother, who seemed to be perpetually getting married, Dylan had made a point of steering clear of anything resembling a serious relationship.

He was self-aware enough to know he was far too selfish to make an excellent partner to another human being. All he was interested in was work, the occasional one-night stand with a willing partner, and traveling when he could take the time away.

Plus, he had his website if he needed a date. That was far easier than any relationship.

Case in point, his little flirtation with his anonymous Sugar Tart.

Since their little back-and-forth three days ago, he hadn't been able to get the thought of her out of his mind. She'd barely filled out her profile on the site, which was a bit surprising, given that most women who signed up were actively trying to find someone to go on dates with and offered lots of information about themselves.

His Sugar Tart seemed more interested in talking to him, trying to get information on who he was, rather than dating. That in itself wasn't unusual—he'd had more than a few people want to know who the owner of the site was, which was one of the reasons he'd used an alias. Typically when he was looking for a date, he used a different name without a picture. The last thing he wanted was to have it readily known that he was the owner of the site and have that come back and have an impact on the family business.

The chance of them losing contracts around the city wasn't worth the risk. And while his family might be more than a little dysfunctional, no one would take very kindly to the idea, let alone the reality, of his little side company.

His dad would see him as little more than a pimp.

And knowing Jonathan, he'd want to sign up.

"Little brother," Jonathan slapped him on the back of the shoulder, "when are you going to settle down? Find some nice girl to spend all your money on."

Ah, the ever-present belief that if you're single, you must be inherently unhappy. It wasn't just his brother who thought this. Dylan's parents would generally bring it up whenever he went out to lunch with one of them. They'd been divorced for fifteen years, but in this matter, they both seemed to feel that because the youngest of the Williams family hadn't tied—and then promptly untied—the knot, he was somehow deficient in life experiences.

Never had Dylan ever felt he was missing out. There were plenty of women out there that he'd had arrangements with: traveling companions, lovers, friends. He'd never had any reason to change his life to "Not happening."

"Why not?" Jonathan used that same tone of voice that also seemed to be a Williams trait. "You're thirty-five, times a wasting."

"I'm thirty-seven, and I'm fine single." He really was fine on his own and had no desire to run out and change his status.

Before Jonathan could jump in for round two of *You really need to get a girl*, Dylan's phone rang. "Sorry, have to get this." Without looking, he hit answer and pressed his phone to his ear. "Yeah?"

"Hi, Mr. Williams, it's Sonya." It didn't matter that his assistant had been working for him for over five years now, she always insisted on letting him know it was her. As though he couldn't recognize her voice by now.

"I've had some e-mails from a reporter wanting to interview you. At least, I think that's what she wants."

It wasn't unusual for him to get media requests as part of his job as CEO of the family company. But he could tell there was something different in Sonya's voice and that this particular request was unusual. "What's going on?"

"Well, she just wanted to know if you'd gone to U of T, and honestly, I couldn't remember what the diploma in your office said, so I just gave her the brush-off. She wouldn't say exactly what the information was for, and she didn't ask me any other questions."

Dylan felt as though he'd been hit in the face with a brick. There was only one person he knew who'd been asking questions about his personal life recently, and that was Sugar Tart. He mentally tried to recall everything he'd said to her online, trying to remember if there'd been anything he could have said that would have led her to make the connection.

He'd been careful—he always was—when he'd texted her. It was probably just a coincidence that a reporter was asking about his background. His family was well known in the city, and he'd been in the media more than once.

Shit, he hoped it wasn't her. She'd hit every one of his buttons, and her flirty, fun nature had brought a smile to his face the moment she'd texted him. They'd had a connection that he'd started to enjoy, probably more than he should. He should have known that the moment his feelings were tweaked, something bad would happen.

"Mr. Williams?"

"Sorry, Sonya. Did she say anything else?"

"Just that she'd be in touch later. I just wanted to let you know in case you got any weird phone calls."

Dylan's frown pulled his face into an uncomfortable position. "Thanks, Sonya. I'll make sure to keep my eyes open. Anything else?"

"I know your father is at the party with you, but he called me about an hour ago to put a meeting on your calendar. Something about a new project he wants you to take the lead on."

Dylan sighed even as the muscles in his neck and back tightened. He was spread way too thin these days, and there was no way he'd be able to adequately run another project. He was barely sleeping, and he'd eaten out for the past several meals rather than cook for himself at home. He loved to cook and wanted more time to just enjoy the life that he'd worked so hard to build for himself. "That's not going to happen."

"I know." Of all the people who worked at Williams Development, Sonya probably was one of the few who understood how worn out he was. "Do you want me to set up a different meeting? I can pull you out with an emergency if that will help? Just let me know, and I'll flag the action in my system."

"I adore you. You're the best personal assistant the world could ever have given me."

"Aww, stop it, boss. You're going to make me blush." She chuckled. "When will you be back in the office?"

"Tomorrow morning around ten." His phone buzzed in his hand, indicating that he'd gotten a message. "I'll let you go. Thanks for the heads-up."

"Yup. See you tomorrow."

Dylan was going to have to make sure that she got a bonus on top of her raise this year. Before he checked the message, he stepped back into the banquet hall and grabbed another glass of wine from a waiter. There was no way he'd be able to do what his father wanted him to do, not without severely impacting every aspect of his life. It was about time someone else stepped up and took charge.

For once in his life, he intended to live it the way he wanted, without having to look after everyone else.

His phone buzzed in his hand, drawing his attention. The message indicator on his phone was from the sugar daddy app, which meant *she'd* sent him another message. If it had been any other day, he would have enjoyed what had become his favorite distraction. But if the reporter was in fact his Sugar Tart, then things would be irrevocably changed between them.

He drained the wine and grabbed another one as he stared at the screen, deciding if he should read it or not. He could be wrong about her, drawing connections where there weren't any. The whole point of the app was to get to know the other person, to fill in some of the holes in their life.

Pressing the button, he quickly read her message. He grabbed another glass of wine from a waiter and drank most of it in one go. What the hell was he going to do? He reread the message, just to make sure he hadn't misunderstood her intentions.

I've been a bad girl. I wanted to know who you were so much that I did some digging. I know who you are. But I don't want you to think that I'm going to blackmail you or anything. I just wanted to meet. Isn't that what we're supposed to be doing on a sugar daddy site? Is there a chance we could get together for coffee and talk?

Dylan couldn't put his finger on why, deep down in his gut, he knew that coming face-to-face with her was going to end badly for him. She'd never given off the stranger-danger vibe, but that didn't mean that she wasn't a con artist of some sort who was looking for a way to make a quick buck. If she was the reporter, then she apparently had an idea of who he was now, which wouldn't end well for him either.

There wasn't anything he could do to stop her from going public with that information. He'd made a promise to himself years ago that if he were ever faced with the choice between blackmail or his identity being released, he would allow it to come out. Then he'd shut down the site.

Unless, of course, he could dissuade her from going any further with her quest to discover who he was. Moving to stand against the wall, he thought for a moment before typing out a message.

You have been a bad girl. Why do you want to know who I am so badly? I have to say it's a bit unnerving to have someone be so determined.

Maybe things weren't as bad as he was assuming. She might be naturally curious or wanting to land the biggest sugar daddy on the site for her own gain. There didn't need to be a big, horrible reason for her wanting to know. Did there?

I'm a reporter.

Shit, of course, it was her. He was about to delete their messages when her follow-up caused him to stop.

A couple I interviewed fell in love on your site. They were so happy that I got my very best friend in the world to sign up as well. She also fell in love, and they're getting married soon. I've talked to several couples (through the app; I didn't hunt them down), who've found their happy ending with a person they love because of your app. I wanted to find out what made your site so different. What was it that allowed people to make these connections beyond sex/time for money? I have no plans to out you, but I'd love to meet, to talk to you about what you've built.

Dylan's head spun as he read and reread the message. Sure, it wasn't unbelievable that some of his clients might have found love beyond their original arrangements on the site, but that had nothing at all to do with him. Jesus, he built the fucking thing because he was *against* long-term relationships. She must be cherry-picking who she was talking to, getting an incorrect impression about what people were doing.

He started to type a response when another message from her popped up.

If you say no, then I'll walk away. I won't do anything to ruin what you've built. It's helping too many people.

Shit. Dylan deleted his message and stared at it again. Laughter from the room pulled his attention from the dilemma unfolding in front of him. It was nearly speech time, which meant he was going to have to get up and say his few words and do…something or other with the maid of honor. A game of some sort. Jonathan stood by Sarah and waved at him to come over.

He'd have to deal with his Sugar Tart at a later time.

Let me think about it. I'll let you know one way or the other in a few days.

He didn't wait to see what her response was and slipped his phone into his pocket as he marched over to the waiting group. His demise was officially postponed.

For now.

Chapter 5

Simone was many things—curious, silly, talked a bit too much when she got excited about something—but mistaken about Dylan Williams being the infamous Candy King wasn't one of them. When she'd called Williams Development and asked his assistant where he'd gone to school, she'd been shocked when the woman went and found out. It wasn't exactly foolproof confirmation of his identity, but it gave her enough confidence to reach out to him on the website and see if he'd bite at her proposal.

She hadn't stopped her research with the nickname from the yearbook, but it was a starting point that held its place. With each new fact she learned, the information always seemed to circle around to him—from his nickname at university to his financial investments, which he'd publicized over the years. But it had been the corporate picture she'd found on the Williams Development website that had sealed it for her.

Dylan Williams was exactly the same height, weight, and age, and he had the necessary skills and connections to pull off a site like this. He appeared older than he had in the yearbook, which wasn't exactly surprising but still gave her pause. If anything, he'd aged extremely well. But there was something in his eyes that caught her attention and stimulated an emotion that she couldn't quite put her finger on. He looked…sad? No, that wasn't it. Stoic? Maybe, though she didn't know enough about his life to know what he'd need to be stoic about.

She'd stared at his handsome face for more than an hour before finally sending him the message on the app. This was the man who'd gotten off at the same time as her while in their respective corporate bathrooms. While everything in his reputation said he was a straitlaced, upstanding community man, she now knew he had a naughtier side that loved to get dirty.

All she had to do was to meet him—ask him the question to his face so she could see his reaction—then she'd know for sure. She'd finally have her Candy King where she wanted him.

As long as he agreed.

A few days had turned into a week and a half, and she still hadn't heard back from him. Simone was impatient by nature, but she didn't want to fuck this up by pushing too hard, too fast. She had no doubt that he'd grant her an interview once he'd had enough time to think. She just had to bide her time and not track him down at a bar while he was conducting a business meeting.

Oops.

In all fairness, she hadn't intended to walk into the bar when she saw him on the street. It was a complete fluke that she'd been assigned to do a story on the library back-to-school programs around the city and had decided to take the subway instead of her car. So when she'd popped out from the station and saw him leading a group of men into a restaurant across the street, Simone promptly forgot about heading back to the office and followed them into the building.

That was why she'd been sitting at the bar of a restaurant she could in no way afford, watching Williams schmooze with a group of business investors. Well, she assumed they were investors because they didn't look very friendly and Williams was doing his best to charm them. *The Candy King doesn't seem to win all the time.*

Simone stirred the melting ice in her glass with her straw, ignoring the growing crick in her neck as she did her best to keep from being too obvious about what she was doing. This was her first official stakeout, and she had every intention of nailing it.

It was fascinating being able to watch Dylan from afar. The way his easy smile seemed to get easier as he poured more wine into everyone's glasses did things to her body that were far from proper. If there'd been a single woman in that group, Simone had no doubt that she'd have been all over Dylan. Simone was finding it quite challenging to keep her distance, especially when his unexpected laugh reached her.

Everyone was all smiles around the table, which meant he'd finally broken through whatever wall had been erected. Dylan's shoulders dropped visibly as he leaned back against his chair.

He wasn't movie-star handsome, but there was sex appeal to the sharp angles of his face, the long bridge of his nose. Simone wanted nothing more than to lick his full lips. She wondered what it would be like to have his face between her legs.

And yeah, probably not the best time to be having sexual fantasies about her mark.

I'm a naughty girl; what else would he expect from me?

God, this was such a horrible idea. She should have turned around and gone in the other direction when she'd spotted him. Nothing good could come of her current obsession with her Candy King. Sure, Carl would give her a hard time if he knew what she'd done with him, but that was online and, as far as she was concerned, her own private business. Nothing she'd done officially could harm the paper or her reputation. As long as she was careful and kept things professional when they met in person, everything should be fine.

Williams laughed again, and Simone couldn't help but glance his way. *You're going to get in so much trouble with this one.*

She tried not to stare, but it was tough not to when he reached up and loosened his tie before rolling his shirt sleeves up to his elbows. God, that was one of her kinks. There was nothing sexier than a man in business attire that was half undone. Images of her undoing the rest of his buttons flashed through her mind. Crossing her legs increased the pressure on her clit, making sitting on the stool a painful tease.

Shit, she was going to have to do something about that as soon as she got home.

"Do you want another?"

She jumped at the sound of the bartender's voice, her hand catching her glass and sending it falling. "Shit!" Water and the sticky remains of her drink sloshed across the bar and covered her purse. "Shit, shit, do you have a napkin?"

The bartender had a cloth in his hand and had mopped up the mess up before the words were out of her mouth. Great, not only had she drawn attention to herself, she really was going to have to buy another drink now. *So much for keeping costs down.*

"I'm sorry. Yes, can I have another?" Simone was thankful for having taken an Uber here because she was far more of a lightweight than she liked to admit. Two drinks, especially the sweet kind, were more than she normally indulged in. "And water. Please."

The bartender left to fill her order, which left Simone alone to examine the damage done to her purse. It was a Kate Spade, one she'd saved up for months to buy before she went to work for the paper. Her mom had told her that if she was going to be a professional and wanted to be taken seriously, it was vital for her to project a specific image. Her friend Kayla had offered to buy her one—a purse worth a few hundred dollars wasn't a large purchase for a woman of her wealth—but Simone knew that, in this particular case, the act of buying the purse herself was almost as important as the image it projected.

It was her first act of independence, the first and only luxury purchase she'd made right out of college. And it was now ruined.

Red syrup darkened the pale green fabric and would undoubtedly leave a stain. Her chest tightened at the sight, and it suddenly became hard to swallow past the lump in her throat. No fucking way would she cry over a damaged purse that she might be able to find a way to salvage. She wasn't twenty-one with no job prospects. She was employed, with aspirations that would take her places. With a sigh, she dipped the cloth napkin into the water the bartender dropped off and began to do her best to clean it up.

"My mother always says that soda water is the way to get stains out."

Simone jerked around, startled for the second time in five minutes, to come face-to-face with the one person she'd wanted to talk to, as much as she tried to avoid him. Dylan Williams stood behind her, his hands on his hips and that teasing smile on his lips. Being this close to him gave her the barest glimpse of throat beneath the fabric of his shirt. His skin appeared naturally darkened and teased her. What would he taste like if she leaned in and licked him right there?

He cleared his throat and nodded toward her purse. "I'm not sure if it actually works, but it might be worth a try until you can take it someplace to get it cleaned."

"Thanks." *Oh shit, this is it and him, and oh shit, I need to say something.* "Uh, yeah. I'll have to try that." *Smooth, you dumbass.*

Dylan slipped his hands into his pockets, which squared his body directly toward hers. "Now that I've helped with that, I'm wondering if there is something else I can do for you?"

Simone's stomach did a little flip. "What do you mean?"

"You've been sitting there staring at me for nearly an hour. I figured you were simply curious or were going to ask me out. But you're not drinking or looking at anyone else. And most women who are trying to get my attention make more of an effort to catch my eye." He cocked his head to the side and smiled. "If you're trying to figure out what my next investment is, you might want to take a table closer to me, instead of sitting here."

"I'm not doing that." She sat up straighter. "God, do I look like someone who invests a ton of money?"

"Based on your reaction to your purse getting ruined? No. Which means you're probably a journalist looking for a story." There was no mistaking the meaning he put behind those words. She could almost hear his silent

"Sugar Tart" at the end of the sentence. Dylan's gaze traveled up and down her body, only to stop at her eyes. "On a different day, I might have bitten on the damsel-in-distress routine." He looked like he wanted to say something else, but the arrival of the bartender at their end of the bar stopped him. "Whatever story you're after, I'm afraid you're not going to find it. Go home, Lois Lane. You're out of your league."

Shock froze Simone to her seat and stole her words. She was helpless to do anything other than watch as he went back to his table and reclaimed the attention of his group.

Well.

That fucking sucked.

Her face heated as the bartender came over with a debit machine. "I take it you want the bill?"

She could only nod, as she fumbled for her credit card. God, maybe Carl was right about this. Perhaps she really wasn't cut out for this type of journalism. If she couldn't even handle getting approached by an attractive man who figured out that she was after a story—one that really wasn't going to be all that hard-hitting—then how the hell would she handle something more difficult?

The answer was, she wouldn't. Keeping her gaze averted from where Williams sat, she grabbed her purse and strode with what little dignity she could muster out of the restaurant.

The moment she stepped outside, noise from Toronto's busy core washed over her, as did the evening breeze. Groups of pedestrians parted around her, like water around a river stone, leaving her feeling isolated and alone.

God, she'd fucked that up in record time. He'd been right there in front of her, talking to her face-to-face, and she didn't ask him the question she'd waited all that time to ask. She'd failed miserably, and there wasn't anything she could do about it. Reaching into her purse, she snagged her cell phone and called the one person she knew would understand. "Kayla?"

"What's up?" Kayla's voice was as smooth and confident as her friend was. "You sound awful."

"I was on a story, and I fucked up." She looked up at the sky and swallowed down a tear. "God, I'm shitty at this."

"Are you kidding me? You're one of the best, if not the best, local reporters this city has." She could practically hear Kayla's eye roll. "Your research is impeccable, and you have a way with people that can convince just about anyone to do anything. You're smart and capable, and if you think you have a story, then there's a story. Don't let one minor setback ruin everything."

Right. It was only a minor setback that the subject of her investigation caught her checking up on him and called her out on it. It wasn't an issue that she was trying to uncover a secret identity of his with the purpose of doing a story on him and because of her clumsiness he was more likely to ignore her.

No, no problem at all.

And yet, she knew Kayla was right, that despite the way he tried to dismiss her, she had no doubt in her mind that Dylan Williams was the Candy King. What she really needed to do was to get the right angle for approaching him again. She needed to make it worth his while to let her in.

"I can hear your brain churning all the way through the phone." Kayla chuckled. "I take it you're good now."

Simone turned to see Williams come out of the restaurant with his group, turn, and shake their hands. He was a businessman, and a powerful one at that. What she needed to do was present him with an offer he couldn't refuse. "Yeah, I think I am."

"Good. Keep me posted, and let me know if there's anything I can do to help."

Simone was only vaguely aware of disconnecting the call, as all her attention was locked hard onto Williams. He was typing something on his phone, probably calling his car service or whatever the hell rich people had these days. In a matter of moments, her best opportunity to get this scoop would be gone and, with it, her best chance at taking the next step in her career.

Screw that.

Simone straightened up, took a breath, and then marched over to Williams. He was looking down the street and only saw her coming when she got to within a few feet. Yup, totally waiting on a car to get him.

Too late to save you from me, dude.

"Mr. Williams, could I have a moment?" She smiled, as she stuck out her hand. "Simone Leblanc. I'm a reporter with the *Toronto Record*, and I was hoping to speak with you."

Williams took her hand, giving it a gentle squeeze that sent a shiver through her body. His gaze was locked onto hers, so it was easy to see his amusement. "How's the purse, *Sugar*?"

She shuddered and blushed at his nickname for her. "How did you know it was me?"

He chuckled. "Believe it or not, I don't normally have multiple reporters digging into my life in the space of a few days. When you told me you were a reporter in there, I put two and two together. Besides, I got the impression you don't give up easily."

"My purse is probably ruined. Which is on me. I haven't quite mastered the art of surveillance." She forced herself to look him in the eye, reminded of the intensity of his gaze in the yearbook photo. "How long did it take for you to realize I was watching you?"

He shrugged, letting her hand go. "Five minutes."

"Damn." She really was going to have to get better at that if she wanted to make a go of being an investigative reporter. "I'd hoped it had been a bit longer than that."

"You have the small problem of being an incredibly attractive woman. Men will notice you far sooner than you'd like."

There wasn't anything off-putting about the comment, nor did it feel as though he was trying to come on to her. Still, she felt a blush cover her face and had to fight not to look away from him. "Thank you. But that won't distract me from my reason for being here. I was hoping I could sit down with you and talk about one of your business ventures."

Williams narrowed his gaze and lowered his chin and his voice. "I thought I'd asked for time to consider your option?"

Okay, here we go. She smiled, nodded once, and let out a little huff. "You did. And honestly, I wasn't planning on talking to you tonight. Shit, I wasn't even a hundred percent certain you were the right person until just now. But I was curious and needed to figure out if you were, in fact, the person I thought you were, and I'm really sorry that I spilled my drink and made an ass of myself. I hope it didn't ruin your meeting."

"They thought I was kind to help you out." He looked around at the traffic, the muscle in his jaw jumping. "What do you want now?"

What did she want? They weren't exactly strangers, despite never having met before. But she wasn't sure if she could completely trust him. Absent the safety of the Internet, Simone wasn't naïve enough not to realize that Dylan could be capable of anything.

She could walk away right now. It was probably the smart thing to do.

Or she could take a risk and see where the story took her.

"Well?" He cocked his eyebrow.

Hefting her purse strap up, she met his gaze and smiled. "I want to know everything there is about the Candy King."

Chapter 6

Dylan's stomach bottomed out on him. There was no way in hell she should have been able to track him down, let alone show up at a place he hadn't planned on being three hours earlier. He'd been beyond careful to ensure that his name wasn't listed anywhere online, and he'd set up a holding company as the owner. But somehow this woman had been able to figure it out, to draw a line between him and millionairesugardaddy. com. As much as they'd texted over the past month, he knew for a fact he hadn't shared anything about himself that would have given anything away.

Had he?

Apparently, given that she was standing right in front of him, a twinkle in her eyes that seemed to give her entire body a shine. She bit down on her bottom lip as she cocked her head to the side. "If you want, I'll walk away. Like I said, I never had any intention of ruining you or your life. I just wanted to do a profile on the Candy King persona, on the site, and on the entire sugar daddy phenomenon in Toronto. I wanted to know what made your site so special. That was all."

She was more beautiful than he'd ever imagined she'd be.

He'd fantasized about her more than once since they'd started their little back-and-forth online. Her voice was deeper than he'd imagined, and every time she spoke, it sent a pulse of desire through him, straight to his cock. Now knowing what she looked like, Dylan was going to have more than a few new fantasies to deal with.

But despite everything, he couldn't afford to take the chance that she'd reveal his identity to the world. That bombshell would cause more problems, both professionally and personally, than he was willing to deal with.

"I'm sorry, I don't think I can help you." His limo turned the corner, and Dylan was able to breathe a bit easier. "I wish you luck with your story."

He stepped toward the curb, mentally counting down the moments until his ride arrived. Simone's fingers wrapped around his forearm, and she gently tugged at him. "I know this is the last thing you want, and that I'd promised you space and time to consider. Is there anything I can do to convince you that I'm not out to cause you problems? I'm really just trying to make a name for myself."

Twenty, nineteen, eighteen..."I don't think you can appreciate the position you've put me in here. If I say yes, I run the risk of you learning too much about me, things that I don't necessarily want to be shared with the general public. If I say no, you have my identity and could easily go public with whatever story you want to put out there, regardless of what I ask you to do."

"I would never...though I guess you don't know who I am, so you wouldn't really be able to trust that." She crossed her arms and cocked her head to the side. "Though in all fairness, you now know who I am as well. And you have copies of all our texts. I'm sure if you wanted to take this information to my boss, there wouldn't be anything I could do to stop you."

Dylan turned and stared at her. Of course, it was his site, and he had full control of the database and the user information. Even where she'd used an alias, it wouldn't take much for him to pull all the data and fire it off to wherever it was she worked. "I guess we're both stuck."

"Only if we allow ourselves to be. I'm a reporter, and I try to be as honest and up front about my interviews as I can be. We can establish parameters, questions or subjects you don't want to go anywhere near, and I promise to back off. This is a huge phenomenon in Toronto, and I think it's something that the public has an interest in."

Shit, he knew this was a horrible fucking idea, even as his mind churned through various topics he'd be willing to discuss with her. He knew exactly what would happen to his reputation and that of his family if his little side project ever came to light. While his views on relationships and marriage were liberal, many of his family members didn't share them. In their eyes, to be single, rich, and good-looking pretty much sealed the fact that you had no choice but to get married. What was the point of having it all if you didn't have a family as well?

Fuck that.

He'd never wanted one. The idea of kids was something that, in equal parts, freaked him out and pissed him off. There were more than enough people in the world that he didn't need to fire his sperm off all over the place in the interests of procreation. There were better, far less selfish people out there who would make better parents than he would be.

Maybe Simone here.

She too was looking at the approaching limo, no doubt gauging how much time she had left for talking. "Look, you started this site for a reason, and it's incredibly successful. People would want to know that, and it would be great for your business. Bringing it into the light would lend it an air of legitimacy."

"It is legitimate." Unconventional, sure. But legal and providing a safe way for people of like minds to connect.

Simone nodded. "But despite that, it's still relegated to the fringes. Maybe having a feature done on you and the site would be a way to pull everything into the mainstream."

"Maybe I like having my business on the fringes. No matter how good a reporter you are, sugar daddy sites aren't something that the mainstream world is going to welcome with open arms."

The car pulled up, and Dylan yanked open the back door. He had two choices: he could ignore her and pray that everything would go away, or he could give her a few minutes and figure out exactly what she was hoping to get from all this. Either option had consequences that he wasn't sure he liked. At least with the second option, he would have a bit of a heads-up.

He looked up at the sky and sighed. "You're killing me, Sugar Tart."

"I promise, you'll enjoy it." Her entire body positively glowed from her excitement. "Come on, it will be awesome. And you can get a preview of the article, so you'll know exactly what's going to print."

Dylan knew that this story was going to happen, with or without his approval. He'd seen what had happened when people didn't participate in stories done on them, and he didn't want to risk any misinformation coming out about him or the site. And having to spend some time with the woman who'd haunted his dreams for weeks now wasn't exactly going to be a hardship.

"Well, Ms. Leblanc, you have a choice. You can get into the limo and drive with me until I get home. I'll have my driver drop you off wherever you want after that. Or you can drop this and never talk to me again."

That took the wind out of her sails a bit. "You want me to come with you to your house?"

He closed his eyes and counted to three in his head. His cock went hard at the thought of her stretched out on his bed. Maybe this wasn't a good idea after all. "No. I'm offering the twenty minutes it will take for my driver to take me home for your interview. That's it. Take it or leave it."

Even the time he was offering her was more than he should be doing. Nothing good would come of him talking to a reporter, no matter how cute and vibrant she was. But he'd been in the business game long enough to know that she wasn't going to let this go now that she'd caught the scent. Better to make the offer, so that if she didn't take it, she couldn't claim that he hadn't given her a chance.

She crossed her arms and cocked her head to the side, her stained purse bouncing off her leg. "That's not exactly ideal."

It really wasn't fair of him, inviting a woman into the back of a car who didn't know who he was or what he might do to her. In this day and age, he knew everyone had to be smart about their safety. "No, I suppose not."

She seemed to weigh her options before reaching into her purse. She pulled something out along with her cell phone. "I'm going to text a friend of mine and tell her where I'm going and who I'm with. Then I'll get in the car with you."

"What's that?"

"Mace." She held it up for him to see. "And yes, I know how to use this. If you try anything, I'll blind you long enough to get your driver to pull over so I can get out."

Despite everything, he was quickly growing to like this woman. Not just the fantasy he'd mentally created, but the flesh-and-blood spitfire who stood before him. "Deal." Holding out his hand, he cocked his eyebrow and gave her a smirk. "Well?"

With a snort, she took his hand and climbed into the back seat, sliding over as far as she could before turning toward him, meanwhile shifting the can of Mace to her lap. Dylan wanted to laugh, but that wasn't going to set her at ease. He slid into the seat beside her and closed the door. The limo pulled away from the curb. "The clock's ticking. How did you uncover my name? I've been careful over the years to make sure that my identity isn't out there."

"Wait, this is supposed to be my interview." She narrowed her gaze, leaning forward. "And you gave me bits and pieces to go on during our texts." She blushed and looked away for a moment. There were some other things they'd done, and it was good to see that she'd been as impacted as he'd been.

"Like what? I need to make sure that I'm more careful next time I'm talking to a potential suitor."

Her back straightened, and she snapped her gaze back to him. "Age, height, weight, hair color. I made the leap that Candy King was a nickname, and with your vitals on hand, I went looking at local universities. I had a whole plan of where to check next, but I happened to get lucky when I ran into someone who knew you at U of T."

"Who?" Most of his friends were still in the city, but he couldn't imagine that any of them would rat him out to a reporter.

"A Professor McKenna. He said he played rugby with you and showed me a yearbook that used your nickname." She leaned in and grinned. "Something about your sweet moves with the ladies."

"I did all right with them." He hadn't bothered to get the yearbooks when he was at university. It wasn't something he cared that much about.

"I bet you did." Her blush hadn't let up. She leaned back against the seat and looked out the window.

Dylan's chest tightened, and it was suddenly difficult for him to sit still. "Okay. You wanted to do a story on me, made contact to get information—"

"Actually, I asked you directly if you wanted to meet. Remember? I was going to tell you that I was a reporter then."

He sighed. "Then when I didn't bite, you took what you knew and went on the search for my identity based on my screen name."

God, she actually looked proud. "Honestly, I wasn't certain that it was even a nickname. Just like ninety percent certain. Maybe ninety-three percent. Because, yeah, it's a silly name, and lots of people have silly nicknames in university or college. I mean, my friends used to call me Boober—you know, the smart Fraggle from Fraggle Rock? I had a roommate who called me that when I did her laundry and organized all her books because I couldn't handle the chaos in our room. She was an animation student and into all things focused on kids, so she knew all the Fraggle names and stuff, so I became Boober." With a snap, she closed her mouth and shrugged. "I liked it when you called me Lois Lane, though."

Dylan wasn't generally charmed by women. Lusted after, admired, or impressed by—yes. But never charmed. There was something about Simone that relaxed him, something so genuine that he knew every word she'd just said was correct. She was one of those people who had a light to them, one that appeared to shine through every pore of her skin, through her eyes and out through her voice. He'd only met one other person like that, and she'd gone on to become his second stepmom.

Nope, not going there.

Simone rubbed her hands along her thighs, sneaking glances at him. "I need to be up front about our texts. I'd never intended for them to get... out of hand. I, ah, yeah. The whole, ah, bathroom thing wasn't planned."

Dylan had wondered if she'd actually done what she'd claimed she'd been doing while at work. The thought of her masturbating in the bathroom had made him so hard, there'd been no way he'd have been able to focus until he'd gotten some relief as well. Being the boss meant there were some perks, and having his own private bathroom was one of them.

Simone clearly didn't have that option.

Dylan sat on his hands to keep himself from acting on the impulse to reach out and pull her in for a kiss. "I'm glad to hear that it wasn't some way to entrap me."

Her eyes widened. "No. That's not something I'd ever do."

"Hard for me to know that. We're strangers."

"Who've gotten off together." She chuckled. "Virtually."

"There's that."

She put the Mace back into her purse and pulled out her phone. "I did have a question for you."

They were only a few minutes from his home now. Soon his little adventure with his Sugar Tart would be over. "What's that?"

"Once I learned who you were, I did some more digging. To get some additional background. I found an interview with you from quite a few years ago. I think you might have just graduated from university." She held out her phone, and Dylan knew precisely which interview it was, just by the picture—and the headline: toronto billionaire bachelor back on the market.

"There's a quote there from you. *While relationships are wonderful, they're not for me. I'm publicly declaring that I'm a bachelor for life.*"

He'd just broken up with his long-term girlfriend, Andrea. They'd dated all through university, and for a brief period of time, he'd believed that maybe, just maybe, he would be different from the rest of his family. That he'd be able to get past the relationship cloud that seemed to engulf everyone. As much as he loved Andrea, her vision of what their lives together had been was so vastly different from his, it was becoming more and more difficult to reconcile those two views. So they'd parted ways amicably, and he'd sworn off all relationships beyond sex from that point on.

She reached out to touch his knee. "You okay?"

How he'd managed to forget about Simone, Dylan wasn't sure. "I'm fine. What do you want to know?"

"Is this the catalyst for you starting the sugar daddy site? The timing lines up with the site's launch six months later."

God, he hadn't given Andrea or their turbulent relationship much thought in recent years. "I assume we're on the record."

"We are. But I can take this off if you want." She cocked her head to the side and gave him a look that told him she truly wanted to make him feel comfortable. "Right now, we're just getting to know one another."

While Dylan might not be into the whole relationship thing, he did love women, exceptionally competent ones. Clearing his throat, he turned to look at the passing Toronto streetscape.

"Off the record, yeah. That was part of the reason."

"What's the other part?"

"Why do you care so much about doing a story on me and my site?" There was something about her that was relentless. If Dylan agreed to do this, he knew there was no way Simone would back down if she caught the scent of something he didn't want to talk about.

Simone sat back with a groan. "Two reasons. First, my editor hasn't been willing to give me a fair shot at the paper. He keeps putting me on local food stories, community festivals, and student sports events. Which are important, and I love doing them, but I want more. Being able to run a story on a site that's putting Toronto's rich in touch with financially strapped students and the love stories that are coming as a result? That would take my career to the next level."

Interesting. She was ambitious and thought his little company was the way to make her mark. That was a first for him. "What's the second reason?"

"My friend is one of your clients—" She smiled. "Kayla is engaged now, and they're so happy. So are Vince Taylor and his wife, Marissa. Those are two that I know personally. I've also reached out to some students on a few different campuses around the city. While not everyone is getting married, more than a few of them have found themselves in stable relationships. I don't know what it is about your site, but relationships rather than hookups are far more common there than on any other sugar daddy site I've investigated. I want to know why."

Halfway through her explanation, Dylan turned to stare at her, completely shocked by what she was saying. The last thing he'd ever intended was for his hookup site to result in marriages. Sure, odds were one or two might work into something long-term, but not whatever it was she was implying. "How many people have you talked to?"

Her smirk was back now that she knew she had his attention. "I was able to interview twenty women and three guys who have signed up for millionairesugardaddy.com. Over half of them considered themselves now involved in a romantic relationship with their sugar daddy."

Dylan's mind screeched to a halt. "You said Kayla? As in Kayla Arnold, founder of Fashion Finds?"

"Yup. She's my very best friend in the whole wide world. And she's getting married to an awesome guy who—" She snapped her mouth shut. "Not my story to tell. Regardless, she used your site, and it made her happy. I want to let all of Toronto know exactly what they have out there. Not just the whole financial aspect of students not being able to afford to live while they go to school, but also that having a sugar daddy doesn't have to be about sex."

God, this was utterly fucked up. "It's nothing more than a hookup site."

"It really isn't."

"I…" How the hell could he explain to her how much he hated even the concept of being in a relationship, how they were all doomed to failure? How could he do that and not out himself, put his and his family's reputations in danger of being destroyed? "The Candy King has his reasons for keeping his identity a secret. Being a part of an interview would cause me a lot of problems."

Simone tapped her fingers along the side of the Mace can. "How about this. Let me follow you around your daily life; you can tell people that I'm simply doing a story on you and your family in your day job. I mean, that's been a thing before, yes?"

"It has. Though I've never had anyone follow me around." It wouldn't necessarily be a hardship having her with him for hours on end, but the practical problems might be more than he could anticipate.

"I'll follow you, and you can tell me why you created the site. What drove you to want to run a business like this, and what makes this sugar daddy site so different from all the rest. I'll write the article, and you can read the whole thing before I submit it to the paper. I'll promise you complete veto power over the article. If you don't like something I've said, if you don't like how I've portrayed you, then I'll bury the story."

This was such a horrible idea, he couldn't even fathom why he was entertaining the thought of the interview. *You're thinking with your dick again, asshole.* "And if I tell you to pull the story and you don't, my reputation could be impacted."

She reached out and patted his knee. "You don't have to hide from me."

"I don't think anyone could hide from you." The limo turned the corner, and he saw that his place was just up ahead. "Let me think about it."

By the time the limo came to a stop, she was visibly shaking with excitement. "You won't regret this."

"I haven't said yes yet." He opened the door, turned, and braced his arms on the car to look down at her. "I might not."

"You will." She let out a happy squeal. "Thank you! I'll get in touch with your assistant to book an appointment."

"Did I miss where I said yes to this?" Had he?

Simone slid across the seat closer to him, forcing herself to tilt her head back to maintain eye contact. "Tell me if I'm wrong. I can tell that you're unhappy. I don't know why, but you are. There's something about this site that's become your way to rebel against what people's expectations of you are. Whether it's because your family is well established, or because of your money, or maybe people are pressuring you to get married or something. I don't know. What I do know is that there's a part of you that wants to tell this story. Wants the world to know that you're not what people expect. I'm giving you that chance."

Dylan's mouth had all but dried up by the end of her speech. She was right in ways that he hadn't fully vocalized to himself. Shit, he really was going to let her do this.

"Where do you want the driver to take you?"

"Just back to where we came from is fine. I'll make my way home from there." She wiggled back against the seat. "I'll talk to you tomorrow, Candy King."

"Good night, Sugar Tart." Dylan shut the door and shuddered.

What the hell was he getting himself into?

Chapter 7

Simone hadn't been able to sleep more than a few hours last night. Her mind kept going over her limo ride with Dylan, and this interview process wasn't going exactly the way she'd anticipated. Not to mention that she didn't have a clue what questions she wanted to ask Dylan this morning, what the best approach to today's interview would be, or whether it should be an interview at all.

Now that they'd met and she'd come face-to-face with her Candy King, Simone wasn't sure if she should go through with this at all.

While she'd been excited about stories in the past, this time she knew things were different. She'd never taken the time or the personal interest in one of her story subjects like this before. And to make matters even more complicated, there was something about Dylan that she couldn't quite put her finger on. He didn't exactly lack in confidence or bravado, but when she'd pulled out the article declaring him a bachelor for life, something in his facial expression changed.

She'd seen that look before, more than a few times. Kayla used to look that way whenever Simone would come over and try to convince her to do something fun. She'd been so lonely, and that was the main reason Simone had encouraged her to sign up for the sugar daddy site to begin with.

So why would Dylan, the man who owned and operated that very same site, have the same aura of loneliness? It wasn't as though he didn't use the site, that he didn't hook up with women when he wanted to. For a man who apparently had no desire to be in a long-term relationship, it seemed weird for him to be lonely.

Or maybe she was projecting. That was a thing she did from time to time.

No, it was better to ignore the seriously sexy Dylan and do what she came to do—interview the Candy King for a profile on him and his less-than-conventional business.

While she lay in bed last night, she'd finally been able to move past wanting to merely prove to Carl that she could do this. She realized that she had a real shot at creating something big, something different. The opportunity to stretch people's minds, to make them understand that sex and relationships were more than what general society deemed essential or normal. This profile would finally give her the recognition she craved, but it would speak to something bigger than herself.

She knew the end result would be something she'd be proud of.

Something her dad would be proud of too.

It had been a long time since she'd talked to him, which was mostly self-preservation on her part rather than anything he'd done recently. As far as she knew, he was back on his meds, going to his therapy sessions, and doing well. Her mom still kept tabs on him, even though they were no longer together. She loved him; she just couldn't live with him anymore, which Simone totally understood. While she wanted him to be proud of her, wanted him to have a positive story he could tell his friends, she suspected that there might be a part of him that would be jealous of her accomplishments.

She'd made it as a reporter when he hadn't.

"Enough of that." Her eyes snapped up to those of the Uber driver's in the rearview mirror when she realized she'd said the words aloud. "Sorry."

"Nervous?"

"Yeah. I have an interview today. I'm not sure how it's going to go."

"New jobs are always stressful. I'm sure you'll do great."

Simone didn't bother to correct him, taking the encouragement in the spirit with which it was intended. "Thank you. I hope so."

"I was always told to picture people naked, but that always made things worse for me. I would get distracted." He then winked at her, and Simone had to force her smile to stay in place.

"Never a good thing." *Please let the stop be soon.*

Thankfully, traffic moved quickly, and before she had to go in search of her Mace, the car pulled into the industrial park and stopped in front of a building. "Here you go."

This didn't exactly look like the sort of place a billionaire would work, but then again Dylan Williams wasn't exactly a typical billionaire. There were plenty of expensive-looking foreign cars mixed in with the domestics, so someone financially well-off was inside. She said her good-byes and got out of the car. Her palms were damp as she clung to her purse strap. She hadn't had any luck getting the stain out, but she wasn't going to meet Dylan without it. At least she wouldn't have to worry about explaining what had happened. Squashing her nerves as best she could, Simone pulled her shoulders back and went into the building.

The interior was as far removed from the exterior as Simone could have imagined. Instead of the standard warehouse look and feel that was typical of buildings in an industrial park, the inside of Williams Development was nearly spa-like. There was a huge water feature behind the stone desk at which the receptionist sat. There wasn't a sound coming from it, but the perpetual flow of water was hypotonic. So much so that Simone hadn't heard what the woman had said as she'd gotten close. "Sorry?"

The woman's black hair was pulled tight into a ponytail, leaving her with an open expression that relayed her amusement. "It's the most calming thing in the world."

"I would never leave my apartment if I had it there."

"I have to be careful. When I'm having a bad day, I'll just turn and stare at it, which isn't the best look when someone comes in." Her smile made her eyes sparkle. "What I asked was, did you have an appointment with someone today?"

"Ah yes. I'm Simone Leblanc. I'm here to see Dylan Williams."

"Is Mr. Williams expecting you?" The woman frowned. "He didn't mention anything to me when he came in, and I don't see your name on the calendar."

"We ran into each other last evening, and Mr. Williams was gracious enough to say he'd meet me to discuss the possibility of an interview." Not exactly a lie. The last thing she wanted to do was screw things up by saying too much to the wrong person before she'd even had a chance to sit down and talk to him properly.

"I'll let him know you're here." She smiled at Simone, though the look in her eyes wasn't exactly one of amusement. No doubt, Simone wasn't the first person to try and get an interview without an appointment.

It didn't matter if the receptionist believed her or not, Simone simply wanted her interview with Dylan, wanted to discover what kind of man he really was and what made the site so special, and then move on to bigger and better things. No more school fun fairs for her! No, she'd be down at city hall trying to determine if the proposed casino on the waterfront was a hoax or if they were really moving forward with the investment.

"Ms. Leblanc."

Simone jumped at the sound of Dylan's deep voice, her hands squeezing the strap of her purse a bit tighter than they had a moment before. God, he really was fucking gorgeous. "Yes, hi. That's me."

He shook his head and waved her closer. "If you'll follow me, we can talk in my office."

Okay, here we go. For real.

The office was the complete opposite of the lobby, devoid of any opulence, including mesmerizing waterfalls. Books lined tall shelves, photos of Williams and other men and women at parties and official building openings filling the blank spots. She paused to lean in and look at one. "Oh my God, is that Rob Ford? Shit, tell me you didn't vote for him." All the respect she had for Dylan would be gone in a flash if he was part of Ford Nation.

"It is, and no, I didn't."

"Why do you have a picture of him here then?"

Williams stepped beside her and looked at the photo. "It was an opening ceremony for one of our buildings, and he was mayor. My dad is also there, as are some of our major investors. Whether or not I agree with their politics, our accomplishment isn't any less important. The people involved are more important than one man and what he did or didn't do."

Simone might not agree, but then again, she wasn't a Toronto building developer. "Well then, I guess we should get down to business."

The scent of his aftershave washed over her as he turned and moved to one of the two seats opposite the sizable black desk that took up a large part of the back wall. "Have a seat, Ms. Leblanc."

"Oh, you can call me Simone."

"Then it's Dylan." He pulled out her chair, and she sat down, acutely aware of the weight of his gaze on the back of her head. Something had changed between last night and this morning, though she couldn't put her finger on it. His tone of voice lacked the teasing notes that he'd had in the limo. "You want to know why I started the site."

"I do. I mean, you're a successful, rich man who could have any man or woman he wanted with a simple snap of the fingers. Why would someone like you want to start a site like that?"

"You saw the newspaper article." Dylan took the seat opposite her, tugging up his dress pants as he did. "Because I don't believe in love."

Simone had her pen poised just above her notepad, ready to make notes, but the moment he spoke, she apparently lost the ability to write. She frowned and leaned forward. "Pardon?"

"I don't think it's that difficult a concept. I don't believe in love. I think the single population deserves a place where they can meet, hook up, exchange money for time or sex or whatever else two consenting adults can agree upon. I don't think people should be wasting their time and money getting married when they're probably going to get divorced."

"That's an incredibly pessimistic view on life." While she hadn't set out to find love, Simone always believed that it came to people eventually. She'd never met anyone who not only wanted to remain single but didn't even believe in love. "Don't you get lonely?"

"Of course. Horny too." His gaze ducked down her body with the briefest of flicks, before snapping back to her eyes. It happened so quickly, Simone wondered if she'd imagined it. "That doesn't mean I need to fall in love with someone. Or get married."

"You created millionairesugardaddy.com so you can hook up with men or women—"

"Women. Mostly."

He's trying to melt my brain. "Mostly women for sex. Because you don't believe in love."

"Yes."

God, he looked so proud of that statement that she didn't know how to respond. This was a bigger story than even she'd realized. "I can't do this interview."

"I'm surprised. You were so keen last night." He stood up and held out his hand. "I'll respect your decision."

"I can't do the interview, because this is bigger than an hour-long conversation. The Candy King needs to have a long-form story. If I simply write that you're anti-love and marriage, too many people are going to brush you off, going to discount everything you say because they won't believe you're that selfish."

Dylan's hand fell back to his side. "Wanting to be single isn't selfish."

"I'm not saying that I agree with it, but that's what people believe. I don't know about you, but I want people to take what you say seriously. To understand the irony of how many of your clients have found love when they've been searching for something that is the complete opposite."

Excitement welled inside her, sending her blood racing. This was going to be amazing. All she needed to do was follow Dylan around, get to know what it was about him that not only made him happily single but how that had morphed into love for other people.

She finally stood, shoving her notebook into her purse as she did. "Okay, so I'm going to start today if that's okay. I'll just shadow you, get to know the type of man you are during the day, and then see the contrast to the man who runs the site. It shouldn't take more than a few weeks, a month at most. I mean, I won't be with you all the time. I'll go back and forth between my job and yours and all that. But it will be great. And I don't know if I'll even have to give your real name at this point, because the interview is like way more than that now. This is going to be awesome."

"No."

Simone was ready for this. "I can sign whatever NDAs you need me to, and I'll even offer my services where I can. I mean, I can answer phones and do some ad copy if you want. That was one of my summer jobs to pay for college. Seriously, it's going to be great!"

"No."

The earlier spark of amusement that had shone in his eyes was gone. The rich brown that had given her warm fuzzies before now chilled her. Simone swallowed, her body instantly tensed. "Really?"

"I know you must feel betrayed or misled, which wasn't my intention. When you reached out to me on the site, I thought we were simply going to have a good time with some online flirting. I never asked for this. I can't have a reporter following me, inserted into my life while I work. I won't have you digging up bits and pieces of my background to help propel you in your career. I won't risk everything that I've built just for your story."

A thousand arguments flashed through her mind as to why he should let her do this. One look at him and she knew none of them would work. None of them would be able to put him at ease because at the end of the day, she was a reporter, and she'd follow the story where it led. Even if—*especially* if—that was to a place Dylan wouldn't like.

She wouldn't sit here and lie to him and tell him that she wouldn't follow her instincts with this. It didn't matter that she didn't know him well; she wouldn't mislead anyone. Even if it wasn't her intention to cause him problems, sometimes things happened.

Moving the purse strap away from the dip of her cleavage, where it had fallen, Simone tried to hide her disappointment. "Is there anything I can say to change your mind?"

"No."

"Well, I won't take up any more of your time." Turning, she strode to the door with as much pride as she could muster. "Thank you, Mr. Williams."

"Dylan."

She stopped and looked back at him, surprised when he looked disappointed. "Dylan."

Then she left.

* * * *

Dylan didn't know if he wanted to punch the wall or chase after her. Neither option was ideal, so instead, he moved to his desk and turned his computer on. It didn't take long to let the tide of work wash over him, to drown out the momentary blip of fun and attraction he'd felt for Simone. Her excitement at wanting to do a story on him and the site was intoxicating, to the point where he almost forgot what was at stake if her little exposé went public.

If anyone knew he was the Candy King, it would make his life hell.

His office door pushed open, and his father marched in as though an army was fast on his heels. "We have a problem."

"When do we not have a problem?" The truth of the matter was they'd been in a good place for a long time. He couldn't imagine what was wrong. "Business or personal?"

"Yes." Dad strode up to his desk and leaned both hands on it to look down at him. "With your brother getting married, we've had renewed interest in the company from a community perspective."

"Fine." The Williamses were one of the more prominent families in Toronto, so that in itself wasn't all that surprising. But from the look on his dad's face, he could tell there was more to the story than that. "What's the issue?"

"I've gotten a sneak peek at the latest quarterly results. We're not going to hit our target."

Dylan was on his feet in a flash. "What? Since when was that even in question? We just hit the forty percent sales mark for the downtown condo building. We should be well in the black."

"We will be. Next quarter." Dad moved to sit down on one of the chairs and closed his eyes.

"What the hell's going on? I saw our last financial report, and everything was well on track." Dylan was about to ask again when he the realization hit him. "It was Jonathan. What did he do?"

"Apparently, he made an executive decision to support a community housing project that Sarah put him on. A pet project of hers that has something to do with a Buddhist temple housing complex that will be used to help people with mental disorders. Noble, but not something the company budgeted for. And certainly not something your brother is able to manage."

A wave of exhaustion hit him hard enough to force Dylan back down to his seat. "What do I need to do?"

Because at the end of the day, he was always the one who had to step in and make sure the projects got done on time and under budget. He was the one who had to ensure that the family image was sparkling so no future plans would be tainted. Dylan was the glue that kept everything together while everyone else went out and lived their lives.

It was one of the reasons he'd started the website, why he'd used the persona of Candy King in the first place. There he could be anything he wanted, do anything he wanted for himself. That was the main reason he hadn't wanted Simone to do a piece on the site. He tried to keep that part of his life secret, not because he was embarrassed, but because he didn't want to share it with anyone else.

Jonathan or even his father would find out and want to use it for their own purposes. Not to mention the potential damage to the family business. No, the sugar daddy site was his alone, and he'd do anything to make sure it stayed that way.

Even if it meant continuing to stretch himself thin.

"I'll talk to Jonathan and see what he's committed to. I'll run the numbers and make sure the budget and timelines work."

"A Buddhist housing complex?" Dad snorted. "It won't fill up, and we'll end up taking a bath."

"We just need to make sure that the community is made aware of options that are available to them. Hell, this might end up not only raising the profile of Williams Development but be a great resource for Toronto."

"I don't know the first thing about how to spin this."

Neither did Dylan, not precisely. But he knew of a particular blond local reporter who would be perfect to help them get the word out. "Leave it with me. I'll take care of everything."

Fate had a horrible sense of humor. Dylan pulled out Simone's business card, which he'd tucked into his pocket the night before. It seemed she was going to get her interview after all, just not the one she'd hoped for.

"I need to make a call."

Chapter 8

As Simone walked down the street to the office, she had to focus her attention on not running into random strangers. From the moment she'd slid out of bed this morning, her brain was otherwise occupied—with her dual problems of Dylan and what the hell she was going to tell her boss.

She'd run through multiple scenarios about how to tell Carl about her massive failure as she'd been lying in bed that morning. Flowers? He was allergic. Food? While usually a safe bet, he'd joined Weight Watchers a few months ago, and she didn't have a clue about the points for his favorite foods. She'd no doubt screw that up too because that was her life these days.

What she didn't want was to have to walk into his office empty-handed and inform him that yes, he was entirely correct about her ability to pull in and deliver a big story.

But that was precisely what she was going to have to do.

She'd played yesterday over and over in her mind, trying to figure out if there was something different she could have done. She'd expected Dylan to be flirty in person the way he'd been with her online. And yes, his physical presence did things to her that she hadn't anticipated; there was no mistaking the mental and emotional wall he'd thrown up between them the moment she'd announced who she was outside of the restaurant. Except for a brief moment in the limo when she'd gotten a hint of the man behind the mask, she felt as though she knew less about him now than she had before she'd tracked him down.

Which was more than a little fucked up.

Something had happened to Dylan Williams that had caused him to shut himself off from forming deep personal relationships. She'd been friends with Kayla through her divorce, so she knew what a broken heart looked like. This was something more, something deeper, a wound he'd had so long that he might not even be aware that it still festered.

Not that any of this mattered, because he'd made it clear there was no way he would talk to her again.

Her office building was just ahead, which meant there was not a lot of time before she had to face the music. So, of course, she ducked into Starbucks and got in line. While she might not be able to bribe Carl into going easy on her, she could at least buy herself a mocha latte to boost her spirits.

Her phone rested heavy in her pocket rather than in her purse. She'd slipped it there so she could feel and hear the vibrations in case she got any notifications. Not that she anticipated Dylan reaching out to her through the app, but there was a small part of her that was still hopeful he might.

Shit, everything had been going so well until she'd tracked him down. She hadn't realized how much fun she'd been having talking to him, being silly, not having to worry about trying to impress him. They were just two people with nothing to lose and everything to gain texting on the Internet.

She missed talking to him.

Over the past few weeks, they'd chatted and teased back and forth throughout the day, from the moment she woke up to just before she went to bed. They weren't long or serious conversations, sometimes not even conversations at all. Quips, jokes, teasing. It couldn't have gone anywhere, not really. She was a reporter working on a story, and he was the subject. All of their interactions up to the point where she'd revealed who and what she was were tainted by that omission. She didn't blame him for pulling away.

But she did wish there was a way she could start over.

Simone's hand slipped into her pocket as she moved forward in line. What would he do if she texted him? Would he delete it, and before or after he read it? Or would he have blocked her by now? Did she even have the right to talk to him any longer, seeing as the entire basis of their communication was based on a lie?

What would happen if she sent him a note right now?

"Welcome to Starbucks. What can I get started for you?"

Simone blinked at the young woman behind the counter before smiling. "Ah, hi. Can I get a grande mocha latte?"

"Anything else? Something to eat?"

I'd love to have a bite of Dylan. "Nope, I'm good."

"Your name?"

For the briefest of moments, she almost said Sugar Tart. "Simone."

Moving to the side to wait for her drink, she looked down at her phone, now out of her pocket with its screen on. There was no message indicator for the sugar daddy app, which meant that Dylan hadn't mysteriously changed his mind. If anything was going to happen, it would be on her to reach out. At the very least, she should probably apologize for having tracked him down when he wasn't interested in meeting her.

Right? That was a thing she should do.

Looking around to make sure no one was reading over her shoulder, Simone opened the app and their message thread, and began typing.

Hey. I just wanted to say I'm sorry for having come at you the way I did. You'd been clear in needing time, and I didn't honor that request. But I'm not sorry that we were able to meet. I—

She paused, not knowing how to accurately express how she felt. It wasn't on him to make her happy, to be her friend—online or otherwise—or to worry about her emotional state. Dylan was a man who'd been up front in his expectations. He didn't want or need a relationship. He used his own program to arrange a sexual contact with women when he wanted to. And that was it. Even if that scenario broke her heart a little bit, that was on her, not him.

With a quick glance to see if her drink was ready, she fired off the rest of the message without overthinking it.

I miss our talks. I miss flirting with you, even if nothing was going to come from it. I miss feeling desirable. You made me feel that, and I want to thank you. It was fun while it lasted. And I want to let you know that this will be the last time you'll hear from me.
Be well, Candy King.
ST

"Grande mocha latte for Simone."

She shoved her phone deep into her purse, grabbed her drink, and bolted for work. She didn't have time to worry about Dylan any longer, not when she had to tell Carl that she'd failed and was going to need another assignment. Following the crowd, she stepped into the elevator and mentally prepared for the crap she was about to face.

Okay. I can totally do this.

Taking a sip, she mentally braced herself as the elevator announced her floor and the doors slid open. She'd gotten three steps before Mark came striding out to the lobby, his blue eyes wide and wild. The second his gaze landed on her, his finger came up, and he wordlessly pointed at her.

"Mark…hi?" Sure, they might not get along on a personal level, but professionally they were always civil. She slowed her approach, suddenly concerned that she was about to get fired. Or worse. "What's going on?"

"Carl needs to see you." Mark's face flushed red, and the muscles in the side of his jaw jumped as he snapped his mouth shut.

"Am I in trouble?" There was no way Carl could have known about her failure yet, and the last story she'd been on had already gone to print. "Is the paper in trouble?"

"Just go see him." He then spun around and marched back to his office.

Simone looked over at the intern—Monica, who was operating the front desk—and frowned. "Do you know what's going on?"

Monica shrugged. "I just got here five minutes ago."

Well, shit. "I guess I better go see Carl."

Simone was more intrigued than scared now, especially after Mark's reaction. If nothing else, it would serve as a temporary distraction before she'd have to tell him the bad news. With her latte in one hand and her other hand grasping her still-stained purse, she strode to Carl's office.

The sound of voices rumbled through the half-closed door as she approached. Carl's was obvious, and the other was familiar, even though she couldn't quite place it. Had her brain been working at full force, she wouldn't have been quite so shocked when she knocked on the door and stepped in.

Dylan stood to the side of the office, his arms crossed and his attention focused on a physical newspaper that Carl was showing him. "Ah, hi."

The second he looked up and their gazes met, a shot of lust pulsed through Simone's body. It was the same reaction she'd had when she'd first laid eyes on him outside the restaurant, a reaction at how overtly sexual this man was. It wasn't merely his looks either. There was a presence to him that exuded confidence and an aura that blinded her to nearly everything else.

Her mouth opened, and she was about to say something when she noticed that he had his phone in his hand. She didn't need to be able to see the screen to know that he'd just read her message. There was a look in his eyes, something possessive and primal, and it was directed toward her.

She sucked in a breath through her nose as she looked from his phone to his eyes. He cocked an eyebrow as he put the phone back into his pocket.

Okay, so that's a future conversation she hadn't anticipated having.

"It's about time you showed up. You're late." Carl snapped the paper shut and stepped forward. "I'm sorry for the delay, Mr. Williams. Simone here is normally far more punctual than this, and it shouldn't reflect poorly on the paper."

What the funky fresh hell was going on? She looked between the men and shrugged. "I…I'm sorry?"

"Good. Now have a seat."

Simone cocked an eyebrow at Dylan when Carl turned his back on her. He flashed her one of his seductive smiles and moved behind one of the guest chairs. "Ms. Leblanc, I was just telling Carl here how impressed I was with your article on the last Toronto Marathon. You did an excellent job spotlighting the multigenerational family that had driven in from the Maritimes to participate. I knew when I saw that story that you were the right person for the job."

By the end of his speech, Simone had to sit down on the chair he'd pulled out for her, more due to shock than anything else. Dylan was here, pretending they'd never met before, talking about a piece she'd written months earlier, and asking her to write something for him. She knew things eventually would start to make sense. Any moment now.

"Thanks." She pulled her purse closer to her body. "What job are you talking about?"

"His company is looking to open a special community building and wants our paper to do a piece on it." Carl sat down behind his desk and glared at Simone. "So that little side project of yours needs to be shut down for the time being. This takes priority."

"Of course." It should have felt overwhelming to have Carl act so aggressive with Dylan standing behind her shoulder. But instead his presence at her back was strangely reassuring. "I'll make Mr. Williams's story my focus."

Dylan stepped to the side and held out his hand. "Thank you, Miss Leblanc. And please call me Dylan."

She stood and shook his hand, her skin soaking in the heat from his touch. "I'm Simone."

"I'm sorry my arrival has changed things for you. But I knew after reading your piece that only you would be able to do justice to the opening of our new center."

There was a ton of subtext behind his words, but Simone was too confused to bother teasing out their meaning. "Thank you. It will be wonderful to sit down with you and learn more about what your goals are for the piece."

There was always an angle when someone approached them to do a community piece. Dylan might not want to be outed as the Candy King, but something obviously had changed from the last time they'd spoken for him to approach her to do this story.

If she were going to be spending time with him anyway, she'd still have the chance to do her article on the sugar daddy site. Shit, if she could produce two stories for Carl, he'd have no choice but to give her better assignments.

And if it meant she had to spend more time with Dylan, then that wasn't exactly going to be a hardship for her.

"Dylan, if you have time now, I'd love to sit down with you and get some background information on your project. It wouldn't take long, and then I could arrange a longer meeting with your office at a more convenient time."

He didn't look away, but something changed in his expression, and for the life of her, she couldn't quite put her finger on it. It appeared to be attraction or maybe pure curiosity on his part—either way, something was going on between them. She was going to have to be extra cautious because she didn't need the complication of a man in her life. If Carl even caught a whiff that there was something improper going on between them, she knew damn well that she'd be the one who'd be punished.

No, everything about this interview—even her side project—had to be 110 percent professional. She couldn't risk the setback.

Dylan took out his phone and checked a few e-mails. "I have a meeting at one, but I have lots of time to get there. Let's have a chat now."

"Are you sure you don't want me to grab Mark as well?" Carl leaned back in his seat, his eyes darting between them. "As a backup. I'd hate for anything to fall through or for you to not get the story you were hoping for."

Simone cringed. Yes, she was used to her boss not showing much in the way of confidence in her abilities to do a good job, but having that vocalized so readily in front of a reader and now client hurt more than she'd ever admit aloud.

"No, Simone's style and ability to tell a compelling story are exactly what Williams Development needs. We need someone who can highlight the human element, and based on what I've read from your other reporters, she's the best person for the job. But I can always go over to the *Star* and talk to–"

"Simone will do an excellent job." Carl was on his feet and ushering them out the door in a heartbeat. "There's an empty conference room down the hall to the left. That would be the best place for you to talk. Simone, I expect you to keep me posted on your progress."

"Yes, sir. I'll make sure it's in my weekly status updates." Her smile firmly in place, she motioned toward the room. "This way."

Dylan didn't say anything until she shut the door, giving them a small measure of privacy, despite the large bank of windows that allowed people to see inside. "Your boss is an asshole."

"He can be old-fashioned. Carl just wants to make sure the paper is getting the best quality of work that it can. He still doesn't quite get the whole online thing, but even he is slowly being dragged into the twenty-first century."

"That sounds like something you've said more than once. You shouldn't have to make excuses for him."

Was she? Simone never even considered that she'd defended Carl. Whenever she said stuff like that, it always felt more like self-preservation. "He's my boss. He's the one who has the final say on what I get to report on. I have to play the game better than my male colleagues just to inch my way and maybe even the playing field."

"It doesn't need to be that way. There are other papers, other online sites that would love to have a journalist of your abilities."

"You don't even know what I write. But thank you for the vote of confidence."

He rolled his eyes. "I wasn't bullshitting him. I went back and read several of your stories last night when I realized we were going to need someone to do a story on the housing complex. I wanted to make sure you really were as good as I suspected you were before I came down here."

Simone shook her head. "You mean this story thing is real?"

"Why did you think I came down?"

"I..." That was a good question. "I don't know. To give me a second shot at doing my story on your site? Because that would be the thing that Carl would have to acknowledge. I'd prove to him that I'm better than food truck and marathon stories."

He sat down on the edge of the conference table, causing his pants to pull tight against his thighs. Simone had to fight to keep from staring at what were clearly well-developed muscles. "Is that what you want?"

God, there were so many things she wanted, things she had no doubt Dylan would be very, very good at delivering. "I want to make a name for myself." *And multiple orgasms.*

He nodded, his gaze dropping to the floor as he frowned. "I read your message."

His voice had softened as his hands twitched. Dylan sucked in a breath before looking her in the eye and smiled. That single look, the naked desire she saw staring back at her was enough to send her heart racing to her throat.

"Yeah, so I wasn't anticipating ever seeing you again. Had I known you were in my boss's office I never, *ever* would have sent that. I mean, I'd hate for you to think—"

"How about we make a deal?"

Get naked and fuck, then go out to dinner? She gave her head a shake. "What kind of deal?"

"The housing development is going to be done in the next three or four months. We're repurposing one of our existing sites for use. You spend time with me, interviewing the people involved, the positive impact on the community, and all that. In those three or four months, I'll agree to give you the information you want on the sugar daddy site. You can profile me, but I do not give you permission to reveal my name. I'll simply be known as the Candy King. Everything else, though, I'll agree is fair game. I'll show you what that world is like and why I've done what I have."

Dylan stood again, and his very presence seemed to fill the room. Simone's heart pounded with every step closer he took until she could barely breathe. Her hands shook at her sides in anticipation of…she didn't know what. Him touching her was out of the question, and there was no way in hell she'd give in to this weird impulse to throw her hands around his neck and kiss him.

No, no, no, that wasn't happening.

His gaze roamed her face before finally coming back to her eyes. There was a foot of distance between them, but as far as that look went, their bodies could have been pressed against one another. She licked her lips. "I can work with that."

"Good. Me too." He held out his hand once more for her to shake. "I'll have my secretary add you to the relevant meetings. And for every hour you spend working on this story, I agree to give you an hour on the website. Deal?"

This time when she slipped her hand into his, there was no mistaking the connection between them. Simone shivered, unable to keep her gaze on his. "Deal. I'll look forward to her e-mail."

She jumped when someone knocked on the window. A group of five people stood out in the hallway, looking in at them. "Shit, someone has the room booked."

Dylan finally dropped her hand and stepped back. "That's fine. I think we're done here anyway. I'll be in touch soon."

And with a smile, he left.

Simone didn't move immediately, even when the people from the hall filed into the conference room. It wasn't until Connie from accounting came up beside her that she also realized she'd been staring after Dylan.

"Who the hell was that, and when are the two of you going out?"

"Dylan Williams and never."

Connie snorted. "I haven't seen that much eye-fucking in years. If you don't do something about that, I'm seriously worried for you."

"Carl would fire me in half a second if he even suspected I'd do something like that."

"You wouldn't be the first person to fall for someone you did a story on. I'm sure he'd adjust."

"Not with me, he wouldn't." Wrapping her arms around herself, Simone looked behind her. "Sorry, I'll leave you guys to it."

Simone headed straight for the bathroom because there was no way she'd be able to focus on work until she cooled the hell off. She was going to have to come up with a plan to check her libido if she was going to survive the next few months.

Because, sexy source or not, she wasn't going to jeopardize her job for anything. Not even for the chance to sleep with Dylan Williams.

Chapter 9

It was probably a bit childish, but Dylan made sure that he didn't see Simone for at least a week after their initial meeting. Sure, he probably could have had her come to one of the planning meetings, if for no other reason than it would have provided good background on what they were hoping to accomplish with the project. He could have, but after their brief exchange in the conference room, he knew there was no way he could see her again that soon. He'd been hard as a fucking rock for an hour after he'd left the paper, to the point where he'd considered jerking off in the bathroom when he'd gotten back to the office. He'd managed to get himself under control before it had come to that, but clearly, he was going to need some space before inflicting Simone on himself once again.

And then there was the app.

While he might not have seen her in person over the past few days, he could feel her presence on his phone. He'd kept every message they'd ever shared, loathe to delete them. He'd told himself it was for his own safety, to have a record of what she'd said just in case he ever needed some protection. It was a lie, especially after the message she'd sent after she thought they'd never talk to one another again.

He'd been looking for an excuse to not talk to Carl for even a few more minutes when he'd pulled out his phone to read whatever message had come through. When he saw it was from her, his curiosity was more than he could resist, and he opened it up.

Arousal and sympathy were an odd combination for him to have experienced at that moment. And yet that was precisely what he'd felt. He'd wanted nothing more than to track her down and pull her into a hug—which was so unlike him, the thought was more than a little terrifying.

Simone's boss was rough around the edges and apparently wasn't convinced Simone knew what she was doing. No wonder she'd been trying as hard as she could to do the sugar daddy story. Though Dylan couldn't help but think it was a shame. Simone had a real knack for getting to the heart of a story. He really had enjoyed the marathon article she'd done, so it hadn't been a hard sell at all when he'd told his dad about his plan.

Having seen her and spent time with her, Dylan couldn't help but want to help her, even if that meant putting his own reputation at risk.

And that wasn't like him at all.

Somehow, he knew that Simone wasn't a threat to him. While she was up front about wanting to make a name for herself, she was too conciliatory, too kind and accommodating to print anything without his permission. The problem was, spending time with her, keeping her in his orbit on a regular basis was going to be hell on his libido.

That woman was able to pull out lustful thoughts from him in a way he hadn't experienced in years. The prospect of amazing sex with her was excellent, but there was something else about her that attracted him. She made him smile, even laugh, in a way that he'd never admit to another human being. Their moments of easy flirting had quickly become the bright spots in his day, and now that they had stopped, Dylan found himself missing them.

Missing her.

And those feelings could only lead to disaster.

"Hey, are you even listening to me?"

Dylan looked over to where Jonathan was standing at the work site. "Sorry. Say it again?"

"We're going to need to gut the kitchen for sure, turn it into something a bit more industrial to be able to handle twelve people." Jonathan strode around the work site, blueprints rolled up in his hand as he spoke over the noise. "I've done up a design that I think will work, but I need you to look at the budget to see if I've gotten too close to the wire."

It had been a long time since he'd seen Jonathan this excited about a work project. His brother was a gifted architect, but since his last divorce, he'd been less enthused about work. Now he was sporting a smile that could power a small city for a year.

"I'm sure you've taken everything into account." Dylan was the numbers guy, which was critical to the project's success, but far less sexy a job. "We'll look everything over at tomorrow's update meeting." He looked at the door, half expecting Simone to be there, waiting for him. She wasn't.

"Is someone late?" Jonathan bobbed him on the head before tucking the blueprints back under his arm. "You keep looking at the door."

"The reporter from the *Record* is supposed to stop by today. She's the one I mentioned last week who's going to help us put a spotlight on this and drum up business so Sarah's dream project gets off the ground."

"Not just her dream. I happen to believe in this as well." Jonathan shook his head, not bothering to hide his annoyance. "It's going to be great for everyone. It's about time we did another project for the city. Toronto has given our family a lot, and we need to make sure we're repaying the favor."

"That sounds like Sarah talking." Not that she wasn't right, but it was utterly fascinating to hear his brother parroting the words.

"It does, but I agree with her." Jonathan's gaze drifted off to the side as he smiled. "She's really helped me see things with fresh eyes. Not only Toronto but our family, myself, everything. It's refreshing."

And if Dylan hadn't seen his brother in love before now, he might believe things were different this time. But this was marriage number three for him, and within a few years, Dylan knew that Jonathan would show up in tears, his heart in tatters because something horrible had happened and he was now on his own.

That was the way of the Williams family, and Dylan long ago vowed never to fall into that trap.

"Excuse me, is Dylan here?"

At the sound of Simone's voice, his cock went hard. Jonathan straightened, gave him a smug look that made Dylan want to punch him, and marched over to Simone. "Hey, I'm his brother Jonathan. I'm the lead on this project. Great to meet you."

Dylan braced himself before he turned around to see her, knowing he would have to be extra vigilant to keep himself in check. It was a good thing he did because the dark green shirt Simone wore clung to her breasts and waist in a way that should be illegal. Not to mention the way the black skirt hugged her hips and thighs. She was professionally dressed, with her blond hair piled high on her head and her black-rimmed glasses drawing attention to her cheekbones.

Her drink-stained purse was draped over her shoulder, a reminder of the night they'd met. Why she hadn't gotten rid of it or replaced it with another bag was beyond him. He wasn't a sentimental person, but the bag must have some deeper meaning beyond a fashion item.

She smiled as she shook Jonathan's hand. "It's wonderful to meet you. I've been reading up on the project, and I have to say I think this is going to be perfect for this community. The world definitely needs more zen in our lives. And people with mental health challenges need to have more safe places where they can live."

It was fascinating to watch her interact with others. She had an easy way about her that seemed to put everyone at ease and drew out their smiles. Except for her boss, Simone seemed to be able to do that with just about everyone. Even he wasn't immune to her bubbly charm. When Jonathan lifted her hand to kiss the back of it, Dylan immediately crossed the room to them.

"Let's not sexually harass a reporter." He took Simone's hand away from Jonathan, rubbing the back of it with his thumb before letting it go.

Jonathan's eyes widened. "I didn't mean to do anything...sorry."

"It's fine. I've experienced worse." She pulled out her phone and held it up. "Would either of you mind if I took a few pictures for my own reference? These wouldn't be used in print or online, but I like to be able to reference pictures when I'm writing up my accounts."

"Fine with me." Jonathan grinned. "I see now why my brother asked you to do the feature." When Simone cocked an eyebrow, Jonathan continued. "You're very organized and forward thinking. He's the same way, which is why he likes you."

Simone blushed as she pushed up on the bridge of her glasses. "Thanks. Um, yeah. So, where are we going to start?"

This would continue to be Jonathan embarrassing her if Dylan didn't step in and take control. He pulled the blueprints out from under Jonathan's arm and held them out. "You need to take these and make sure you have everything double-checked before the city engineer gets here. I'll take Simone around and show her what we're starting with. We can meet up tomorrow at the office." He made sure that his tone of voice left no room for Jonathan to argue.

"Sounds good." Jonathan's grin widened. "It was wonderful to meet you, Simone. I'm sure we'll see a lot of one another over the next few months."

"Thanks. Good to meet you too."

Dylan handed the blueprints back to his brother and quickly led Simone in the other direction. "Sorry about that. He's a bit much some days."

"It's fine. Seriously, he didn't do anything wrong." She looked around the space, her gaze passing over the exposed brick and beams. "This place is amazing."

Dylan liked to think of himself as pragmatic, the one who could see the value in any project presented to him. This building had the potential to be a unique jewel in their family crown if it was done correctly. The problem with these old warehouses was you never knew what you were going to find when you started to open the walls. The project could go from manageable to bank-breaking with a single discovery. And there was no way a Buddhist commune would be able to afford to cover the costs if they got out of hand.

"It has potential." He just needed to make sure everything was under control. "While we are really just retrofitting the place, there are still a lot of moving parts we need to consider."

Simone stopped at the foot of the metal staircase that led to the second floor. A beam of sunlight splashed across her shoulder and down her arm, accentuating her skin. Dylan almost reached out to touch her, to feel if her skin was as soft there as he imagined it would be. He wanted to press his nose against the hairline just behind her ear to see if she smelled as sweet up close as she did from afar.

When she turned and met his gaze, her blush returned. "An hour here means you owe me an hour to talk about the site." Her throat bobbed as she swallowed. "When do I get to claim it?"

Fuck, the site again.

It was a solid deal on her part, one he shouldn't have proposed. But despite knowing it was a bad idea, he couldn't help but want to spend as much time with her as he could. Besides, what harm could come of promoting the sugar daddy site? If anything, it would increase his exposure and business. He'd be even more prosperous, and she'd get the exposure she'd craved.

Right, this was all business. Smart business. Nothing more.

"What are you doing tonight?" If she really wanted to know what it was like to be in a sugar daddy relationship, then who was he to deny her the experience.

"Nothing."

She reached up and touched the side of her neck. His cock twitched.

"I was going to head home after we were done here. Watch Netflix and eat leftover pizza."

"I'll pick you up, take you to supper, and answer your questions about the site. A few at least."

She lit up at the word *supper*. "I'll never say no to food. Though it sounds like it's going to take more than an hour."

"We'll talk about this project too. Just to keep things fair." Shit, it was far too easy to tease her, to slip into an easy back-and-forth that made him smile. "I'll pick you up at seven?"

"Ah, sure." She looked down at the floor. "But we'd better get started here, or else you'll have to pay for an extra-long meal later."

He really should be enjoying the idea of that, and yet...

"This way, Ms. Leblanc. Let me tell you about my brother's crazy idea."

* * * *

Simone burst into the lobby of her apartment building, thankful beyond belief that Kayla was already there waiting for her. "Oh my God, I have a date with a millionaire."

Kayla cocked an eyebrow, her painted red lips twitching into a smile. "Really?"

She'd expected her friend's teasing, but it wasn't exactly something she had time for right now. Grabbing Kayla by the hand, Simone pulled her onto the elevator. "You can pick on me upstairs as you help me figure out what to wear."

Her apartment building wasn't huge, nor very posh, but Simone loved it. There were only ten families in the whole place, and the rent had been firmly set long ago, so she didn't have to worry about the price going up so much that she couldn't afford it. The people who lived here had been around for years, and they'd formed a de facto family. Everyone knew Simone and, by default, Kayla. So when they marched past several of her neighbors, she didn't need to worry about offending anyone when she was less than pleasant.

"Date problems, Mrs. Lee." Simone sighed loudly even as her elderly neighbor laughed. "I needed the expert."

"It's a sad day when you're considering me the expert." Kayla gently pulled her hand free and came willingly into Simone's apartment. "Though I'd be mortally offended if you hadn't called me for fashion advice."

"I have the ear and eyes of the founder of Fashion Finds on speed dial, and you think I wouldn't call you?" Simone snorted. "I'm neurotic, not an idiot."

Simone kicked off her shoes and continued straight through to her bedroom. She knew Kayla would take her time, probably get them a glass of wine on the way, but Simone had jumped headfirst into panic-land. Regardless of how causal Dylan had been about dinner tonight—how it was nothing more than an opportunity for them to work on the two stories—Simone couldn't help but hope something more would come from this.

Not sex, because that was crossing a bunch of professional barriers that she wasn't willing to pass. But establishing a good working relationship with him was going to be critical to her success over the next few months. And if she was able to do a little bit of flirting and maybe set the groundwork for a relationship when all this professional stuff was over, then she was going to be sure she had on the sexiest dress she could find.

Kayla did, in fact, come into her bedroom with two glasses of wine and handed one to Simone before sitting on the edge of the bed. "Give me the short version, please."

"Dylan Williams." She pulled out a red dress that showed more cleavage than Simone possessed and tossed it to the floor.

"I've met him a few times. Nice man, is anti-relationships beyond sexual encounters. He's apparently great in bed, though that's not firsthand experience."

"He's the Candy King." She threw an emerald green pantsuit to the floor. "Though if you tell anyone that, I'll probably get fired and sued. Not necessarily in that order."

Kayla began coughing, and Simone had to quickly rescue her wine and make sure she was okay. "Dylan Williams is the owner of the sugar daddy site?"

"Oh. Yes. I guess I might need to give you the long story."

"Yes please."

It didn't take long to fill her in, but by the time Simone was done, Kayla couldn't stop shaking her head. "Why do you want to push this? If he doesn't want his identity revealed, you can't do that."

"And I'm not going to. Even without his real name, the story is going to help move me out of these fluff pieces and into something real." Simone sat down on the bed beside Kayla and took a drink. "Carl doesn't take me seriously, no matter how hard I work or how good my stories are. If I'm ever going to make it big, I need to get a boost."

Kayla shook her head. "You were always so happy doing those community pieces. What changed?"

Simone was back on her feet in front of the closet. "Nothing changed. Can't a girl simply want to achieve more in her life?"

"I'm the last person who's going to judge you. But that wasn't my question. Why do *you* want more? The last time you spoke about your job, you were thrilled to be the voice of the little person. Something changed, and I want to know why."

She really didn't want to know, because if Simone told Kayla that she'd been embarrassed at the paper's internal awards ceremony last month—where she'd received not a single acknowledgment for the work she'd done since her arrival three years earlier—she would only tell her to brush it off.

But it hurt, working her ass off and barely getting a pat on the back while her colleagues seemed to fly past her professionally. She'd never expected to get rich or famous being a journalist, but she'd at the very least hoped she'd have gotten *something* to recognize her accomplishments by now.

And yes, she wanted to be able to show her dad that she was doing great. That she was living the dream he hadn't been able to accomplish himself. The community pieces were fun, and she got to learn about the ins and outs of the city, usually while being fed some of the best food Toronto had to offer. But every time she showed her dad another article with her name on the byline and it wasn't some hard-hitting exposé, she saw his disappointment. It would be nice if once, just once, she could see a spark in his eyes and know that he was proud of her.

Kayla had become a billionaire when she was in her early twenties, so it wasn't exactly like she understood how Simone felt. She'd accomplished everything she'd set out to achieve and far more.

"Simone?"

She glanced briefly over her shoulder. "Can you help me pick something out?"

Kayla sighed, got up, and came over to the closet. It took her three seconds of looking to pick out a cute floral-print dress that came down to Simone's knees, clung to her waist and chest, but was professional enough that she wouldn't have to worry about the image she projected. "This one will look sweet on you."

"Thanks." She took it from her, holding it tight to her chest. "I hate being left behind. I hate being told that I have talent, a spark that everyone can see, but then never getting to that next step with my career. I'm...tired. And lonely. And I just want something to go my way for once. If I can break this sugar daddy site story, then I'll at least have a chance."

Kayla pulled her in for a hug. "If it's what you want, then I'm here to help you however I can. I just want you to be true to yourself."

"Yeah well, being true to myself doesn't exactly pay the bills." Taking the dress off the hanger, she did her best to push down the unexpected melancholy. "Let me put this on, and you can tell me how I look."

"I'll be here drinking your wine."

Simone went into her bathroom but didn't bother to shut the door. It wasn't anything Kayla hadn't seen before. "Do you know why Dylan has sworn off relationships? He's good-looking and rich, so I'm sure he's had his fair share of fortune hunters to deal with."

"I don't know him well, but I have an associate who dated him for a while."

"Yeah?" Simone shimmied into the dress and even managed to zip it up with little difficulty, before going to work on her hair. "And?"

"He told her up front that all he could offer was sex and a good time. It wasn't anything personal; he simply didn't believe that long-term relationships could work and he didn't want to put himself out there like that." Kayla came into the bathroom and leaned against the door frame. "You look great."

"Thanks." She didn't bother to freshen her makeup, simply adding a bit of lipstick. "That's a pretty sad outlook on life."

"Speaking from experience, it sounds like he's had his heart broken and doesn't want to risk it again. I know that was what I felt after Christoph cheated on me."

"But then you met Devin." They grinned at each other in the mirror. "How's your boy toy anyway? I really am sorry that I showed up the other day and woke him up."

Kayla waved off her concerns. "He's excited about the new school year starting. How he was able to get a long-term teaching contract already, I have no idea. I've never seen a grown man that excited about buying school supplies before in my life."

"He's precious. And he makes you happy, so I will forever love him." With some luck, someday she'd find something or someone that gave her an equal amount of joy.

Maybe Dylan had the right idea. Basing relationships on sex had the advantage that he and the other person could be up front with what they wanted, allowed the individuals to move on without guilt if things didn't work out, and meant that they didn't have to worry if their jobs ended up taking priority.

"I wonder if Dylan uses the sugar daddy site himself?" Kayla cocked her head to the side and tugged down the front of her dress. "He's a man who likes sex and avoids commitments. He must have dipped into that particular pool."

And there was her blush again. No matter how close a friend Kayla was, there was no way in hell Simone was going to admit that she'd tracked him down using the site herself. "I'm sure he does."

Kayla coughed. "You signed up for the site. That's how you found him."

"Of course, you…yes, I did. But that doesn't mean anything."

"It means that you're a sugar baby!" Kayla laughed and shook her head. "I love this."

"A bit too much."

"Come on. Given how you pressured me into signing up, I think it's only fair that I get to tease you. Besides, you might find someone for yourself."

Simone wasn't about to dwell on that because it was ridiculous to think that she'd be one of the lucky ones who'd find love on a sugar daddy site. She'd only done what she had needed to chase her story. That was it. Nothing else. And as soon as this whole thing with Dylan was over, she had every intention of deleting her account.

Kayla, the one with the practical experience with both the sugar daddy site and the falling in love part, was little help. She adjusted Simone's necklace and gave her a from-behind hug. "Never stop being yourself. The world is a better place for it."

Simone snorted. "I guess I'm ready."

"You'll knock him dead."

"I just want to make sure I get the story. That's all this is about." If she happened to get a few good meals out of it as well, then all the better.

Because as much as she wanted to think about being a sugar baby, Simone knew she really did need to be true to herself. And that meant being the best damn reporter she could be, and not mooning over some wealthy businessman.

Simone nodded at herself in the mirror. "Okay then. Let's do this."

Chapter 10

Dylan loved to drive. One of the first things he'd bought when he was out of university and had come into his own fortune was a sports car. Then he bought another when he realized he had more disposable income than was healthy for a single man. His current pride and joy was a Tesla Roadster in cherry red that screamed midlife crisis, even though he was only thirty-seven. He loved the speed, loved the feeling of control, and especially loved taking people who'd never been in a car like this for long rides.

He didn't have a clue if Simone was a person who knew anything about cars, let alone if she enjoyed them. She'd shared a lot over text—favorite movies (*Babe* and *Mean Girls* because who could pick), songs ("Crazy = Genius"), food (gumdrop cake that her mom bakes every Christmas) —but they hadn't gotten around to cars. With each revelation, he found himself mentally taking another step closer to her. It had been a long time since he'd been interested in the private life of a woman, the small details that friends learn slowly over time.

He *shouldn't* care one way or the other what her preferences were, not if he was going to keep his self-proclaimed bachelorhood safely intact. But he couldn't help but want to make her smile, want to see that infectious enthusiasm she had bubble forth and spread. It was part of the reason he'd made a stop before coming over to the address she'd texted to him earlier.

When he pulled up in front of her building, he couldn't help but do a mental evaluation of the premises. As with a lot of older buildings in Toronto, he could immediately see some improvements that needed to be made, that would not only improve the value of the building but would also make life easier for the tenants. Because he was looking at the front door and calculating what changes would need to be made to ensure better safety, he saw Simone the second she stepped outside. There was another woman with her, a dark-haired, thin beauty who looked vaguely familiar, who gave her a hug before sliding into the back seat of a limo that was waiting a short distance away.

Dylan slid from his car to come around to the sidewalk where Simone now stood. "Was that Kayla Arnold?"

"Yup." Simone gave the limo a little wave as it pulled away. "She's my best friend in the world."

"I remember you mentioning her name that first night, but I guess it didn't exactly register." It seemed Simone had more experience with people in his social circles than he'd realized. He wasn't sure if that was a good thing or not. "Are you ready for dinner?"

"Sure." She looked down at the car and smiled. "No limo?"

"Believe it or not, not all billionaires like to be chauffeured around. I only use the company limo when I need to make an impression on a client. Otherwise, I bomb around in this baby."

She ran her hand across the roof and peeked in the window as she smiled. "My dad is a big fan of these. He took me to see one in the Yorkdale Mall once. I didn't quite get the appeal then. Plus, you know, sitting in a car in the mall is kind of lame when you're fifteen."

"Well, you're in for a treat then." Their gazes met, and they grinned simultaneously. "Get in."

Dylan loved that he didn't need to try and impress Simone, that their interactions had to do with work and nothing personal. He could relax and be himself in a way that he usually didn't do, even when he was spending time with his family. Simone knew all his secrets and didn't seem to mind that there was a darker side to him. Well, to his business practices. Dylan wasn't precisely the brooding type.

He turned the car on and realized that Simone hadn't been in an electric car before. "I'm going to warn you, this thing goes fast very quickly."

"I like fast."

"That's surprising." Joy spread through his chest, and he wanted to laugh at the look of excitement on her face. "Are you ready?"

"Oh yeah." She clapped her hands as she looked around at traffic. "Let's do this."

The minute there was a significant lull in traffic, Dylan hit the gas and pulled onto the road. Simone let out a surprised squeak as she was thrown against her seat back by the force of the momentum.

"Shit, it's so quiet!" Then she laughed.

It only took a few seconds for them to catch up to the traffic, and Dylan had to slow back to a reasonable speed, but the momentary burst and Simone's reaction were worth the potential speeding ticket. His heart swelled, and impulsively he reached over and gave her hand a squeeze. "The 401 is a dangerous place for this. Someday I'm going to get in trouble."

She squeezed his hand back, as though it was the most normal thing in the world. "I'd have my license suspended within a week. Holy shit, that's insane."

In the quiet of the car, Dylan could only focus on their breathing and the touch of her skin on his. The smell of her perfume washed over him and made his chest tighten from the sweetness of it all. He didn't dare look at her face, couldn't bear it if she was looking at him with anything other than indifference.

Because Simone was precisely the type of woman who would be a temptation to him if he gave in. They might even have a good time together until the inevitable moment when one of them did or said something that would drive a wedge between them. He gave her hand another little squeeze before returning his attention back to the road.

"I have to be honest. I was thinking about taking you to some fancy restaurant tonight, but we don't have to. Do you have a preference?"

Simone bit her bottom lip and smiled. "Honestly, I'm a big fan of food and will eat just about anywhere." She chuckled. "My mom's a pastry chef who works in a bakery. Most of my best childhood memories center around food. I'm a bit of a fan of eating as a result."

"I think that's great. I love the ritual of eating out, of selecting something special to eat."

"Or getting the same thing at a restaurant every time, just because you love how it makes your soul warm."

Dylan couldn't stop from smiling. "I've never heard it described that way."

"I've been told my views on eating are different."

"If you have a place you'd like to go, someplace special, say the word, and I'll take you."

She hesitated, her cheeks flushed. "Somewhere we can talk about the project and the site will be fine. And I promise we can use code for that, so anyone who happens to overhear won't know what we're discussing."

Right. The site.

Dylan nodded, a plan beginning to formulate. "I have an idea."

He snapped down the blinker and made a left turn, taking them along a side street. "I have a friend who has a restaurant downtown. We can use one of his private party rooms."

"Do you need to give him a heads-up?"

"Naw. He's always trying to get me to come in to eat. I have an open invitation, mostly because he wants to use me as a guinea pig for new meals."

"Interesting." She shifted in her seat and pulled her phone from her stained purse. "Well, we might as well talk about the project."

"I have a question first."

"Sure."

"Why haven't you gotten rid of that purse yet? It's clearly ruined, yet you keep bringing it to work and events. Why not switch it up with something else?"

Simone tugged the purse closer to her body. "Ah. It's my good luck charm. I bought it with my first paycheck from work, and I promised myself I wouldn't get rid of it." She ran her hand over the drink stain. "And honestly, I can't afford to replace it right now."

"I'm sorry that I had anything to do with it getting ruined."

She shrugged. "I'm clumsy and have been since I took my first steps. I'm surprised I haven't done something like this before now."

It didn't take them long to reach the Cork and Pig. His buddy Park started the restaurant with a loan from Dylan right after he'd graduated from culinary school. It was Dylan's first business investment without the support of his family, and Park's success had been the beginning of Dylan's fortune. The sugar daddy site had quickly followed, and now Dylan didn't have to worry financially about anything. He could look after his friends and family, help with their dreams, and ensure they got the best start they could with what they wanted in their lives. There was an absolute joy he got from being able to provide for others, even if he didn't get anything in return.

Maybe Simone needed a practical example of what it was like to have a sugar daddy.

Maybe.

He got out of the car and moved around to open her door. Holding out his hand, he couldn't help but look into her eyes and see her excitement. "Have you heard of this place?"

"Heard of it? Shit, I did a whole series on the best places to eat in Toronto last year. I tried to get in here, but they were so booked up, even my press credentials didn't help." She laughed. "I have a co-worker who is going to be crazy jealous."

Simone was quite a bit shorter than him, the top of her head coming just up to his chin. Her blond hair wisped out of whatever was holding it in place, and he couldn't help imagine what she would look like just out of bed, tousled and sleepy.

She adjusted the strap of her purse, lifting it up a bit higher, even as she squeezed it. Nope, he wasn't going to let that go a moment longer.

"Before we go in, I have something for you. It's an apology for the other night." He went to the trunk and pulled out the fabric bag and hoped he wasn't about to screw this up. "I know this isn't quite the same as what you bought yourself, but I feel I owe you."

Holding the bag behind his back, he held it out for Simone, watching her gaze, and prayed this was the right thing to do.

Simone frowned as she took the gift, her eyes growing wide when she saw the logo. "You bought me a Kate Spade?"

"That's what your purse is, right?" Shit, he thought that's what she'd said. "The styles have changed, but the saleswoman told me it was the 'in' purse for the season. I had to trust her on that one."

Simone blinked rapidly as she pulled the blue and yellow purse from the bag. "Oh. That's lovely. Thank you, but you didn't have to do this."

"Your purse was ruined because you were nervous about surveilling me. It's not the same as you buying one for yourself, but I figured it was the least I could do."

Simone opened her mouth to speak, but instead only smiled. "I'll be sure to switch things over to it when I get home." She opened the car door and put it on the seat. "We should go in."

There was something off in her demeanor that didn't sit right with him. "Sure."

They fell into step as they strode across the parking lot to the Cork and Pig. It had been a long time since he'd been here, and Park really had been after him to come and eat. If nothing else, he'd be able to check this off his to-do list.

The old building had been refurbished as part of the restaurant's start-up, and it was one of Dylan's pride and joys when he'd first started out. Lots of glass, exposed metal painted black, and wide-open spaces. A fire was lit, casting shadows and light across the refurbished wood floor. The hostess smiled at them as they entered the restaurant.

"Welcome to the Cork and Pig. Do you have a reservation?"

He didn't often play the *I'm rich and important card* when he went out to eat, but tonight was going to be the exception. "I don't. I'm a friend of Park's. Is he in tonight?"

The hostess smiled, not looking overly impressed. "May I ask your name?"

"Dylan Williams."

She pulled out a book and checked a list, her eyes growing wide when she found his name. "Mr. Williams. Yes, you're on the VIP list. Please come with me, and I'll get you seated."

Simone snorted as she fell into step beside him. "Must be nice to be a VIP."

"It doesn't happen very often."

"I somehow find that hard to believe."

They went up some stairs to a loft area that overlooked the main restaurant. There were only three tables up here, along with a private bar and what looked to be a side kitchen. Knowing Park, he'd intentionally created this area as his own personal playland, where he could feed and chat with friends, family, and those who he was looking to win over. Not that he had to work very hard doing that these days.

Dylan made a point of pulling out Simone's seat for her, taking a moment to let the scent of her shampoo and perfume wash over him. His cock pulsed, reminding him that after tonight was done, he was going to have to go home and take care of business.

The hostess disappeared, only to be replaced with a waitress who smoothly moved in to hand him a wine list. "Good evening, Mr. Williams. My name is Marta, and I'll be your server tonight. Do you need a moment to look over the wine list, or do you have a preference that I can get started for you?"

He glanced over at Simone, who looked amused. "Are you a wine person?"

"Never met one I didn't like." She licked her lips, and the sight of her pink tongue sent a jolt through his body. "I'm more of a white person."

"Might I recommend a Penfolds St. Henri Shiraz? We have one out back, and it will go beautifully with tonight's meal." Marta smiled at them both.

"Sounds good." Dylan handed her the menu as the doors to the kitchen pushed open to reveal Park striding out. "There's the super chef."

"You asshole! It's about time you showed up to let me feed you." Dylan was barely on his feet before Park pulled him into a hug. "How are you doing, and why didn't you tell me you were coming?"

"It was a bit of a last-minute idea." He pulled back as Simone stood. "This is Simone Leblanc. She's a reporter with the *Toronto Record* and is helping me with a story on a new venture."

As good as Dylan liked to think he was with women, Park's ability to charm someone was far superior to his own. He moved gracefully beside Simone, took her hand in his, and placed a kiss on the inside of her wrist. Her eyes widened, and she sucked in a small breath as he pulled back. "Charmed. Welcome to the Cork and Pig. I hope you don't mind me spoiling you with more food than is proper to eat."

"I've wanted to come here for ages. I'm so excited." Simone spoke in a breathy sort of way that would have been better suited for the bedroom. "Thank you for having us."

"Are you kidding?" Park winked at her. "I should thank you. I've been harassing Dylan to come here for ages. If you're the reason he finally broke down, then I'll have to be sure to have your name added to the VIP list."

The blush that sprung high on Simone's cheeks added to her natural glow. "Wow. Thank you."

"Okay, sit. Marta will bring you some wine, and I'll personally work on your meal tonight. I don't get to work the kitchen as much as I used to, so this will be a treat for me as well."

As quickly as he'd showed up, Park grinned and marched back to where he'd come from. Dylan couldn't help but chuckle. "Nice to see that he hasn't lost his spark."

"He's…intense." Simone picked up her water glass and downed half the contents. "And quite the charmer."

"At university, Park got all the girls. He was a horrible wingman because he inevitably was the man going home with the girl I had my eye on."

"I'm sure you had your fair share of dates." She reached up and tucked her hair behind her ear. "Or was that one of your motivations for starting the site?"

Okay, he could either make up some shit that would play well for the story on why and how he'd started the millionairesugardaddy.com site, or he could lay everything out for the first time ever. Simone wouldn't know the difference, and he didn't precisely owe her anything. But this might be a chance for him to vocalize some of his frustrations about love and dating, and the pressure society put on people, fairly or not.

Wrapping his hand around his now-sweating water glass, he enjoyed the cool touch as he tried to sort through his thoughts.

"The site, believe it or not, has nothing to do with being rich. That seems to be the thing that I see online the most. Why would men and women who have more money than they know what to do with want to buy a person's company? For me, it wasn't that I couldn't find a date or companionship. I couldn't find someone who wasn't looking for love. I was tired of everyone expecting me to date, find a woman who I loved and who loved me, get married, and have the requisite number of children. They couldn't understand that some of us are happy being single and that we only occasionally want to hook up with someone for sex. Or to go to the movies. And nothing more."

Simone hadn't spoken during his little tirade, nor did her expression change. She didn't look angry or confused—if anything, she was riveted. He didn't say anything else while Marta came over and filled their glasses.

Simone smiled at her and took a sip as soon as she was able. "So, you never want to get married?"

"No, I don't. Does that surprise you?"

"Not really. I don't particularly want to get married myself. Not because I have any deep-seated relationship issues. It's just not a priority for me."

"Does your family give you a hard time about that? I mean, you're an attractive and successful young woman. But I get the impression it's harder on women who are career-focused and don't want a family."

"My parents have other things they're focused on." Her gaze slid away to the breadbasket. "I wonder what your friend is going to make for us?"

Warning received loud and clear—avoid the family. "Knowing him, it will be something strange that I won't be able to pronounce."

As her lips turned up in a smile, it struck Dylan that Simone was an extraordinary woman, one he wasn't going to get out of his head anytime soon. He might not want to get into a long-term relationship, but he was still a healthy man with an active sex drive. And given the amount of flirting they'd done online, he was in far more danger of falling into bed with Simone than he'd been with any other woman in recent months.

God, she had a way of pushing his sexual buttons. Sitting here looking at her, all he could think of was what might be going on in her head, what teasing thought she'd just had to cause the little look of wonder that crossed her face. Did she like someone going down on her? Was she into kinky sex or more of a missionary girl? Either worked for him. He'd been with women who could make missionary seem like the most exciting thing in the world.

And kink could feel like a boring rerun if done with the wrong partner.

He'd done his best to keep his gaze from roaming beyond her face, but the allure of her cleavage and the tightness of her dress were more than flattering on her. She was downright sinful. "What's your fascination with the sugar daddy site? What is it about the arrangement that's caught your attention?"

"As I told you the other day, the rate by which people fall in love because of your particular site is higher than average. I can't help but wonder what it is about what you have set up, what's special that makes these connections more than simple hookups?" She leaned forward, making the side of her neck a temptation.

"Is that it?"

"What else would there be?"

It was Dylan's turn to lay on the charm. He slid his hand across the table and let his fingers brush Simone's. "I couldn't help but wonder if you wanted a sugar daddy of your own."

"I…what?"

"Isn't that one of the reasons you signed up for the site in the first place?"

"What? No. I was just trying to track you down." Her face was flushed, and it traveled down her throat toward her breasts.

Dylan doubled down, wanting nothing more than to tease her in person the way he had online. "I'm sure there's a part of you that wants to be spoiled by someone else. That wants to feel special in a way that you know you deserve and that no one else seems to see."

Simone's eye had gone wide, but she hadn't pulled back from his touch. Emboldened, he continued and covered her hand with his. "What better way to understand what it's like to have a sugar daddy than to actually have one."

"What are you saying?"

"For the next three months, let me show you what it's like. Be my sugar baby."

Chapter 11

Simone's brain hadn't stopped spinning since Dylan had made his proposal. Of course, the moment he'd said it, Marta had come back with their appetizers, and that had effectively killed their conversation. She'd switched over to questions about the housing project, which were safe, still relevant to cover, and far less confusing.

Had she wanted to have a sugar daddy?

No, not really.

No?

No.

Most definitely she hadn't wanted to put herself into someone else's control, to be at their beck and call whenever they were lonely or wanted someone to fuck. Though if Dylan kept looking at her the way he'd been doing tonight, she might have to reconsider that particular point.

Shit, she really needed to keep things professional, needed to make sure nothing happened that would jeopardize her story or her position at the paper. Though Carl might turn his nose up at her, she couldn't imagine him having a problem if a relationship of sorts developed between her and Dylan. As long as it didn't impact her professionally, and as long as she used what happened between them merely to extort Dylan, everything *should* be fine. Maybe. Perhaps. If she wanted to take the next step and sleep with him.

Did she want to have sex with Dylan? One glance at the way he was smiling and laughing with Park when he'd brought out dessert only made him look that much more attractive. It was when he was relaxed, caught off guard, that he was his most appealing to her.

And really, it was only sex.

She really did like sex.

Simone snatched up her wineglass and finished the tiny amount that remained. Her stained purse was by her feet, the ruined fabric a constant distraction in the corner of her eye and a reminder of the gift waiting for her in the car. No, she really shouldn't accept the purse from Dylan, mostly for ethical reasons. Besides, it wouldn't replace the meaning of the one she'd bought herself, even though the thought behind it was sincere. He'd cared about her feelings, how upset she'd been, and he'd wanted to do something about it. Not many people would have done that.

"Ms. Leblanc, I hope you enjoyed your meal, even if you did have to spend it with this stick-in-the-mud." Park clapped Dylan on the shoulder.

"Shit, dude, how old are you? Does anyone even say that anymore?" Dylan rolled his eyes.

"Just me."

Simone made a point of swiping her finger across the remaining chocolate on her plate before sticking it in her mouth. "This is the best thing I've ever eaten in my life. And if it's okay with you, I'd love to do a little story for the *Record*. I've run several pieces in the past on the best places to eat in Toronto, and while I'm no food critic, I'd love to do a write-up."

"I'll never turn down kind words in the paper." He winked at her. "And I'll be sure to add your name to the VIP list. Any woman who can hold her own with this jackass is welcome here any time."

"I appreciate that. Thank you."

"And on that note, I better get Simone home." Dylan stood as he shook Park's hand. "Thank you, buddy. That was amazing."

"You better come back sooner next time. I don't want to have to chase you down."

The good-byes finally wrapped up, and before Simone knew it, Dylan had his hand against the small of her back as they headed toward the stairs. It would have been easy for her to break the contact, to walk a half step faster so he wasn't able to touch her. But something was reassuring about the touch, something she wasn't ready to break just yet. So she kept pace until he let his hand drop, leaving his warmth clinging to her skin.

She hadn't been able to get out of her mind his offer of him being her sugar daddy. Even if it was only pretend, something was alluring about his proposition. In truth, it would be the best way to get information on what that sort of relationship was like. She knew part of the deal was the negotiations, and that sex didn't have to be a part of the arrangement. And given that she wasn't really looking for someone to wine and dine her, she wouldn't even put that up for consideration.

Even if she wanted nothing more than to strip Dylan naked and lick up and down the length of his body.

Ha! And I was worried about accepting a gift from him. I think we have bigger issues.

The walk back to his car was quiet, and the air between them simmered with an electric charge. God, what the hell was she going to do? Agreeing with his proposition would no doubt land her in a pile of unwanted trouble. But the thought of saying no felt as though someone was turning a knife in her gut.

She wanted this. Wanted to spend time with Dylan and learn more about him. More importantly, there was a not-so-quiet part of her that was always whispering in the back of her brain—*do it. You deserve to be happy, to be spoiled, to be fucked the way you want. You don't need to be proper or to do the things others always want. Do this for yourself.*

The temptation was far too real.

Dylan opened her door, and she slipped into the car, moving her new purse to her lap as she sat. The thin protective bag couldn't entirely hide the beautiful blue color of the leather below. She'd never had someone give her a gift of this caliber who wasn't Kayla. And she really didn't count, mostly because her best friend was generous to a fault to just about everyone. Simone ran her hands over the new purse and pulled it tighter to her body.

When Dylan slid behind the wheel, his gaze slipped over to her, and he gave her a little smile. "Ironically, I've never had a long-term sugar baby. The few women I dated through the site weren't interested in anything beyond one or two dates. They were looking for money and were willing to act as a date for some of my business dealings that required me to socialize."

His fingers flexed around the wheel, and he turned his face away from her to look out at the road. Simone couldn't look away from his profile, the slope of his slightly prominent nose, the way his ears poked out from beneath his stylish hair. She didn't know what to say, didn't think she needed to respond, as Dylan appeared to be working through something as well.

He looked down at where his hands gripped the wheel. "I get the appeal though. Having money and wanting to spend it on someone who not only needs it but also genuinely appreciates the gifts. It feeds into a man's savior complex, gives us that primitive rush of 'Look how well I'm treating this woman. I'm providing for her when no one else did.'"

"You could do that with someone you're dating as well. It doesn't need to be a business transaction."

"But that's the rub, I don't want anything beyond that. I don't want marriage and kids. I don't want to grow old with someone or watch as our relationship falls apart. I don't want to end up resenting someone else, because I've seen firsthand when that happens, and it's horrible and hateful and not the type of man I want to be. I'd rather have something beautiful, short, with clear expectations. And when the time is ready, we both move on with fond memories."

Simone's heart pounded in her chest as a trickle of arousal spread through each cell of her body. "That sounds interesting. And a bit lonely."

"Only if you let it be." With a slowness that telegraphed his intentions, Dylan lifted his hand from the steering wheel and placed it on her thigh. "I made you an offer earlier. You can say no, and it won't change a thing. I'll still do both stories for you. I'll ensure that your articles are the best they can be and that your boss is happy. But if you want to know, if you want to see what it's really like, I would like that too."

The weight and heat from his hand seeped through the thin fabric of her dress and seemingly into her soul. It became difficult for her to breathe, and her breasts were suddenly far more sensitive. Swallowing hard, Simone had to force the words from her. "I probably shouldn't."

"Don't want to, or are you worried about what others might think if they ever found out?"

"The latter."

He began to rub his thumb against her thigh. "Do you always worry about others? Have you ever just done something for yourself and said 'fuck it' to the rest of the universe?"

"I haven't." She sucked in a sharp breath and squirmed in her seat as her arousal grew. "I've worked too hard to give in to impulses that don't serve to move my career forward."

"Life isn't just about your career, Sugar Tart."

"That sounds hilarious coming from you."

"Are you saying no?" He lifted his hand from her thigh, letting it hover. "I certainly don't want to force anything on you, and I'll back off right now."

Did she want him to stop? She knew that many of these relationships operate exactly the way he described; they were transactional and with clear guidelines. But there was a growing minority of these long-term relationships that seemed to have emerged, and those real-life fairy tales were alluring in a way she couldn't quite grasp.

Do it.

"I get to set the rules." She swallowed down a nervous laugh. "I get to say how far I'm willing to go and what to do. And this can never, ever come out in public. My boss...well, he would fire my ass so fast it would make your head spin."

"I promise. All of that. Whatever you want." His hand returned, bringing with it the promise of so much pleasure. "Can I tell you what I want?"

Simone nodded, before forcing out a little, "Yes."

"I want to slide my hand under that skirt of yours, right here and now, and make you come. I want to hear your cries and smell your arousal. I want to get fucking hard as a rock and then take you home. I want to jerk off thinking about this when I get there, reliving every sound you made in my head."

By the time he'd finished speaking, Simone couldn't hold back. Pressing her head back against the seat rest, she lifted the purse to her chest and spread her legs. "Oh shit."

Dylan chuckled and, with ease, slid his hand beneath her skirt and up between her thighs. The press of his fingertips against her panty-covered clit was immediate, as though there was no barrier between them. She squeezed her eyes shut hard, knowing there was no way she was going to last long.

"You don't have to hold back." He deftly slid his fingers beneath the elastic band of her panties and teased her pubic curls, continuing on his search. "You always seem so guarded. Let go, relax. Let me take care of you."

God, she was going to die right here and now before she even came.

The first moan to escape her was soft, and the sound surprised her. Dylan moaned his approval and rewarded her with a gentle press of his fingers against the top of her clit. There was no holding back her surprised gasp, as the pressure of his touch was more electric than she'd anticipated. Opening her legs a bit wider, Simone tried not to think about the people walking by on the sidewalk, or the fact that anyone could very quickly figure out what they were doing and take a picture, or laugh and make comments. Nothing mattered beyond Dylan's touch and the fast-approaching orgasm.

"That's it. God, your face is so fucking beautiful when you're turned on like that. I'm going to fucking smell you in here for days. Yeah, more. Just like that. I'm going to fuck you with my fingers now. I want to feel you come. I want to smell you on my hand when I go home."

Simone couldn't keep up with it all. When he did as he said and pressed a finger into her pussy, she lost the ability to think, to hear, to worry about her reputation or if this was a good idea or not. All that mattered was the rhythm Dylan set with his hand and chasing her release.

Her body took over as she began to match his rhythm, rolling and bucking her hips in time with his thrusts. She wanted to touch her nipples, to have him suck on her breasts, but that would be too obvious to anyone passing by. Dylan turned his hand, shifting the pressure deep inside her and triggering the one thing she wanted. Heat and pleasure exploded from her pussy, and she was able to suck in a breath before letting out a long, low moan, and she came hard against his pumping hand.

"Ah fuck. Yeah. Come on, sweetheart. You're so fucking hot." Dylan didn't stop until she gasped and tried to pull back. Only then did he slow and eventually come to a stop, before finally pulling his hand free.

Simone opened her eyes and turned to watch him, her breathing coming out in short, sharp pants. "Wow."

"I need to take you home now." He swallowed, his gaze locked onto hers. "Then I'm going to go home and do exactly what I told you I would do."

Her brain was too far gone to do anything about that statement, so she merely nodded. "Okay."

Dylan pressed down on the front of his pants before sucking in a breath of his own and turning on the car. "I'm going to get a fucking speeding ticket for sure."

"Don't do that." She chuckled, finally able to fix her clothing and get herself to look as though she hadn't just had a mind-blowing orgasm.

"Tomorrow. We'll make all of the necessary agreements tomorrow. But for now, just know that for the foreseeable future, I'm going to look after you. You'll be treated like a queen. And sooner or later, this will come to an end. Agreed?"

"Agreed." She didn't have time for a relationship. But an affair? That was absolutely something she would do. "Tomorrow."

"Yup." Dylan gave her one last look before putting the blinker on and pulling the car into traffic.

Chapter 12

Dylan had a problem, one that he wasn't sure he was going to be able to solve correctly. He knew that starting an affair with Simone was one of the worst things he could possibly do, but that didn't seem to matter to the part of his brain that couldn't let go of what had happened between them last night. He had done exactly what he told her he was planning on doing; the second he'd gotten back to his home he went immediately to the bathroom, pulled down his pants, and jerked off as quickly as he could manage. It wasn't a moment he was particularly proud of, but sometimes retreat was the better part of valor.

He'd fallen asleep quickly that night but had woken up far earlier than he usually would have, his brain latching on to the idea of Simone being his sugar baby. This wasn't exactly the sort of thing he had planned when she had caught his attention at the restaurant a few days earlier, but there was no way he was going to be able to walk away from it now. The time had come for him to put his mouth where his money had always been. It was time for him to have a sugar baby of his own.

He knew Simone was going to be at the planning meeting that had been arranged for later on this afternoon, and he needed to make sure that he had his thoughts in order before he saw her again. There is no way he would be able to concentrate on what needed to be done if all he could think about was the sounds she made as he fucked her with his hand last night in the car. Dear God, the noises that came from that tiny little body that looked so prim and proper. He never would have imagined how arousing everything had been. Even thinking about it now was enough to make his cock hard, a distraction he really didn't have time for.

"Did you hear a word that I just said to you?"

Dylan looked up from his computer, his gaze landing squarely on his father, who was looking more than a little amused. "Pardon?"

"I was asking you about your brother's budget for the new building. Do you think he's actually taken everything into account, or am I going to have to make sure that I have additional discretionary funding?"

"For once I think he's actually managed to get everything together in one place. Though I'm sure it would be smart to make sure we have a backup plan. This *is* Jonathan we're talking about."

"Yes, I suspected as much. Your brother can be a bit absent-minded when he is in love." His dad leaned forward, his gaze narrowing on Dylan. "Speaking of which, when was the last time you went out to do anything that wasn't related to work?"

"Last night, in fact." There'd be no sense in giving him any of the gory details, but he knew damn well that if he didn't say something, his father wouldn't let it go. "I was out at Park's restaurant. I ate, drank, and was merry, exactly what you would want from me."

"I also want you to get laid occasionally."

"Jesus Christ, Dad."

"What? You're a man in your mid-thirties. Of course, you're going to be having sex. I'm surprised you haven't found some woman to settle down with before now. Unless you're not into women, in which case, you know, I will love you no matter what."

"Yes, I like women, and I know that you would love me no matter what. But that hasn't exactly worked out for anybody else in this family. You have all collectively been divorced longer than you have been married."

"I understand that we haven't set a perfect example for positive relationships, but that doesn't mean it's not worth trying to have one of your own." His dad sat up straighter, his head cocked to the side. "I hope it isn't because your mother and I didn't get along that you have decided to live on your own. I had always assumed that you preferred to be single."

Today was turning out to be a day full of surprises. Dylan hadn't realized that his desire to be alone was even visible to his father, let alone accepted by him. "I do prefer to be single. But I never thought that you and Mom would be okay with it."

"Well, your mother wouldn't be, that's for damn sure." His dad rolled his eyes. "That woman is determined to have grandbabies sometime in the next ten years. I hope to God either you or your brother can make that happen. I don't want to have to listen to her complain if it doesn't work out."

While there were many things that Dylan was willing to do to make his family happy, having a child was not on that list. Even if he were to, say, stumble into a relationship with a particular blond reporter, he couldn't imagine ever having children. He admired people who were able to raise a family, especially in today's current climate. But he lacked the patience to be a father. He was also happily selfish and would never want to subject a child to even the barest hint of resentment. It was better to leave the parenting potential to his brother and to merely spoil any nieces or nephews who might arise.

"Well, I better leave you to it." His dad stood up and started to head for the door. "We have that management meeting this afternoon, so I'll see you then."

The meeting reminder quickly brought up the image of Simone in Dylan's head. She was going to be here, and he would have to make damn sure that any business between the two of them was resolved before she came face-to-face with his father. No doubt his dad would pick up on the subtext between them. "There's going to be a reporter there today. The one from the paper who's going to do a profile on the new housing complex. Jonathan's not exactly sold on the concept, but it's exactly what we are going to need if we are going to make this successful."

"Your brother's just going to have to follow your lead on this one. He doesn't exactly have a track record that will allow him to argue with your point. Is the reporter cute?"

"Dad, you can't say shit like that anymore." No, he wasn't discussing Simone's looks, cute or otherwise, with his dad.

His dad held up his hands. "I'm sorry, I forgot. I'm trying not to be an asshole, but it's hard to forget the old rules of engagement."

"It's really fucking simple, Dad. Women aren't there for your pleasure; they are there to do a job."

"I know. I'll make an effort."

His dad left the office, and Dylan made a mental note to warn Simone before she arrived. His dad really did mean well, though he had a bad habit of being a flirt. As much as his dad didn't speak well of Jonathan, he was more likely to be the one with a sexual harassment suit filed against him than his brother.

Speaking of Simone...

He pulled out his phone and quickly opened the sugar daddy app. Her scent had lingered in his car; he'd been aware of that the moment he'd slid behind the wheel this morning. As he indulged in the memory of her pleasure, he recalled that he had wanted nothing more than to relive the situation, with her permission to take things to the next level. He wanted to strip her naked, lick up the side of her body, suck her nipple hard into his mouth until she was a moaning, thrashing mess beneath him. He wanted to feel her body squeeze around him, wanted to explore the pleasure and give it back in return.

He pressed the message button and let his thumbs hover above the keyboard. But what the hell do you say to somebody you sort of had sex with and barely knew the first thing about? His mind spun as he tried to come up with something to say until he finally decided to stick with the basics.

Good morning. Well, that was a start. *I wanted to make sure that everything was okay after last night.*

She hadn't given any indication that there was a problem, but, then again, emotions had a way of rearing up once a person was out of a particular situation. There was no way to know if she had really wanted his advances, even though he had given her every opportunity to say no. His phone buzzed, and the light came on, indicating a new message. Dylan held his breath for a moment before waking his phone back up.

Hey. I was just thinking about you.

Well, that was something. *Good things, I hope?*

Ah, kind of had last night on repeat in my head. That was something.

At least he wasn't the only one. *Same. Is that a bad thing?*

Nope. Well, unless you have a problem with it, and then I don't know what I'll think.

He could picture her on the other end, her phone in her hand and that cute little confused look on her face as she pushed the bridge of her glasses so they rode higher on her nose. She no doubt had that adorable blush coloring her cheeks, and she was probably squirming in her seat. Simone appeared to not be able to sit still for longer than five minutes at a time. It would be fun to take her somewhere, to do something that would have the two of them running around. He'd rarely dated anyone who had the energy to keep up with the things he liked to do.

He smiled down at his phone. *I have no problems. I just wanted to make sure you were okay.*

Okay? Dude, I haven't come that hard in years.

Dylan laughed out loud. *Good to know I haven't lost my touch. And maybe you'll be up for a repeat?*

Well, I have been thinking about your offer. I don't exactly know what to do about it.

You can always say yes. I'd like you'd say yes.

There was a pause that stretched out for several minutes, making Dylan far more nervous than he had anticipated. But when her words finally came through, his heart rate increased, and unexpected excitement surged through him.

Then I better say yes. As long as we have some rules ahead of time. I don't want either of us to regret this decision or to get into any third-party trouble.

He didn't want to do anything that would put her job in jeopardy, he really *had* enjoyed her articles on food trucks around Toronto. The local paper needed people like her, people who could put a human touch on things going on around the city. Simone had a gift for seeing the humanity in everything and everyone around her. Even a jaded sugar daddy like himself.

Simone, I promise you no one but the two of us will know about this. You'll get to be in charge of what you are willing to do and where you are willing to go. Sex doesn't have to be a part of this, but I won't say no if it's something you want. It was best for him to be up front with her regarding precisely what he wanted.

We'll have to see on the sex thing. Maybe you can take me on an adventure first. It seems like all the best relationships have adventures.

From the people who he knew used his site, he did realize that these relationships were more than about sex. If Simone wanted an adventure, then he would figure something out. There were more than a few things they could do in Toronto. *I'll be sure to come up with something.*

I'll hold you to that. And I'll see you at the meeting in a few hours.

Dylan tucked his phone away and tried to think of what would qualify as an adventure for this exciting, slightly hyper woman. Because if he was going to do this, if he was going to play the part of sugar daddy, then he was going to do it the very best way he could.

* * * *

Simone sat at the back of the conference room, a silent guest at the housing development project meeting, her notebook open and her hands cramped from all the writing she had done. She knew that half of this wasn't going to find its way into her article on the housing complex, but it was all necessary information to help her paint an accurate picture about what they were trying to accomplish. Plus, she had needed the distraction.

Dylan was sitting only a few feet away from her at the head of the conference table. He had made a point of greeting her the same way he had greeted everyone else, with a firm handshake and a slight nod as he welcomed her.

"It's wonderful to see you again, Ms. Leblanc."

"Yes, it's great to see you as well."

It had been good form, but it also had been the most sensuous handshake she had ever shared. There was no way she was going to be able to look at him throughout this meeting and not think about what he had done to her last night in the front seat of his car. She hadn't been able to get the memories of his touch, of his voice, of his unspoken need from her mind. She had barely slept and hadn't been able to eat this morning, her nerves were acting up so strongly. How the hell was she going to be able to pretend that there wasn't something going on between them over the next few months?

So she had chosen the chair farthest away from him and made a point of keeping her gaze locked onto her sprawling handwriting instead. At least this way she would get something accomplished.

"I think our biggest challenge is going to be ensuring that the local neighborhood is willing and able to accept a housing complex that looks after people with mental health challenges. Even if these people are completely self-sufficient, that doesn't mean that they don't experience prejudice when it comes to their daily lives." Dylan's voice filled the room, his passion for the project obvious.

She knew, based on what he had told her before, that it was his brother, Jonathan, and not Dylan himself who had started this project. Clearly, something had changed along the way, or else Dylan tackled these projects with the same enthusiasm he had shown when he seduced her in the car— fully committed, and with expertise.

Jonathan sat off to the side, his gaze locked on the table and not his brother. "I told you I have that under control. We will engage in community outreach, and make sure that everyone is aware of what we are trying to do."

"That doesn't mean that they will accept it." Dylan tapped the table with his finger, drawing everyone's attention. "That is one of the reasons why I have asked Ms. Leblanc from the *Toronto Record* to be here."

Everyone in the room looked her way, and the pressure of their gazes was practically physical. She smiled and gave them a shy wave, hoping her presence wasn't going to cause more problems than it would correct. "Hello."

"I don't understand why you're the one taking the lead on this." Jonathan pushed back from the conference table and crossed his arms. "I have made sure that the project plan is complete and accurate. This is my baby, and I want to run with it."

"I'm just here to help. I don't want or need the credit for this project." Dylan looked around the table, his lips pulling down into a frown. "I think that's everything for now. Jonathan, you and I should have a quick chat before you head out."

Simone closed her notebook, knowing full well that she was included. Sugar daddy contracts and adventures would have to wait until a later time. But as she walked past Dylan, he reached out and gently touched her forearm with his hand. The brush of his skin against her sent a chill through her body.

"Do you mind waiting outside my office for a minute? I shouldn't be very long, and then we can chat."

"Yep, that should be fine." And she walked out into the hall, picking a direction that she hoped would lead to his office.

She couldn't understand the tension between the two brothers, but it was clear to anyone with a heartbeat that Jonathan wanted to be the one in charge, rather than his brother. There was obviously more to the family history than what she had first assumed. The reporter in her wanted nothing more than to dig until she pulled up the story that was obviously there. But the woman who was trying to get to know Dylan better, who was more than happy to play the part of sugar baby to get the bigger story, knew better than to go down that road.

There was no secretary outside his office, only his nameplate on a door. It would be easy to go inside, maybe even take a look at his desk, but she wasn't that brave. If Carl knew she had such an opportunity, he would probably prod her on until she got the information she needed. Maybe she wasn't cut out to be an investigative reporter?

As she waited in the hall, she leaned against the wall and wondered what exactly would come of this sort of relationship. Kayla had been the one to spoil Devin, invite him to the CN Tower for supper, and take him to her high school reunion, where they ended up falling in love. The transaction had become so much more, but Simone could only wonder if that was unusual—if her friend, who usually had terrible luck in love, just had gotten lucky.

Simone was not usually that fortunate.

Pulling out her phone, she opened up her latest game obsession, Homescapes, to see if she could finally break through level 554. She was on attempt number three when the sound of voices echoed down the hall, quickly followed by a door slamming open to reveal Jonathan marching down the corridor. She took two steps forward as Dylan followed his brother.

"Jonathan!" But his voice did nothing to stop his brother from leaving. "Goddammit."

"Everything okay?"

"My brother's just being a jackass." Dylan put his hands on his hips as he turned to face her. "I know we haven't had our talk yet, but I was wondering if you wanted to get out of here? If I have to sit behind a desk, I'm more likely to punch my computer monitor than I am to get any actual work done."

God, this was probably a horrific idea. "I have my car here. Is that going to make a difference?"

"I can always drop you off later if that's what you want." There was something off in Dylan's tone of voice, a note of frustration that she hadn't heard before now. "Right now, any distraction."

For the life of her, Simone didn't know if he meant that *she* was the distraction. "Where are we off to?"

Dylan looked down at his watch, then pulled his phone from his pants pocket. "I have an idea. How do you feel about surprises?"

Simone shrugged. "Depends on if it's pleasant or if I end up with a pie in my face."

"That happens?"

"I have interesting friends."

"I promise you, no pies. But definitely, there will be hot dogs and beer." He held out his arm for her to take. "If you will come with me, I promised you an adventure."

Simone smiled as she slipped her arm around his. "I look forward to being wowed."

With any luck, this would be the beginning of something exciting.

Chapter 13

It had been a long time since Dylan had shown up for a baseball game. The Blue Jays were not necessarily the most consistent team, but he did love them, and always had, since the days when his dad could only afford the five-hundred-level tickets. He had left his ball cap in the downstairs closet, not anticipating a spur-of-the-moment trip to the ball field. He had no idea if Simone was into baseball at all, but he made sure to buy her as much paraphernalia as he could manage to shove into her arms as they walked through to their seats.

She currently sat beside him with a Blue Jays cap on her head and wearing a Jays shirt that she had changed into in the bathroom. She'd been excited when she realized where he was taking her, and that excitement was utterly infectious. It was the first time in ages that he was thankful for his season tickets and his financial freedom to purchase them in the premium dugout section.

"I don't even remember who is on the team this year." He took a long pull of his beer and debated whether he should get them some hot dogs. "I've been so busy this season I haven't been able to take advantage of coming here in the middle of the day."

"Are you insane?" Simone was sitting on the edge of her seat, looking everywhere except at him. "We're actually not doing that bad this year. Our bullpen has pulled us out of more than one mess. I mean, we're playing the Yankees today, so God only knows how that's gonna go."

"I had no idea that you were into baseball. I just wanted to do something a little different today." The fact of the matter was that Dylan was tired of the daily grind. It really had been a long time since he had taken advantage of his tickets, or anything else for that matter. His life was little more than going to work, coming home, working on the website, and then crashing.

"I love baseball." Simone turned around, sending her blond ponytail flying around her shoulders. Her eyes were wide and her excitement palpable. "I've only been to one or two games and never in seats like this. But I watch the games with my dad—on the weekends mostly."

Every time she mentioned her father, there was something in her tone, a longing of some sort, that was obvious to Dylan. Having grown up in a family where what you were able to do for the family company was almost more important than who you were as a person, he recognized a kindred spirit. For whatever reason, Simone wanted something more from her relationship with her father than what she currently had. Not that he was about to ask her anything about it. They weren't exactly at that stage in the relationship.

"Well then, I'm going to count on you to let me know what I need to know for today's game. And if you want to meet any of the players afterward, just let me know. I can pull some strings, and we can take some pictures and get some autographs."

Simone's eyes widened even more. "Dude. That would be amazing. Not that I want to bother them after a game. They might be tired or not want to have anything to do with a fan, especially if they've lost."

"Have faith. They haven't lost yet. And most of the guys are pretty good about meeting fans."

Having a date for a ball game was an entirely new experience for Dylan. None of the women of his acquaintance were into baseball, and his brother wasn't keen on coming anymore. It had been something they had shared when they were younger—the love of going to a game and spending time with one another—but somewhere along the way their relationship had drifted apart, and so had their trips to the Jays games.

Most of the women he had spent time with over the years were not into sports at all. Over the years, he had tried to take a few dates to a game, but it had always ended with them leaving early and him making it up to his date with an expensive meal. If he was on the lookout for a long-term relationship, finding a woman who enjoyed baseball and hockey would be at the top of his list.

Not that he had a list. Because he wasn't looking for a long-term relationship.

And never would.

"Please stand for the singing of our national anthem."

Dylan stood up, but Simone was on her feet faster than he'd ever seen another person rise. She was practically vibrating as she looked around and took her cap off. "This is so strange. I keep expecting to hear the television commentators tell me what I need to know. It's like a strange void, anticipating a voice that never comes." She turned to look at him, and for half a second, he wanted to reach down and brush her hair behind her ear. "I kind of like it."

He kind of liked her, and that was going to be a problem.

The first Yankees player stepped out to take the first at-bat. Simone sat back down on the edge of her seat and drank some of her beer. "Strike him out!"

The pitcher couldn't accommodate Simone's request, and the batter hit a double.

"Dammit." Simone sat back down with a sigh. "Though it would be boring if they actually made this an easy game."

"We wouldn't want that, would we?"

Simone leaned all the way back in her seat and half-turned to face him. "So why don't you come to baseball games very much anymore? If I had seats like these, I would never leave the Rogers Centre."

"As I said, I don't really have anyone to come with. Half the fun of a baseball game is spending time with other people."

"So, what do you do for fun?" Simone rested her chin on her hand and looked up at him with genuine curiosity. "Do you honestly do nothing but work? I find that so strange, especially given your side project."

"I told you I wasn't normally one of my own customers." Until now, that was. "And I'm not into—"

"Long-term relationships. I know, I know." Simone leaned a little closer to him, and for a moment, it felt as though they were the only two people in the stadium. "Don't you get lonely? I mean, I'm not really much for dating myself, but I also find it difficult to be alone. Maybe that's just me."

Dylan really wasn't a fan of being on his own; it was one of the reasons he'd enjoyed spending time with his brother at the ball games. But dating wasn't necessarily the solution to that particular problem. More often than not, it created more issues than he wanted to deal with, and Dylan would often feel lonelier on a date than if he was spending time with someone for some other purpose.

But to verbalize something like that made him sound crazy. What kind of person didn't want to be alone and yet refused to seek companionship?

"I'm human; of course, I get lonely. But in my experience, having a partner doesn't always solve that problem. My parents ended up hating one another by the time their marriage was over. My brother is about to walk down the aisle a third time. Even my grandparents didn't stay married. Every time something would fall apart, I was the one who had to help the parties put the pieces back together again. I was their shoulder to cry on. It's not the sort of thing I would want to put myself through."

Again. He had done this once before; he had gotten his heart broken, and he would be damned if he would suffer again.

"That's one of the most heartbreaking things I've ever heard." Simone shook her head and turned around as the next batter walked to the plate. "The irony isn't lost on me, either."

"What's that?"

"That the man who runs one of the most successful sugar daddy sites on the Internet, a site that has the strange tendency to create long-term relationships based on common interests and not sex, is one of the loneliest people I have ever met. Kayla wouldn't believe me if I told her."

"But you won't, right?"

Simone sat straight up, totally ignoring the fact that the Blue Jays pitcher had struck out the current batter. "Oh my God, no. I just, she's my best friend, and I have this terrible habit of telling her everything. But no, I won't say a word to her about you or your alter ego."

There was a strange look on her face, and Dylan wasn't sure if she was lying to him, or if she was worried that she would be unable to keep her promise. "I'm going to hold you to that."

The rest of the game continued without any further discussion of relationships or sugar daddy sites. They did talk on about the housing project and the best way they could position it in the paper. With each consecutive meeting, Dylan was becoming more invested in the success of this venture. Simone also seemed to genuinely care about what they were trying to accomplish.

"I can't imagine it's easy for people with mental health challenges to find a place where they feel safe and don't have to worry about their personal problems spilling out into their living arrangements."

"I've been doing some reading on these types of co-op homes in different cities around North America. When they're done right, not only are they a boon to the community, but they help these individuals become more successful. That is the sort of thing that I want to have the Williams label attached to."

Simone smiled, and she reached out and gave his hand a squeeze. "You're a good man, Dylan. And not exactly who I thought you would be."

"What was that?"

"I don't know? Maybe I thought you were possibly a bit of a sexual deviant? Maybe?" She blushed and pulled down the bridge of her ball cap, which partially covered her eyes. "You could still be, I guess. And that might be interesting too."

Dylan was many things, though he'd never been accused of being deviant when it came to his sexual desires. He wasn't precisely vanilla, but he wasn't going to be shocking anyone in the tabloids with his exploits. Still, he was the guy who had finger-fucked her in the front seat of his car parked at the side of a busy downtown street. He could ratchet things up if he needed to. And there was something about Simone that made him want to, made him want to try to live up to the image of him that she had had before their meeting.

He wanted to be the Candy King for her.

Maybe he needed to take a chance, to give in to some of his wilder impulses. If she was willing, why couldn't he be her sugar daddy? Why couldn't he spend his money on her, buy her things that she wanted, merely for pleasure's sake? It might not lead to anything long-term—nor would he want it to—but, for once, the void inside him might be filled, even if for only a short time.

The crack of cork hitting wood filled the air, causing everyone to leap to their feet. The Blue Jays were at-bat, and the batter had just knocked in a double. Simone was jumping and screaming along with everyone else. Her face was flushed, her glasses had slid down her nose, and her blond hair was bouncing behind her as her unbridled excitement exploded. Falling into bed with her would not be his worst idea.

Before she retook her seat, Dylan reached out and took her hand in his, giving it a gentle squeeze. "What are you doing later tonight?"

She bit down on her bottom lip and looked away from him. "Other than checking in with the office? I'm pretty much free from this point on. Somehow I'm going to have to justify a baseball game to my boss."

"All you need to tell them is that you were following the story where it led." He cocked his eyebrow.

"That will work. Carl would sacrifice his own mother if it meant getting a good story." Simone snorted. "As long as I bring him the story, everything will be fine."

"Once the game is over, why don't you come back to my place?" Dylan let go of her hand and reached for his beer. "Only if you want to. We haven't even discussed the details of our potential arrangement."

"That is definitely something we would need to work out." Simone ran her hands across the tops of her thighs. "Guidelines would be critical.

This isn't exactly something I would want to do long-term. I mean, I'm not exactly someone who would be signing up for the site."

"I get the impression that you're not the first person who has said that." Despite rarely being a client himself, Dylan was more than aware of the expectations of the people who came to the sugar daddy site. Very rarely did people come to it who didn't need something—whether money, companionship, sex, or merely a warm body to sit beside and talk to. All of those reasons were valid; all of those reasons, and the people they were important to, mattered. There had to be a mechanism in society that wasn't based on the principles of matrimony.

He tried to pay attention to the game but couldn't take his eyes off her. "Are you okay with doing this? Really?"

Her gaze dropped to her lap as her face scrunched up. "You know what? I am." When she finally looked over at him and smiled, her whole body seemed to glow with excitement. "It's easy to see the appeal to this sort of thing. We will have guidelines, clear expectations. My anxiety won't kick in at a moment's notice to tell me that you don't want to really be with me because you're just using me for sex. I already know that part. I can simply enjoy our time together until we're done."

When she put it that way, Dylan couldn't help but smile. "Okay then."

Simone quickly drank the rest of her beer as the announcer came over the PA system once more. "Blue Jays fans, everyone, welcome the Home Hardware cleanup crew."

"I wanted to be one of these guys when I was younger." Simone cheered as the group of men and women raced onto the field, brooms in hand, sweeping dirt off the bases and grooming the infield. "I thought it would be the best job in the world."

Dylan chuckled even as Simone whistled at the crew.

"The irony is that I hate cleaning."

One additional point that he would have to file away about this fascinating woman.

The next hour and a half passed quickly, and it was tense right up until the ninth inning. Simone had given up all pretense of being a calm, rational human being and began screaming and hollering as the Blue Jays had two men on base. With only one man out, there was a chance they might be able to pull this one off.

Those hopes were dashed when the batter hit a low fly ball to center field and the runner on second was thrown out trying to get to third. The crowd moaned, and Simone pulled her ball cap from her head. "Fucking Yankees."

"We're having another one of those seasons for sure."

Simone turned to face him. "Is that offer to go back to your place still open? I think I could use the distraction after this."

Dylan's cock grew hard, and for a moment he had to catch his breath. "If that is something that you want to do, the offer still stands. We can discuss...specifics."

Simone might blush easily, but that didn't seem to mean she was shy. She grinned as she reached for her brand-new purse. Putting the strap over her shoulder, she shoved her new Blue Jays cap into it and sat up. "As a journalist, I appreciate specifics. Clear guidelines, word counts, definitions, things like that."

He had no doubt that there were hidden meanings to each one of those words, but for the life of him he couldn't figure them out. "I'm more of a hands-on guy. More a doer and less of a speaker. I like physical examples, hands-on learning."

"Well, I think our two learning styles might be compatible. At the very least, they'll make for an interesting conversation."

He was absolutely numb from the teasing at this point and grabbed her hand, tugging her along behind him. "It's gonna take us forever to get out of here. God only knows what traffic is going to be like."

"Horrendous. Traffic is always horrendous." She moved up alongside his body until the side of her breast was pressed against his arm. "We may have to sit in the car for a while. I'm sure we can find something to do."

Jesus Christ, she was trying to kill him.

It took them a half hour to make their way from their seats back to where he had parked the Tesla. The parking garage was full of laughing people, families and friends enjoying themselves despite their team's loss. There was a buzz in the air, a mix of excitement and summer relaxation that clung to every person they passed. Usually Dylan would be one of them, laughing and carrying on, but not tonight. Tonight, the only thing he could focus on was Simone and all the things that he wanted to do to her when they got back to his place.

He helped her into the passenger seat before making his way around to the driver's side. With each step, he berated himself for mentally stripping her naked and sliding his hard cock inside her. There was still every possibility that she would not want to have sex with him, and he was going to have to be on his best behavior until he knew for sure.

The moment he closed the driver's-side door, he turned to look at Simone and realized that he could see her erect nipples through her bra and T-shirt.

Okay. Clearly, she was either cold—highly unlikely in this heat—or she was just as excited about the prospect of sex as he was. Unless there was another reason a woman's nipples get hard; he was a dude, after all, and sometimes he wasn't aware of everything that happened to a woman's body.

Simone chuckled. "I know this goes against pretty much everything I have ever been taught as a journalist, and I might even get fired if my boss found out. I know that we haven't even discussed the particulars of what it would mean for me to pretend to be your sugar baby and that I am under absolutely no obligation to have sex with you. All that said, unless something strange happens between now and when we get to your place, that's probably what's going to happen. Unless you don't want to. And maybe I'm being presumptuous, that's absolutely something that I have been in the past." Her eyes widened again, and her voice lowered. "You do want to have sex, right? I'm not imagining that, right?"

Dylan burst out laughing. Probably not the wisest decision, given her obvious distress, but he couldn't exactly stop, as his laughter was based on the expression of real panic mixed with arousal on her face. "If that is something you want to do, I am absolutely on board."

Simone sighed and leaned back against the seat. "Oh good. I've been known to jump the gun."

"You don't need to worry. My *gun* appreciates the enthusiasm."

And with that, Dylan put the car into reverse and mentally calculated the fastest way he could get them home.

Chapter 14

Simone did not know what to expect when she'd agreed to come back to Dylan's place, but taking an elevator to the penthouse of a condo building that looked out over Lake Ontario wasn't exactly it. Over the years, she had driven by these buildings so many times that she had lost count, but not once had she even considered stepping foot inside them. And going up to a penthouse? She wasn't exactly in the pay grade that would allow for such as a visit.

It was easy to forget that Dylan was incredibly wealthy. How rich she wasn't exactly sure, but she knew the family was worth billions. Add in the money that he would be earning from the website, and she knew that Dylan wasn't exactly hurting financially.

The elevator dinged, and the door slid open, revealing a short hallway that led to a single entry. Simone looked down the hall and noticed one other door at the opposite end of the building. "So, you just have one neighbor?"

"Yes. My brother actually owns that unit. His ex-wife, Lidia, lives there right now. He still owns it, but he lets her stay there rent free as part of their divorce settlement."

"That's one hell of a settlement."

"Lidia is one hell of a negotiator. And despite everything, Jonathan really did care for her. He wasn't about to cause her problems just because he was impossible to live with."

Amicable divorces were not exactly the norm. She would have to give Jonathan bonus points for not being a complete asshole, even if he wasn't exactly thrilled that she was on board with the project. "Why is he so against me doing a piece on the condo building for the paper? I would think he would want as much positive exposure as he could get."

"It's not you that he has the problem with. Jonathan hasn't had great luck organizing projects, and Dad tends to push him to the side and lets me take the lead. You were my idea, so Jonathan would be a bit resentful."

The last thing she wanted was to get into the middle of a family feud. She would make a point of walking carefully between these family lines.

Not that any of that mattered at the moment. She watched with excitement and a tiny bit of fear as Dylan opened the door to his condo. Fresh air rushed out into the hallway, greeting her with relief from the heat outside. As she walked into the room, her sneakers squeaked against the tile floor.

Windows lined the side of the living room, giving her a perfect view of the lake. The sun was setting, and a golden glow filled the room. Shoving off her shoes, she followed Dylan into the kitchen and gladly accepted a beer from him.

"I thought we would start with something simple." He cracked open the bottle and took a drink, moving to sit opposite her. "I'd rather not do this in writing, but I will if that makes you feel any better. I want everything to be clear and obvious, so neither of us feels trapped or deceived."

Simone couldn't take her eyes off his throat as he swallowed his next drink of beer. The muscles moved, his Adam's apple acting like a sensuous tease. He'd worn a light blue, button-down shirt even to the ball game, and she wanted nothing more than to pop every button that held the fabric together. After they were alone, with no prying eyes to watch or pass judgment, there really wasn't any reason why Simone had to behave.

"Simone?"

"Right! Yes, rules. I mean, I don't need them written down. But yes, we should have them. Rules are important."

Dylan cocked an eyebrow. "Are you nervous?"

"I don't get nervous." She snorted, hating that she did that whenever she got nervous. "I'm excited."

"Excited to be my sugar baby? Or excited to see if I'm as good with my dick as I am with my hands?"

"Yes." She smiled and put her beer bottle down. "It's been a while since I've had good sex."

"Thank you for assuming that I'm capable of good sex." He winked at her. "I take it very seriously."

Of that, Simone had no doubt. "So, what does it mean to be a sugar baby to Dylan Williams?"

"It can mean anything you want it to mean. But I think for your article it's important to have the full experience." Dylan stood, coming around beside her close enough to touch, but not touching. "I'll give you money to buy things, whatever you want. I'll take you to shows, the ballet, to the most expensive restaurants in the city. You'll be pampered and cared for the way that only a man with more money than he can count can afford to do."

Simone was barely able to breathe by the end of his little speech. Never in her life had she been treated that way. Even with her friend Kayla, there were limits to what Simone felt comfortable asking for; she never wanted to be seen as taking advantage of her friend's money. But with Dylan, this was something very different. "That might be crossing a few lines for me professionally. I'd be accepting payment to write a story on you. More than a few conflicts of interest there."

"Then I won't give you cash. If anyone asks, we're simply friends enjoying one another's company, and I'm treating you. No one should have any issues with that. If you don't use my real identity in your story, then no one will be the wiser."

"There aren't any rules about me spending time with someone I met on a job outside of work. I guess that would be fine." She chewed on the inside of her cheek for a moment, needing the slight pain to distract herself. "And what about sex?"

"It doesn't have to be on the table if you don't want it to be. Just like my site, this isn't about sex. You're not prostituting yourself. It's simply an exchange—your time for my money. What we do beyond that is nothing more than an agreement between two consensual adults."

Dylan reached up and took the end of her ponytail in his hand, gently threading the hair between his fingers. Simone sighed, loving the feeling of being petted. "For tonight, for right now, I would very much be interested in having some hot, sweaty sex."

A small growl escaped Dylan. "There is nothing hotter than a woman who knows exactly what she wants."

"What I want is for you to stop talking and kiss me."

The words had barely left her mouth when Dylan reached up, cupped her face, and kissed her hard. There was no hesitation as he pulled her hard against him and plunged his tongue into her mouth. Her hands balled his shirt, as she held him close, refusing to let anything ruin this moment. For nights now, she'd wondered what it would be like to kiss this man, to feel his heat against her, the press of his tongue against hers. He was a contradiction of hard angles and gentle touches. While his hands held her close, she felt his body shift against her and the sudden press of his erection against her stomach.

Simone sucked in a small breath at the contact, wanting to see exactly what he was hiding. Letting go of his shirt, she slid her hand down across his stomach to the band of his pants, hesitating only for a moment before running her fingers along the hard ridge of his erection. It was Dylan's turn to sigh as she squeezed his cock.

"I might have to walk back my earlier statement about my abilities and good sex if you continue to do that."

"We wouldn't want that to happen, would we?" Simone tugged on the zipper of his pants and slid her hand inside, worming her way beneath the band of his briefs. "I'll be careful."

"You're going to kill me."

Simone chuckled as she dropped to her knees, only to realize that the height would be off and she wouldn't be able to reach his cock from this angle. "Shit. I think we're going to have to move to a couch or the bed. I'm too short for you."

Dylan tugged her back up to her feet. "This way."

His bedroom was easily double the size of hers back in her tiny apartment. The blue and brown color scheme suited him, though she couldn't imagine him picking out the bedding or paint on his own. The plush carpet cushioned her feet as she strode behind him, trying her best to keep pace with his long strides.

"Welcome to my lair." He spun her around and tossed her on the bed in a single motion.

Simone giggled as she bounced with her landing, the new T-shirt pulling tight across her breasts. "You don't strike me as much of an ogre."

"I'm a beast." He growled as he climbed up on the bed, positioning his body above her. "And I'm here to eat you."

"God, I hope so." Her last sexual encounter had sucked ass. The guy didn't do that eating-out shit, and unsurprisingly, she was left wanting. "Though I believe I was in the process of trying to get a peek at that cock of yours."

When Dylan smiled down at her, his entire face lit up. "Well, you're the one calling the shots."

In a single move, he flopped onto the bed as he grabbed her and rolled her on top of him. Simone laughed again, not remembering the last time sex was this fun. Her hair flopped over her shoulder and dangled in the space between them. With a flick, she dropped it onto his chest as she worked down his body, flicking open the buttons of his shirt on her way to the opening of his pants.

It only took her a moment to unzip him and free his still-hard cock from the confines of his briefs. The sight of his swollen shaft had her mouth watering with anticipation of what was to come.

"Hello, Mr. Williams." Simone dipped her head lower and licked the head of his cock. "It's a pleasure to meet you."

"The pleasure…is definitely all mine." He reached out and captured her hair, wrapping the strands around his hand.

While she loved banter during sex, Simone had been dreaming about this moment from almost the second she'd first laid eyes on him. The last thing she wanted was for one of them to say something and make things awkward. Closing her eyes, she sucked as much of his cock into her mouth as she could manage, until she was scared she might gag. Only then did she increase the suction and pull back slowly.

"Fuck." He bucked his hips as she reached his crown and tugged on her hair gently. "You're really good at that."

"I'm just getting warmed up. Help me with this." With effort, they worked together to pull his pants down, fully exposing his groin to her. "Oh yeah."

"Fair warning, I'm going to stop you before this goes too far. As much as the idea of coming in your mouth is a temptation, I want to feel your pussy squeezing me. I want to taste you when you come in my mouth."

Simone wrapped her hand around his shaft and took a steadying breath. "You're good at the sex talk. I'm not good at that."

"You're good at other things. Like"—he sucked in another breath when she ran her tongue up the length of his cock—"that."

Now that she'd committed to sex with Dylan, Simone was going all in. She licked and sucked on his cock, shifting lower to tease his balls with her tongue before going back up to the crown of his shaft to scrape her teeth gently across the sensitive skin. With her free hand, she teased his balls and went even lower to rub her nails across his asshole. Not all men enjoyed that, but Dylan widened his legs, giving her better access.

Maybe he really wasn't as vanilla as she'd first thought.

She continued to tease his asshole with her finger as she set a steady rhythm on his cock. Simone loved giving head, even more so when the recipient uttered a constant litany of sounds, like Dylan was doing. Her clit pulsed as her arousal grew with each passing moment. She squeezed her legs tight together, increasing the pressure on her pleasure center.

His cock throbbed in her mouth, its girth increasing slightly. Dylan tugged her hair as he sat up. "Stop, stop, stop." He leaned over her, his breath coming out in sharp pants. "Enough."

She couldn't stop her grin. "Too much for you?"

"You have a wicked mouth." He rolled them once more, so he was now on top of her, his hard, wet cock pressed against her thigh. "But so do I."

He pulled her T-shirt off over her head but didn't bother to undo her bra, instead pushing it up to free her breasts. Her nipples went instantly hard in the cold air, eliciting a moan of her own.

Dylan moved his mouth to her left breast, maintaining eye contact with her as he sucked the swollen peak into his mouth. Simone fought and lost against keeping her eyes open, letting them roll back into her head as his tongue teased her sensitive skin. With each flick of his tongue, she could feel a complementary pulse of pleasure in her clit until her pussy was wet with her arousal.

She carded her fingers through his short hair, encouraging him on. "You're so fucking good at that."

"Mmm." He switched breasts and increased the suction.

With his free hand, he went to work on the front of her pants until his fingers found her clit. Shit, he wasn't the only one who was close to orgasm. She rode out the rising pleasure as long as she dared before pushing down on his shoulders. "If you want to taste my come, you better relocate."

Dylan pulled back with a pop, pausing just long enough to place a quick, hard kiss on her mouth. "Yes, ma'am."

Simone hadn't had a man strip her that quickly ever in her life. Her new Blue Jays T-shirt went flying across the room to land silently somewhere, while her pants and panties were shoved to the floor. Naked and completely exposed to him, she stretched her legs wide, giving him full access to her body. "Have at me."

Dylan wasted no time, shifting lower, so his mouth was only a few inches from her clit. "I've been thinking about doing this since that night in my car. I didn't want to wash my hand, wanted to keep your smell with me as a reminder for as long as I could."

"That's gross." She laughed, turning to look away from him, not wanting him to see how much the sentiment meant to her.

"Hygiene is critical." He then dipped his head and sucked her clit hard into his mouth.

Simone moaned and bucked her hips forward as her hands flew to the back of his head. "Shit."

"Mmm." He rapidly flicked his tongue across her clit, quickly followed by pressing two of his fingers deep into her pussy.

Her ability to speak evaporated as he fucked her once again with his hand. As horny as she'd been up until now, it only took a nanosecond for her orgasm to threaten to explode. Dylan sensed her impending release and pulled back, slowed down, and generally frustrated her. "Oh no, you're not getting off easy."

"Not a good time for puns." She sucked in a deep breath and tried to get herself under control.

"It's always a good time for puns." He turned his fingers, so they now pressed against the top of her pussy, sending a burst of warmth through her. "You're fucking delicious."

Whatever reply Simone intended to come up with quickly left her mind when Dylan pressed his thumb against her clit and rubbed in a circle with his fingers deep inside her. Every cell in her body threatened to explode from the intensity of the pleasure. She squeezed the bedsheets in her hands in a vain attempt to hold her body down on the mattress. With her feet braced, she lifted her hips as her orgasm slammed into her, and a cry ripped from her mouth.

Dylan moaned low and deep as he increased the pressure on her clit. He worked her orgasm with his hand until she was left a gasping mess on the bed.

"You make the most delicious sounds." Dylan sucked her juices from his fingers.

Simone forced her eyes open, in awe of what he was doing. She'd never been with a man who enjoyed sex as much as Dylan clearly did. She couldn't imagine why he was single, why he would want to be single, given how good he was at this. She was also surprised by her own greed at wanting him again.

"Condom?" She swallowed, her throat sore from her orgasmic cries. "Tell me you have one."

Dylan got off the bed and marched over to the nightstand, where he pulled out a roll of condoms from the drawer. "It always pays to be prepared."

It took him little effort to strip away his pants and briefs, leaving him gloriously naked in front of her. Dylan was every bit as big as she had hoped and dreamed he was. Her excitement at what was about to come was almost more than she could handle. She hadn't known him long, but that didn't mean she hadn't fantasized about what it would be like to sleep with a man like him. Someone in control, someone who knew what they wanted and wasn't afraid to take it.

Someone who wanted her.

Dylan opened the condom wrapper and rolled it down his shaft quickly while maintaining eye contact with her the entire time. "Take your hair out of that ponytail."

It took her a moment to force her body to comply with the request, yet it felt good the minute she freed the hair from its elastic confines. She still had her glasses on, not wanting to miss out on the opportunity to see his expressions as they fucked.

Crawling up the bed to cover her body with his, Dylan licked the skin as he moved. Pausing when he reached her breasts, he sucked her nipple into his mouth, teasing her with his teeth and tongue. She took his head in her hands, scratching her nails along his scalp at the back of his neck, encouraging him on.

She felt the press of his cock against her opening, and she widened her legs. He didn't push into her all at once, entering her body with short moving thrusts until finally he was seated fully inside her. He braced his body on his forearms so that he could look down at her, his gaze flicking across her face.

"You're fucking gorgeous." He bucked his hips, increasing the pressure against her sensitive clit. "I want to feel you come around me."

She didn't want to moan, but she couldn't stop, and she squeezed her legs around his hips as she leaned up and nipped at his chin. "Challenge accepted."

Setting a steady rhythm, Dylan took her mouth in his and kissed her long and deep. One hand found her hair, tugging and touching everything he could find. The other hand moved along her body, caressing the side of her breast, her arm. She did her best to keep her eyes open, but there was no way she could, given the pleasure that was coursing through her body.

She wasn't typically one to have multiple orgasms during a sexual encounter, but there was something very different about Dylan. He seemed to sense what her body was feeling, how close she was to orgasm. Once again, the familiar tingle of pleasure began to build deep inside her. Her nipples rubbed against his chest hair, a continuous tease that she was not used to. She began to buck her hips against him in rhythm, increasing the pressure against her clit and pushing her closer to release.

"Close." She swallowed hard. "Harder."

Dylan pressed his face against the side of her throat and increased the force of his thrusts. He kissed and licked at the sensitive skin at the juncture of her shoulder and neck. He was speaking, though she couldn't make out the words. It sounded like he was moaning *yes* and *more* and *beautiful*.

This was more than she had ever felt before; it was overwhelming physically and mentally. Her orgasm was close, but she knew she needed help to push it over the edge. She tried to reach between their bodies to touch her clit, but he pulled her hand away. Leaning back, he sucked his thumb to wet it, before pressing down once more on her clit.

That was all it took. Simone squeezed her eyes shut as her orgasm washed through her once again. This time the pressure of Dylan's cock deep inside her intensified her release. It must have been too much for him to handle because the next thing she realized he was crying out and slamming into her as hard as he could.

It was all too much for her, and the moment he finally settled, relaxing on top of her, she turned her head and let her exhaustion win out.

Either seconds or minutes passed—Simone was uncertain—but eventually, she felt Dylan move, sliding from her body and placing a kiss between her breasts. "Let me clean you up."

He disappeared then, leaving her cold and shivering on the bed. She reached for the covers she was lying on and pulled them around her body, missing his warmth and his touch.

Dylan chuckled upon his return. "You look like a burrito."

"Mmm." She snuggled deeper into the covers.

"Here, I'll clean you up a bit." He tried to pull the covers away from her, but Simone fought against him.

"I'm cold. Come cuddle."

"I'll cuddle if you let me in."

It was hard to argue with that logic. With a sigh, she lifted the covers and let him climb inside. She was only a little surprised when she felt the wet facecloth at her back.

"Do you need the cloth?" He kissed her shoulder.

"Not right now. Just you."

She heard him toss it somewhere on the floor behind them before he wrapped his arms around her once more. It didn't matter if this was just sex; it didn't matter if neither of them was interested in a relationship. Right now this was the one place in the world Simone wanted to be.

She would figure everything else out later.

Chapter 15

Dylan had a problem.

Simone was wrapped around his body like a second skin, snoring away. Her hand rested lightly on his chest, moving up and down in time with his breathing. Strands of her blond hair were draped across his shoulders and along the side of his arm. Her leg was bent at the knee across his, and she'd tucked her toes beneath his thigh. She looked completely at peace as she slept, and the last thing in the world he wanted to do was wake her up.

The problem was that he had to pee.

Desperately.

Simone let out a tiny little snore that made him smile but only served as a reminder that if he didn't do something soon, she would continue to sleep for God only knew how long, while he'd probably pee the bed.

It was a bit of a no-win situation.

As carefully as he could manage, he slowly squirmed his way out from beneath her, pausing when she moaned and tried to grab hold of him once more. Shit, she was a clingy sleeper. Knowing there was no easy way out, Dylan decided to go with the Band-Aid method and moved quickly, hoping the result would be painless.

"Mmm." Simone frowned in her sleep, and he couldn't help but chuckle at her annoyed expression. "Sleepy."

"Then sleep." He pushed her hair from her face. "I'll be back."

It didn't take long to relieve himself, get cleaned up, and locate some additional wine for them. It was probably too late to have another glass, but he felt relaxed for the first time in ages and didn't want the sensation to wane. With their drinks in one hand and the bottle in the other, Dylan made his way back to the bedroom.

Simone was still snoring away, now curled up in the spot where his body had been only a few moments earlier. Rather than disturb her, he sat in the chair off to the side of the room, moving it so he could easily watch her sleep as he looked out the window into the night sky.

This wasn't what he'd expected when he'd made the offer to be her sugar daddy. Yes, he'd had sex with other women, but not once did any of them fall asleep in his bed. They'd gotten dressed as they talked, laughed. The women, more often than not, had to go to class the next morning and didn't want to have to deal with getting home too late. Dylan would send them some money, get them an Uber, and that would be it.

It was strangely different with Simone. Not only had she fallen asleep, but he also had no urge at all to wake her up and send her on her way. It wasn't as though he had any specific emotional attachment to her; it was more what she looked like curled up in his bed, and how close they'd come to the multitude of dreams he'd had about this moment over the past few weeks.

Strangely, she looked better than he'd imagined.

Dylan was nearly finished with his wine when Simone stretched and rolled onto her side, facing him. She blinked her eyes open, yawning in a way that wouldn't have looked out of place in some sort of cute-ass anime. "Was I sleeping?"

"For a while now." He smiled at her look of panic. "It's fine. I'm a bit of an insomniac."

"I'm not normally someone who does that after sex." She rolled onto her back, pulling the sheet up across her breasts. "I love to sleep. This bed is heaven."

Dylan got up and made his way over to the mattress, where he sat down and offered her some wine from his glass. "It better be, considering what I paid for it."

"I've had the same mattress since before I left home. Someday I want to buy a queen and get some really nice sheets for it."

"Why don't you?"

"I have other things that I need to spend my money on." She shrugged and sat up enough to take another sip of wine. "This is good."

"I have another bottle in the wine fridge if you want another glass."

"I better not, considering it's late." She lifted her head off the mattress and frowned. "What time is it?"

"Three fifteen."

"Holy shit!" She threw back the sheet and was on her feet, wide-eyed. "I had no idea. I'm so sorry. I can leave right now if you want."

Dylan chuckled, stood up, and wrapped his arms around her naked body. "It's fine. A bit late to head out now, unless you really want or need to."

"I just...I didn't mean to..." She growled. "My brain's not working."

Guiding her back to bed, he pulled the comforter from the floor and wrapped it around her. "Go back to sleep. I've got some work I can do on the computer. I'll come to get you in the morning, and I'll take you back to your place."

He started to pull away when she grabbed his arm and tugged him to the bed. "Or we could have sex again?" Her sly smile went straight to his cock. "I mean unless it's too late for you?"

"Never." Without giving it much thought, he kissed the side of her neck and proceeded along her jawline until he reached her mouth. "As long as it's something you want."

She spread her legs, and his hard cock nearly slipped inside. "I hope you have another condom."

"Shit." He didn't want to leave her, but he wanted to push inside her even more. "Don't move." It didn't take him long to find another condom packet, open it up, and slide on the protection.

Simone watched him, looking as sleepy as she did aroused. This wasn't going to be a crazy bout of sex, but instead, the lazy kind Dylan preferred, even if he didn't usually say anything.

"Now, where was I?" He moved back on top of her and gently pushed his cock into her warm body. "Right about there."

Dylan had had more than his fair share of sex with women over the years. Many of his partners were exciting and adventurous, which led to excited and adventurous sex. Rarely did he share moments with women that were slow, lazy. His cock throbbed from their earlier round of sex; it wasn't sore exactly, but it reminded him that they'd already done this once. It was a physical reminder to take his time, to enjoy the moment with her.

Simone's body was pliant, soft, and took him in quickly. She wrapped her arms and legs around him, lifting her mouth to suck on his earlobe. That was something new, and Dylan moaned his appreciation against her neck.

"I don't think I can come again," she whispered against his ear. "Don't bother waiting for me."

Pulling back so he could look her in the eye, Dylan frowned. "You can't because your body is telling you that you can't? Or you can't because no one has ever given a shit enough to try for you?"

She turned her face, resting her cheek against the pillow. "Does it matter?"

"Yes. One is a physical limitation, and I'll assume you know your body well enough to tell me what it's capable of, and I will leave you alone." He leaned in and nipped her jawline. "The other is a challenge."

She chuckled, a low throaty sound that went straight to his cock. "What if I say I don't know? I've never had anyone try, but I'm not sure if I can either."

"Then I'm going to go down on you to see if I can make some magic happen. And if it doesn't feel like things are going to work out for you, then we'll come back here."

She bit down on her bottom lip and nodded once. "Sure. We can try that."

His excitement was more than a little surprising, yet Dylan wasn't about to question why. A beautiful woman in his bed wanted him to go down on her. Who the hell was he to argue with such a thing?

With a grin, he pulled out of her and kissed his way down her body. Her breasts posed a bit of a distraction, but Simone didn't seem to mind. He sucked her nipple into his mouth, dragging the peak between his teeth several times until she began to moan and squirm beneath him. Only then did he switch breasts to start his ministrations once more.

Shifting his hand between them, he fingered the curls on her mound, teasing and tugging at them as he sucked her nipples. Simone opened her legs wider, giving his hand better access. Yeah, this was precisely what he wanted, the best type of intimacy he could have with a woman.

With a final kiss to the breast, Dylan continued his downward journey until he reached her pussy. The scent of her arousal, mixed with the heat of the sheet over his head, was enough to make his head spin. With a flick of his hand, he sent the sheet flying away, giving him a clear view of her entire body.

She was watching him through a narrowed gaze, her lips parted and swollen from where he'd been kissing her moments earlier. Maintaining her gaze, he lowered his mouth and licked a single, slow path from her pussy opening to the top of her clit. Simone's body shuddered beneath him.

"You like that?"

She nodded.

"Good." He did it again, this time pausing at her clit to flick the nub with his tongue. "Think we can make some magic happen?"

His eyes widened, and her lips parted further, but she didn't say anything. Well then, he was going to have to try and see what he could do. Closing his eyes, he pressed his finger into her pussy and began to slowly fuck her with it. He timed the flicks of his tongue with each thrust of his finger inside her, wanting to build a slow, steady wave of pleasure inside her. The faster a rhythm he set up, the wider Simone stretched her legs. She began to buck her hips in time to his thrusts, even as her body grew more rigid.

No, no, no, he didn't want her coming that fast. Especially not after she didn't think she'd be able to come at all. He slowed the pace until she moaned her disapproval.

"Don't worry. I'm not going to let it go away." He nipped at her inner thigh, knowing what he wanted to do next. "Let's try something else." He moved, so he was now lying flat on the mattress beside her. "Come sit on my face."

Simone's face went red. "I've never done that before."

"The angle gives it a slightly different sensation. Plus, you can control how much or how little I lick you. Come on."

It took her a moment to shift around, then straddle his face with her thighs. Not only did it give him the best view of her body, but it also provided him better access to her. Simone looked far too serious for a woman who was about to come. She gripped the headboard as she watched him as she lowered her pussy to his mouth.

Dylan licked her for a moment before she pulled back with a laugh. "Oh, this is fun."

"You've really never done this before?"

"Nope." She lowered herself down once more. "But I think it's going to go permanently on my list of things I want my sex partners to do."

He reached up and cupped her ass cheeks with his hands, providing him with a bit of leverage he needed to be able to eat her out properly. This time Simone didn't pull back, didn't stop him from licking and sucking her clit. He moaned as he pressed his face hard against her, devouring every inch of her pussy that he could reach. His fingers flexed against her skin, and the temptation to tease other parts of her was too much for him to resist.

Opening his eyes, he looked to see if there were any problems as he moved his hand to press a finger lightly against the rim of her asshole. Simone sucked in a breath, and her eyes widened, but she didn't pull away, nor did she tell him to stop.

Well, all right then.

He didn't have any lube, so he didn't dare push inside her, but that didn't stop him from teasing the sensitive opening. As he'd done with her nipples, he timed his sucking and licking of her clit with the press of his finger against her asshole. After a few minutes of that, Simone reached up and pinched her left nipple as she pressed down harder against his face.

"Close." She managed to gasp out, even as her face scrunched up in concentration. "Don't stop."

There was no way in hell he'd do anything but keep going, not until she came all over him. Thankfully, it didn't take long. Within another few moments, the first rush of her juices flowed down his chin as her thighs clenched hard and she cried out. Dylan grabbed her by the hips and held her body tight as she continued to come. He wanted to pound into her, wanted to fuck her hard and fast, to follow her into pleasure's embrace as quickly as possible.

So the moment she relaxed against him, slumped forward toward the headboard, Dylan sat up and flipped her onto her back, her head now toward the foot of the mattress. Checking to make sure the condom was still in place, he thrust into her with a single buck of his hips.

Simone's gasps turned into moans once more. Her pussy clenched around his cock, practically vibrating from her recent orgasm. God, there wasn't a better feeling in the world than fucking a woman who'd just come. Dylan pressed his face to her shoulder and pounded into her, chasing his own orgasm. His balls tightened a split second before he felt the first wave of pleasure pulse through him.

His whole body went rigid, his vision darkened, and the only things he was aware of were his mind-blowing orgasm and the sweet scent of Simone's body. Finally, the waves of pleasure subsided, and he collapsed on top of her.

When she started gasping for air, he mentally shook himself and slid beside her. "Sorry."

He felt her smile against his shoulder. "It's good. More than good. It's really awesome."

"You're going to fall asleep again." Opening his eyes, he looked down at her tired face. "What time do you need to be up in the morning? I'll set the alarm."

Simone sighed. "What's tomorrow?"

"Friday, July twentieth."

"I'm having breakfast with my dad." There was something off in her voice, a note that shouldn't be there after just having had an orgasm. "I think I'm meeting him at ten, so I better be out of here by eight, so I can go home and get changed."

Reaching over, he grabbed his phone and set the alarm. "You have breakfast with your dad a lot?"

"Nope." She pulled her arm back and reached for the sheet. "I better try and get some sleep."

"Sure." This was the second time she'd changed the subject from her family. If he were smart, he'd back the hell off and give her the space she clearly needed. It wasn't as though they were in some sort of relationship. He shifted to his side so he could spoon her. "This okay?"

She grabbed his arm and pulled him closer. "Yup."

"Good night, Sugar Tart." He kissed the top of her shoulder.

Her body shook slightly as she chuckled. "Night, Candy King."

Tomorrow he'd figure out what was going on with her family. And what, if anything, he could do to help.

After all, he was her sugar daddy.

Chapter 16

Simone sat down in the booth of the diner, her thighs sticking to the pleather seats as she slid into place. Her body still pleasantly ached from last night's adventures with Dylan. Even though she'd showered and changed the moment she'd gotten home, she swore she could still smell him on her, could feel the touch of his hands on her body.

God, the things he did to her, both mentally and physically, were amazing. It wasn't as though he'd done anything weird or kinky, but he seemed to know exactly what she wanted or needed even before she did. That was one of the reasons she hadn't wanted to talk about her dad. It wasn't merely because they weren't really a couple or anything and she didn't need to unload that on him.

No, she was mostly scared that he'd be able to see what was wrong. And that the problem was her.

She looked around, but her dad still hadn't arrived. That in itself wasn't unusual. Even when she was a kid and her parents were still together, he wasn't exactly known for his ability to be on time. More than once, she'd been forgotten at school after play practice or an art project session. It had only gotten worse when her parents had divorced, but at least then her mom was faster to come to the rescue.

Simone made of point of never letting it get to her. Her dad suffered from severe depression and anxiety, and it wasn't exactly something that was in his control a lot of the time. Leaving the house some days proved to be the most challenging thing he'd have to do. Who the hell was she to criticize him for being a little late?

When he hadn't shown up after ten minutes, she pulled out her phone, intending to play a round of her current game. Somehow, she'd missed the notification that she'd received a message from the sugar daddy app. There was only one person in the world she spoke to through that, and she was shocked that he was interested in talking to her so soon.

With a quick look around, she opened the app, smiling almost as soon as she saw the message.

Hey Sugar.

I had a great time last night. And not just the after show. It's been a long time since I've attended a ball game. Thanks for bringing some excitement back into my life.

That got me thinking. If I'm going to be your sugar daddy, if I'm going to treat you the way a normal sugar baby would be treated, then I want to take you shopping.

After all, you need the full experience.

Sexy clothes. Lingerie.

A new mattress.

Anything your heart desires.

Remember, it's for research.

CK

Oh. Dear.

Simone's hands began to shake as she imagined what it would be like to go shopping with someone like Dylan. What it would be like to not have to worry about money or not having to debate the quality of a product versus if she could afford to put it on a payment plan?

Incredible.

But there was also a fine line between conducting research for a story and taking money from someone who was the subject of her story. Was Simone acting as a reporter investigating a trend, or was she Dylan's sugar baby and this was a natural part of their relationship? Would anyone care enough about her or the story for it to be an issue?

What would happen if their arrangement continued past the story? What would it mean for their relationship, if she could even call it that, for things to stay the same? What if she fell in love with him? He'd been so very clear about his expectations; how could she think he'd ever want more?

"There she is."

Simone shoved her phone in her purse at the sound of her dad's voice. "Hey." Looking up, she was happy to see that he looked clean and had recently shaved. "You look great."

"I feel great." He leaned in and kissed the top of her head before sliding into the seat opposite her. "Sorry I'm late. I was working on a project and lost track of time."

There was a brightness to his eyes that set off a warning bell in Simone's head. "You have a new contract?"

"Yeah. Don't worry, it's not a long one. I got a graphics design contract to create a new logo and website template for a local grocery store." He smiled at her as he grabbed the menu. "And that means that breakfast is on me."

She should be happy that he was apparently in a good place right now. Work came sporadically for him, as did his ability to complete a contract. His depression tended to go in manic waves, and he was clearly on an upswing. She'd have to let her mom know because he usually reached out to her when he'd inevitably start to crash. "That's awesome, Dad. But breakfast is on me. Remember, you paid last month."

He looked at her, frowning. "Did I? Well, it doesn't matter. You're my baby, and I can treat you if I want."

"Not if it means you don't have enough money for rent, it doesn't. Besides, you're my dad, and I like treating you too."

He rented a room in an apartment with three other men. It had taken him a long time to find a spot that not only was in a good neighborhood but also didn't break the bank. His disability payments gave him a monthly check, but it wasn't always enough. At least she could earn a decent wage, even if that meant she couldn't afford to go on cruises and vacations the way Kayla did.

Things could always be worse.

The waitress came and took their orders—eggs benedict for her, pancakes with sausage for him—and left them each with a mug of coffee. Simone's phone buzzed in her purse, no doubt another message from Dylan. She really didn't want to be thinking about him right now.

Her dad swallowed down his piping-hot coffee without a second glance. "What are you working on these days at the paper? Any more food stories? That editor of yours is completely wasting your talent on those ridiculous community stories."

She knew he was genuinely curious about what she was working on and was proud of her, but there was always something off when he asked her about her projects. She'd always assumed that there was a certain degree of jealousy, but maybe she was reading too much into it. He was her dad after all.

"Actually, I have something going on that might help give me the break I've been hoping for." Cupping the hot mug of coffee between her hands, she raced through all the things she wanted to tell him, deciding on the easiest. Best not to mention anything about the sugar daddy story and keep things boring. "I'm working with Williams Development on a story about a new housing development they're doing. It's a housing complex for people with mental illness, but also a Buddhist retreat. It's going to be pretty cool."

"Religions are rarely kind to those of us who're different upstairs." He tapped the side of his head with a smile. "Sounds interesting."

She hadn't considered her father's needs as a person who'd been struggling with mental health issues or how he'd react to the prospect of a place like this. "You know, it would be really great to get your perspective on this. You're the type of demographic the development company is targeting. It would be a great angle for the story."

The waitress dropped off their breakfast with a smile and pulled a bottle of French's ketchup from her pocket. "Need anything else?"

"The bill." Her father spoke the words sharply.

The waitress frowned down at Simone before pulling the paper bill from her pad and placed it facedown on the table. "You can pay at the front when you're ready."

"Dad, what's wrong?" Sometimes it didn't take much for him to do a one-eighty on her emotionally.

"Demographic? An angle? Is that all I am to you these days?" He stabbed his egg with his fork and shoved it into his mouth.

"Of course not." Shit, she'd really fucked things up. "But you have a unique perspective that the developer wouldn't have. It might really help other people, the ones who might be living there, to have input from someone who can see things from another perspective."

Every thought that flitted across his face was painfully easy for her to read. He'd been hurt by her words, and yet she could tell that he wanted to be a part of what she was working on. It was the first time she'd even considered involving him in one of her stories, and she did so mostly because Carl had drilled into her that the stories were about the people, places, and events, not the reporter.

But this time, maybe she needed to put a bit more into herself into the piece. In a way, it was no different than what she was doing with the sugar daddy story. Except, less sex.

She leaned across the table and tentatively took her dad's hand. "It might be fun. We'd get to work together on a piece. You can even help me write it if you want."

His chewing slowed until he swallowed slowly. "It's been a long time since I've written anything."

"It's like riding a bike. You never forget."

"You're kind but lying. Still. It would be nice to spend a bit more time with you."

"This will be great!" Excitement exploded in her chest as she squirmed in her seat. "I'll have to check with the development company, but I'm sure Dylan won't mind. Like I said, you'd be doing them a favor in the end. Maybe even help them avoid some pitfalls that they wouldn't necessarily consider."

"They might say no."

"They might, but that doesn't mean I still can't use you. I can do an interview with you as someone who might use their services. They can't stop you from giving an opinion."

Her dad chuckled finally, returning her hand squeeze. "Many have tried, but no one's been able to yet."

"It's settled then. I'll talk to Dylan about you helping, but regardless, you'll work on the story with me. This is going to be great."

Despite his smile, her dad didn't quite have the sparkle in his eyes that he'd had when he'd first arrived. "I have no doubt."

The rest of breakfast was far less eventful, and Simone did her best to steer their conversations away from anything work-related. That left books, movies, and television shows to discuss. Which meant she had to do a bit of fibbing when it came to things her dad liked. She'd told him once that she loved reading a particular author. He then went out and bought everything that they'd ever written, hoping to discuss them all with her. Of course, there was no way she could keep up with him, and to this day, she would say she was currently reading a book when she wasn't.

God, she was a shitty daughter.

Her phone buzzed in her purse a few times, diverting her attention every time. She didn't take her phone out, but she couldn't help but look over, wondering if it was Dylan texting her again. For all she knew, he was planning on taking her somewhere fancy to eat again. That'd be awesome.

"Do you need to get that?"

She snapped her gaze back to her dad. "What? No. It's fine. Sorry."

"You clearly want to check. Go ahead."

She hated doing that to people, but especially him. "It can wait."

He smiled and stood. "It's for a story. I can always tell when you've become fixated on something. You're a lot like me that way."

"Dad, I'm—"

"It's fine. I need to head out anyway." He picked up the bill from the table. "And it's my turn. You can get it next month."

"You said that last time." She stood and gave him a hug. "Thanks, Daddy."

"Anything for my little girl. Go check your phone, and let me know about the story."

"I will. Stay good, and let me know if you need anything."

It was hard watching her dad walk away from her and pay the bill for breakfast. She'd grown up worried about him, made painfully aware of his mental health challenges from too young an age. While she hadn't exactly taken it upon herself to make sure he was okay, she certainly had always tried to make him happy.

It was one of the reasons she was trying as hard as she was to make a name for herself. Yes, she was doing it based on her own desires, but also to make her dad proud.

Her purse buzzed again, and this time Simone reached down to retrieve it. There was, in fact, only one additional message from Dylan, though her work e-mails were currently blowing up. Who knew that leftover donuts in the kitchenette at work could cause such a stir?

But when she opened the message on the sugar daddy app, she suddenly forgot how to breathe.

There was a picture attached. A half-naked picture of Dylan. At least she assumed it was him because he'd intentionally taken it from the neck down. His clothing was gone, and his lower half was covered with a towel, giving her a glimpse of his toned chest and stomach, and the hair that led to his groin. The message beneath it was more than enough to fire up her arousal.

Had to shower. Jerked off thinking about you and our night and made a mess. Let me know when to pick you up.

Jesus fuck, he was trying to kill her. And she'd die happy if he kept sending her pictures like that. She pressed a hand to her cheek to feel her flushed skin before taking a breath and typing out a response.

I was having breakfast with my dad, and you send me something like that? You're a bad, bad man.

The waitress was hovering around, glancing Simone's way. She must want to clear the table and seat the next guest. That meant Simone needed to get the hell out of here and probably go to work. That was the reasonable, adult thing to do. On any other day, she wouldn't even consider doing something different than her normal routine, but today was turning out to be above average.

Today might even be her first day to conduct some unique research.

The phone buzzed in her hand as his response came through.

You haven't even learned the half of it. Let me take you shopping, and I'll show you.

A bubble of laughter burst from her, which immediately sent her to her feet and out the door. Embarrassment was a powerful motivator to move sometimes. Only once she was outside did she type a response.

Shopping for what?

Sexy things.

Lingerie?

We can start with that. Maybe some sex toys. If you're into that sort of thing.

Was she? Sure, Simone had a vibrator and knew how to use it, but that was the extent of her sex toy knowledge. She couldn't imagine what else he'd want to use or to do with those toys, but she was willing to find out. It was all in the name of research, after all. Simone started walking toward the subway station, typing as she went.

Where should I meet you?

Switching programs, she fired off a quick message to work, letting them know that she wouldn't be in the office today, that she was out in the field conducting research. Of course, she got three orders from co-workers asking her to bring back food from whatever food truck she was researching today. Typical.

Dylan's last message stopped her dead in her tracks and brought a smile to her face.

I'm in my car on the way to get you at the restaurant. Look for the Tesla.

Dylan was on his way to come get her. And then they were going to go buy sex toys. Simone's head spun as much as her arousal surged. Turning around, she went back to wait, hoping beyond hope that this little adventure wasn't going to blow up in her face.

Because the idea of using sex toys with Dylan was a temptation she couldn't resist.

Chapter 17

Dylan wasn't exactly sure what had possessed him to suggest they go out and purchase sex toys together, but now that they were in the middle of the store and he was watching Simone wave a giant silicone dick around the aisle, he was forever grateful. This was the most hilarious thing he'd ever personally witnessed.

"Oh my God, this thing would break a woman." She grinned before beginning to pretend to fence with the neon pink dick. "Totally useful as a personal defense weapon."

"You're a terrifying woman." Plucking it from her grasp, he gave it a good look. "This might be fun to play with."

"There's no way in hell I'd ever be able to put that inside me." She rolled her eyes, took the dick from him, and put it back on the shelf. "Not to say that I'm not interested in something. It just needs to be the right something."

Dylan had never been in a sex store with a woman before now. Not that he had any issues with it, but none of the women he'd dated had been interested in meeting up at a store like this. Typically, they'd enjoyed it when he'd bought clothing or toys for them and brought them to their dates. It was very much transactional, and this wasn't.

It was dangerously close to something he'd do with a girlfriend.

Which meant he needed to mix things up, change them around so whatever they ended up doing together was as far away from a relationship thing as he could possibly make it. With that in mind, he began to walk up and down the aisles, looking for the ultimate *thing I want to do with a sugar baby* item. It wasn't until the third pass that he noticed a box on the bottom shelf.

"What's that?" Simone stepped beside him after he retrieved it.

"A strap-on." And a pretty decent one at that. It came with multiple attachments of varying sizes. That was something he'd always wanted to try, but he hadn't brought up the idea with any of his partners before now. "Looks to be a good-quality one."

He was well aware that Simone was staring at him, mouth open. He didn't know the types of men she'd been with in the past, but he'd always been more than a little adventurous in the bedroom. At the very least, he was willing to experiment to see if a possibility was something he might enjoy. No sense in discounting something until you knew if it pushed one of your buttons.

Simone looked around the store, then leaned in a bit closer to him. "You mean you want me to use this on you? Right, like we don't need that for me, so you would be the only one it would make sense to put it... into. Oh my God, you want me to fuck you?" Instead of her voice getting louder as it usually did when she was surprised, Simone's voice dropped to a barely there whisper.

Dylan couldn't help but laugh. "You sound surprised."

"Well, yes. I mean, guys aren't normally into that sort of thing. Right? I mean unless they're gay, and then all power to them. But any straight guys I've been with are all freaked out by the thought of someone going near *there*, let alone putting anything in...I mean...yeah."

"There's a little thing called the prostate that more men need to be aware of. It doesn't make me attracted to men just because I like to have powerful orgasms." He turned to face her, keeping his face as impassive as he could manage. "Do you have a problem with me wanting to do something like this?"

He was taking a chance even discussing his sexual kinks with her, given that she was writing a story on him and the site. But if she wanted to have the full sugar daddy experience, that meant she needed to see everything—all of him, for good or bad. But more than that, it was the first time in a long while that he'd spent time with a woman he didn't mind sharing a private part of himself with. There was something so utterly open and authentic about her that he knew, beyond a doubt, that she wouldn't betray him.

Maybe he was a fool for thinking that, but there he was.

Simone gently took the box from him and looked it over. "No, I don't have a problem. I've just never been asked to do anything like this before. Shit, I've never had a guy ask me to do anything other than give him a blowjob, and that wasn't exactly all that earth-shattering. Honestly, I'd be scared that I'd hurt you."

"Nothing that a lot of lube and careful preparation wouldn't take care of." It was sweet of her to be so worried about him. Not exactly the sort of thing he normally experienced with a sugar baby, let alone one of his lovers. "If we ever did something like that, we'd go slow and make sure we were both comfortable." He put the box back on the shelf, only slightly disappointed that she didn't seem ready to play. "Let's keep looking."

They'd grabbed a basket on their way in, and it didn't take long for him to fill it with a variety of different lubes, a couple of sex games, and other novelty items. The store had lingerie as well, but the quality seemed cheap, not the sort of thing he wanted to get for her. No, only the best for Simone on their shopping trips. He had his back to her, looking at some movie DVDs when the weight distribution dramatically changed in the basket. He looked down and was surprised to see the strap-on box sitting front and center. He looked at her, lifting his eyebrow in a question.

"You went and mentioned it, and now I can't get it out of my head. I can't imagine I'll find too many guys who'd be interested in doing this, so I might as well take advantage." She shrugged. "It sounds like fun."

Her blush covered most of her face, giving her an innocent look, but he damn well knew she wasn't innocent. Excitement bubbled inside him, and his cock grew uncomfortably tight in his pants. "This is going to make my afternoon meeting interesting. I'm not going to be able to concentrate."

She winked at him. "Good thing I'll be there as well. I'll keep you on track."

Shit, he'd forgotten that she was attending the development meeting today. While he might have the ability to keep his cool in social situations, having Simone there and knowing what they were planning on doing afterward was almost too much for him.

He might have to go jerk off in the bathroom again.

What was his life coming to?

Simone looked down at her phone. "I'd actually forgotten about the meeting. I've been finding it hard to focus on stuff since we started our little arrangement. I don't know what that says about me."

"It means that you're a dedicated reporter who's giving her story her all."

"Yes, but probably not the right story. I need to make sure that your development project is front and center, or else Carl is going to give me hell." She bit down on her lower lip and looked away. "We better go pay for this stuff and then head out."

It didn't take a genius to realize that there was something else going on with Simone. She'd been a bit off when he'd picked her up at the diner, but he hadn't wanted to ask about her breakfast with her dad. Family was a subject she'd sidestepped every time he brought it up, and the last thing he wanted to do was upset her.

"Sure, let's head out. We can grab a coffee before the meeting. We'll probably need it."

It wasn't until he'd paid for their purchases—ignoring the smirk the woman behind the counter gave him at the sight of the strap-on—and they were outside that he reached down and took her hand in his. "Are you okay?"

"Yeah." She gave his hand a squeeze. "Breakfast was a bit exhausting."

Okay, maybe family discussions weren't entirely out of the question. "Everything okay?"

She opened the passenger door to the Tesla and climbed in, not saying anything else. Maybe she wanted some privacy to talk, or perhaps she was merely trying to find the right words. Either way, Dylan wasn't about to push her on this. He got into the car, turned it on, and waited briefly before pulling out into traffic. "Did you want a coffee, or are you—"

"My dad has severe depression and anxiety. It was the reason my parents divorced when I was a kid. He'd always wanted to be a journalist, had even started school, but he'd dropped out when he couldn't make it through the classes. It's one of the reasons I chose to do what I do and why I want to make a name for myself."

Usually when Simone started on one of her rambles, she was all bubbly and cute. This time, she spoke every word with a graveness that nearly broke his heart. Without looking, he reached over and gave her hand a squeeze. "That must be a hard burden to bear."

"It's not a burden. Not really. But I worry about him all the time. He's renting a room in an apartment, doesn't have a lot of privacy, and struggles to pay his bills. I got to thinking about your project and how it will help people like my dad. Then I wondered if there was an opportunity for someone like him to help out. Be a consultant of sorts. When you get to the phase of planning the interior."

He could tell that bringing that up was difficult for her. His own family might have problems when it came to staying together, but they didn't have the challenges of mental health that Simone's dad did. Maybe Sarah's ability to persuade Jonathan to create this housing community wasn't a crazy idea after all.

"I'm not asking you to hire my dad. That isn't the sort of thing I'd do. But I'd like to use him in the story, as one example of a potential beneficiary of your project. It would let me give him a chance to play the part of journalist, and it would also show him that there are organizations in Toronto that care about people like him."

It would also have the unintended side effect of entangling him and Simone even more than they already were. When he'd read her first message, he could never have guessed that it would lead them both to here. "Let me talk to my brother, but I think that makes a lot of sense. We'd need to have a consultant of some sort offer advice and input about what people with mental health issues might need from our facility. This is a great way of killing two birds with one stone."

"What's the other bird?"

"Helping you and your dad."

Dylan never considered himself a selfish person, and other than the sugar daddy site, he rarely took anything for himself. Doing this for Simone was an excellent way to not only make someone else happy but to also give himself the satisfaction of making someone happy whom he happened to like.

As a friend and lover. That was it. He'd have done the same for someone he wasn't sleeping with or about to get fucked by.

It was completely normal.

Their conversation drifted back to the mundane as they made their way to the development site. It was nice knowing Simone was going to be with him for the rest of the afternoon, and that they could continue to spend time together tonight. They didn't have to even do anything sexual; it was nice knowing that he had a companion to spend time with, even if they didn't have specific plans.

And that was the rub of being in a relationship. There were elements of it that he liked the thought of—companionship, sex with someone who knew what you liked—but the potential downfall, the inevitable breakup wasn't worth it in the end. At least it never had been in the past.

Maybe Simone was different. Maybe because neither of them was actually looking for anything beyond sex, this time things would be different.

Maybe.

Or maybe he was buying into her whole *People who meet on your website are different and fall in love thing* a bit too much.

Looking over at her as she spoke about the project brought a smile to his face. Even if he wasn't interested in love, that didn't mean they couldn't be friends with specific benefits. There was nothing off or weird about wanting to spend time with someone who had a similar outlook on life and relationships. If anything, they could help protect one another from the inevitable onslaught of people wanting to know when they were going to be in a relationship.

It was a win-win.

"I'm looking forward to seeing what you guys have managed to plan for the project." Simone held the bag from the sex shop a bit tighter. "It really is something special. I'm thrilled to be a part of it, even if it wasn't what I'd originally set out to report on."

"I am too."

Simone cocked her head to the side as she looked at him. "That doesn't mean I'm forgetting about our deal. You still owe me a story on your site."

"And I plan to honor that deal." Especially if it meant he got to continue to enjoy their extracurricular activities. "Even if we don't do anything else sexually. You hold on to that bag, and if and when you want to do something, you let me know."

"Okay." She smoothed out the plastic bag and shifted her gaze out the window. "I'll let you know."

"Good. Okay." God, he shouldn't be nervous or excited about the prospect of doing anything with her. Their relationship was merely one of mutual need, and nothing more. They'd have fun, make a few memories, and then move on. And that was all he wanted or needed from his life. Hot sex with a beautiful, intelligent woman and some laughs.

Yup, that was all. Because asking for anything else wouldn't end well for either of them.

Chapter 18

It was bizarre having spent the last few weeks with a bag of dildos in her bedroom and not having used them. Not that they'd been bought for her, but Simone was undoubtedly one of the principal parties involved.

Dylan hadn't pressed matters, respecting her choice to not move forward with anything sexual since their little excursion to the store. Not that they'd had a lot of spare time since then. At the planning meeting, Dylan streamlined their development project so it would be done within three months rather than four. That caused Simone to adjust her own timelines for the story. And when Dylan brought up the idea of working with someone who would directly benefit from the housing development, assuring that the needs of the people they were hoping to help were adequately met, she was able to suggest working with her dad.

After that, the entire thing became a bit of a whirlwind.

Thankfully, tonight she had nothing on her plate and was able to stay home and relax. With a glass of wine in one hand and her phone in the other, Simone sat down on her well-worn couch and pulled up one of her games. She loved the distraction, even if she sucked at the actual execution of the game. Unfortunately for her, she used up her lives far too quickly and now would have to wait twenty minutes before she could try again.

It was a beautiful fall Friday night, and she was at home alone.

With a sigh, she took another sip of wine. In the past, she would have reached out to Kayla and planned a girls' night out, but she was off with her fiancé on a business trip. And while Simone did have other friends, there wasn't really anyone who she felt she could just pick up the phone and call on a whim.

She didn't even want to think what that said about her life.

With another glance at her phone screen, she saw the shortcut for the sugar daddy site. It had been a while since they'd used the app, opting instead to talk in person or via standard texting. Their conversations mostly dealt with the project or her dad, rather than their sugar daddy arrangement. Simone missed the online flirting, their sexy back-and-forth that generally got her libido all fired up.

She didn't have a clue as to what Dylan was doing tonight. She actually hadn't spoken to him for a few days, despite their multiple contacts about business. No doubt, he was out tonight having dinner and drinks with friends. Or maybe he was at a club, hitting up a potential date for the night. Someone he could take back to his place for a good time. Just because he'd asked her to be his sugar baby didn't mean that they'd agreed to be exclusive. They really hadn't talked much about the expectations on either of their parts. As far as she was aware, she could go out to a club and party all night with hot dudes until they made her an offer she couldn't—

Yeah, that was never going to happen.

But she had no reason to believe that Dylan wouldn't do something like that.

Why that idea tended to make her jealous, Simone wasn't sure. Dylan had been perfectly clear from day one that he didn't believe in relationships; it was the whole reason he'd started the website to begin with. Just because they'd had sex didn't mean that she had any claims on him. If anything, she really should be pushing more to get further details for her story on him.

If she were to message him tonight, it had nothing to do with her own loneliness and everything with her need to take advantage of her free time to pursue the story.

Right?

Yes.

Pressing the icon for the app, she typed out a quick message, smiling at her own words.

Hello, your Highness.

I was curious to know what the other half gets up to on a Friday night? Women? Wine? More than a little taste of sugar? Your Sugar Tart is home alone. All alone and looking at my bag of toys.

We should do something about that. Maybe play twenty questions and see where that leads us.

ST

There, that should get him talking. If nothing else, she could use it as a way to get some answers out of him. But Dylan didn't respond as quickly as she'd hoped, leaving her to drink another half glass of wine in silence.

She really needed to get a life. Perhaps she should sign up for a regular dating app, see if there was anyone out there who wouldn't mind her quirks, who would want to get pulled around the city so she could try out new restaurants, go to concerts or plays or whatever she saw that happened to catch her attention. There was, no doubt, someone out there who would take her by the hand as they sat on a blanket at the park, listening to a choir or group. Someone who would tease her, flirt with her, talk dirty to her all night long until they ended up at their place to have sex.

Someone like Dylan.

Simone groaned, letting her head fall back against the cushion. She really was setting herself up for a fall if she thought for even a moment that a relationship with Dylan was going to work out. He'd been more than honest about how he felt regarding them, not to mention that his entire business model was based on avoiding long-term relationships at all costs.

Her phone rang, and she sat up so fast the alcoholic buzz had her head spinning. But when she opened the app, she couldn't stop smiling.

What's your favorite color?

At least he was starting off with something easy. Not that she was going to do that for him.

Green. What's your favorite sexual position?

She laughed out loud when he came back with an answer almost instantly.

Doggy. How many times can you come in one night?

Clearly, he was willing to play the game.

I've managed twice only a few times. How many times have you used a dildo on yourself like the one we bought?

You need to date better lovers. Not very much, maybe three or four times. Not many of my female lovers are into that.

Simone bit her lip and asked her next question.

So, you've had male lovers?

A few over the years. I generally prefer women. Is that a problem?

Nope, I've just never been with a bi man before.

You have now.

Her phone rang in her hand, and she jumped at the suddenness of it. Dylan's name flashed on the screen, sending her heart rate flying. "Hello?"

"I thought this was easier than the app. Too much typing."

She settled deeper into the cushions. "It is. Are you home?"

"At the office. I had some paperwork on the housing project that I wanted to get done before I could head home."

Figures he'd be a workaholic. "I bet you haven't eaten anything yet."

"Not yet. How did you know?"

"Kayla's the same way. I got used to bringing her food whenever I knew she was working on a big project." Simone pushed away the unexpected wave of disappointment that washed over her. "Her fiancé does that now."

"You sound disappointed." He made some sort of noise on the other end. "What's your address again?"

She pulled the phone away from her ear and looked down at it for a moment before answering. "Why?"

"I'm ordering delivery. I won't be far behind it."

"I thought you were working?" She sat up, her gaze landing on the umpteen piles of clothing around the place that would need to be quickly cleaned up if anyone was coming over.

"I was, but you're right. I need to eat, and I won't if I stay here. Plus, maybe we can break in some of our purchases from the other day. If you're up for that."

A choir of angels exploded in signing inside her head. "I'll text you my address."

"I'll be there within the hour."

Simone spent the first twenty minutes cleaning her place, and the second twenty cleaning herself. Her slight buzz had long worn off by the time the doorbell rang and the food was delivered. The young man at the door smiled. "It's been prepaid. Enjoy."

She had just enough time to set out the food, grab plates, and set out the bottle of wine that came with the meal before the doorbell rang a second time. Dylan smiled as he stood there, hands in his pockets, his dress shirt lacking a tie and unbuttoned. "Hey."

"Come in." The moment he entered, she looked around and was instantly embarrassed at the impression her little apartment made. "It's not exactly a condo looking over the lake."

"It's a great location in a good neighborhood. You can't ask for more. That smells so good. I had Park make something for us. He wanted me to thank you again. This is the most food I've bought from him in months."

Simone chuckled. "I do love food."

"I do appreciate that about you."

"My mom is a professional pastry chef. When my dad would have bad depression days, the three of us would pile into the kitchen and bake stuff. Well, Mom did. Dad and I tried to help but mostly just made a mess. Then we'd eat everything, and for a little while things would feel better." She hadn't thought about that for a long time. "Eating and food have always been a positive family thing for me."

"Then you're in for a treat."

Her brain was on fast-forward as she led him to the table and the meal. She knew that, for the next little while, they'd sit here, make small talk, and have a glass of wine. During that time, her mind would be doing mental gymnastics while she pondered the thought of fucking him with a strap-on.

He pulled out her chair for her. "Madam?"

Okay, so she could sit down and do this, or she could take matters into her own hands. Ignoring his gesture, she walked over to him, cupped his face, and kissed him hard. "I think we really need to have sex first. Because I've had a strap-on in my room for a couple weeks now, and I have to do something with it before I go insane."

Dylan's grin made her heart glow. "I love a woman who knows what she wants."

Simone utterly ignored the word *love* in that sentence, took him by the hand, and led him to the bedroom. "I have no idea what I'm doing, so you'll have to tell me."

She had a mountain of pillows on her bed that she used when she read at night. It took Dylan half a second to push them all to the floor, turn her around, and have her sit on the edge. "I'm going to be honest, I haven't been able to stop thinking about this since we bought this thing. I also know I won't last long once we get started, so it's best if we do a few other things first."

He encouraged her to lie back before he pulled his shirt and socks off. Simone watched, fascinated by his body, the muscles moving beneath his skin. The dusting of hair that covered his chest and stomach curled enticingly, and she had to fight to keep still and not reach up to play with it. "You're really fucking hot."

He arched his eyebrow for a moment before winking. "You're pretty amazing yourself."

Why did this fantastic and handsome man swear off relationships? He was kind, generous, and funny. In the short time they'd known one another, Simone couldn't see any reason why anyone would reject him, break his heart. Yet she knew that's what had happened to him.

Thanks, lady, for ruining it for the rest of us.

Though when he deftly removed her pants and panties, before spreading her legs and dropping his face to her pussy, Simone couldn't help but feel as though she were the luckiest woman in the world. The anticipation had her arousal so high, she knew there wasn't any way she'd be able to hold back her orgasm. She placed a hand on his head, taking a moment to stroke his hair as he put kisses along the inside of her thigh. "I think this is going to be quick for both of us."

"A quick one for you is good. The strap-on has a vibrator for you as well. You'll be able to come again."

Simone cried out at the first hot touch of his tongue on her clit. Dylan clearly was as turned on as she was, because unlike their first time, he was far less controlled, less concerned about dragging things out. No, this was all about the main event and making sure they both got to enjoy it as much as possible.

Without worrying about the speed, she relaxed as much as she could and let the sensations wash over her. Dylan used both of his hands to push her thighs wide open, his fingers flexing against her flesh as he sucked on her clit. The flicking of his tongue was steady, unrelenting, and before Simone knew what was happening, her orgasm was on the periphery of her awareness.

"No, no, no. That's too quick." She closed her eyes and turned her head to the side, not knowing if he could see her pouting. "Slow down."

He did as she asked, but the damage was already done. Despite only the occasional licks across her clit, Simone knew that she wasn't going to be able to hold back much longer. "Shit."

Dylan lifted his head. "Want me to stop?"

"I'll fucking kill you." She sucked in a breath before leaning up to look at him. "Make it hard so I can fuck you."

A soft growl echoed in the back of his throat before he dropped his mouth to her clit once more. There was no pretense any longer on either of their parts. Dylan was unrelenting with his mouth until Simone knew there was no stopping her release. She tried to hold off, but within a matter of seconds her body seized up as her orgasm slammed into her. "Fuck!"

The pleasure didn't seem to want to stop. Over and over the waves rolled as she pressed her pussy up against him as hard as she could. As quickly as it happened, the pleasure stopped, and she collapsed back against the bed. For several moments afterward, the only thing she was aware of was the pounding of her heart and Dylan moving around her room.

When she finally had the energy to open her eyes, she saw that he'd retrieved the sex shop bag from her dresser, where she'd placed it earlier. He'd pulled out the strap-on and the big bottle of lube. "You okay?"

She smiled, giving him a thumbs-up.

"Good. I need to clean this in the bathroom and lube up a bit." He grinned. "I find the first time I do this with someone it's best if I do that in private. Hate to freak people out."

The mental image of him putting lube up his own ass nearly had her come again. "Don't be long."

It was, in fact, a good ten minutes before he came back to her room. He'd taken off his pants and briefs and was now gloriously naked in her bedroom. She couldn't help but stare at him, unable to process that a multimillionaire was in her apartment getting ready for her to fuck him with a dildo.

And that's why sugar daddy sites are a thing.

She pushed herself to a sitting position as she pulled off her shirt and bra. "So, what do I need to do here?"

Dylan looked like a kid at Christmas. "Stand up. You'll need to step into the harness, and we'll adjust it for you. There's a vibrator that should give you some extra fun."

This was more complicated than Simone was used to when it came to sexual encounters, but she was more than willing to learn. Especially if it meant she got to make Dylan come hard. The long silicone phallus had more weight than she'd expected, as it hung between her legs. "This is the weirdest fucking thing. How do you guys live like this?"

"We survive." He winked at her as reached between her legs into the harness. "There's a little button right about here." He flicked it on, and an egg inside the harness began to vibrate against her clit. Dylan turned it off quickly. "When you're ready, you can turn that on. I'd wait until you get this thing inside me though."

Oh my God, what am I doing? "Okay." She swallowed hard and nodded toward the bed. "So now what?"

"Now, I'm going to get on my back while you make sure that there's lots of lube on that cock." He handed her the bottle and gave her an earnest look. "Lots of lube."

Simone had only had anal sex once in her life. The entire production had been far too uncomfortable for her to ever want to do again. Maybe if she'd been with someone as careful as Dylan, she might have enjoyed herself.

A thought for another time.

As thoroughly as she could manage, Simone coated the dildo. It wasn't as thick as her vibrator—or Dylan himself, for that matter—so she hoped it wouldn't cause him any discomfort. Clearly, this wasn't his first time, and seeing as he was the one who bought it, he would know what he could handle.

Giving herself a moment to collect her thoughts, she finally looked over at Dylan, who was now stretched out on the bed. "Okay. I can do this."

"You can. And I'll be all the more thankful for it." He beckoned her over. "Come here. I'll talk you through it."

Simone was not usually someone for role reversals, so the act of stepping between a man's thighs and placing the tip of a cock to his ass was enough to give her pause. That was until she looked down into his eyes and saw how much he wanted this. Without putting much thought into it, she slowly pressed the cock into him, inch by inch.

"Take it slow. Pause every inch or two, so I can adjust." He closed his eyes, and a strange look of relaxed concentration washed over him. "There you go. A bit more."

It took them a few minutes to work the dildo in, but eventually, she was able to move in long, smooth thrusts. Dylan's cock was hard and leaking against his stomach, bobbing and jerking with each thrust she gave. The sight was more than arousing, as was the bumping of the harness against her clit.

Right, the vibrator.

She paused long enough to reach in and flick the switch, before resuming her fucking. "Shit, this is hot."

Dylan moaned. "Can you stroke me?"

Simone wrapped her hand around his cock and fell into a rhythm of stroking him as she thrust. It didn't take long for a flush to cover his chest and throat, and beads of sweat to form on his forehead as his hips bucked up to meet her. She could tell by the way his body shuddered beneath her that he was close to coming. She increased her thrusts and did her best to hold off coming herself.

The first spurts of come splashed across her hand and his stomach before Dylan cried out in release. Simone stared in awe and amazement as his come coated her hand and his skin, knowing that she'd done that to him. It was all too much for her as a powerful orgasm hit her. Her body bowed over him as she rode out the waves, scared to move too much for fear of hurting him. Only after the world threatened to go black on her did she turn off the vibrator and slowly pull out of him.

She didn't bother to take the harness off and flopped on the bed beside him. "Wow."

Dylan began to laugh. "Yeah. You could say that. I haven't come that hard in a long time."

"I can't believe I just did that to you?" Simone closed her eyes, unable to stop smiling. "I need a shower."

"Me too." He rolled on his side. "Mind if I use yours before we eat?"

"Go for it. The towels are under the sink."

She watched him pad to her tiny bathroom, as her mind slowly came back to life.

He didn't want to run away from her. He let her do something to him that she knew was intensely personal, and he didn't want to rush out the door. How the hell was she supposed to keep from developing feelings with him if he kept being so fucking amazing?

This was going to be a problem.

Chapter 19

Dylan's body, mind, and spirit hadn't been this happy for well over a decade. In the two weeks since he'd shown up at Simone's and let her peg him, he'd begun to question his self-proclaimed commitment to bachelorhood. Because, really, a woman who would do that for him and then ask him what he thought about the state of Toronto city politics in the next heartbeat was a woman he could very quickly see himself falling in love with.

And he didn't know what he'd do if that happened.

For the past two weeks, they'd gone out to dinner at some of Toronto's best restaurants, had attended an evening at the Toronto Symphony, and had some of the best sex of Dylan's life. Not to mention their conversations. Simone was knowledgeable on a wide range of topics, everything from the current Blue Jays roster to fan theories on how *Game of Thrones* was going to end to the drama surrounding the latest Toronto city council proposal on how the hell they could fix the city's transit system. She was able to debate, to listen to opposing opinions, and eloquently get her point across without belittling others.

She was perfect.

It was terrifying.

Sounds of the contractors working brought Dylan back to reality as he had to redouble his attention on the state of the renovations. Jonathan was supposed to have met him here today to review the next stage of work. They'd set an aggressive timeline for getting things done. Jonathan had wanted to have the building to a point where he could present it to Sarah as a wedding present. Dylan didn't think that was going to be possible, but he was trying his best.

Even though the building had been mostly completed, due to a previous development that had fallen through, they needed time to ensure it would meet the needs of the intended users.

To that end, Simone was bringing her father by today, someone who would be the ideal candidate to rent a room in the complex. She still didn't like talking much about her family, but Dylan did know that her dad suffered from significant depression and anxiety and had been seeing a therapist for years. Living in a zen environment with access to free daily yoga and meditation might help someone like him.

Hell, it might help Dylan too. He'd have to see if Sarah would mind him slipping into a class or a support group every now and again.

The sound of the door opening drew Dylan's attention. Simone was there, walking beside a man who didn't look much like her, but from his gestures and the way he moved, Dylan knew this was her father. He crossed the room and held out his hand. "Simone, Mr. Leblanc, thanks for coming." He didn't know what she might have told her father about him, so he figured it was best to keep things professional so as not to invite any unwanted questions.

"Dylan, this is my dad, Gerald. For the story, I was hoping to get his perspective on the building. That kind of personal touch will be great and will encourage others to inquire about your rooms." She blushed and didn't quite meet his gaze. "Dad, Dylan here is the lead for the project."

"Nice to meet you." But he didn't shake Dylan's hand. "I thought this was supposed to be some zen shit."

So that's where Simone got her straightforwardness. "It will be when we're done."

"What's in this room?" Gerald walked forward into the common room.

Simone shrugged. "He's a bit on edge. I don't know how long he'll stay."

Dylan gave her hand a squeeze before turning his attention to her dad. "Right now, it will just be a big space. I thought maybe people would want a television or something."

"No." Gerald looked around again. "There should be a waterfall. And no talking. If you're going to make this a Buddhist thing, then be respectful. Meditation, quiet. It's loud enough in my head, I don't need fucking commercials chasing me off to my room all the time."

Shit, he hadn't thought about that at all. "Good point. I'll make a note, and we'll see if we can get a water feature here."

Gerald turned around and narrowed his gaze. "Really?"

"Yes."

"Just like that? Some asshole you've never met before walks into your building and tells you to shut up and put a waterfall in, and you do it?"

"That was the whole point of inviting you here. This isn't a typical apartment or condo building. It's to help an exceptional group of people."

"Why? Sorry, but the average person doesn't usually give a shit about folks with mental health issues."

Dylan looked over at Simone, who was trying very hard not to look as though she weren't hanging on their every word. "Honestly, it's a wedding present from my brother to his bride-to-be. I didn't think it would work. So I'm doubly glad Simone invited you here. It's important for me to see that there's a real need for a place like this."

If it helped someone like Gerald—and, by extension, Simone—then maybe Jonathan wasn't so out to lunch with his idea after all.

"Are you the one who's brought a smile to my daughter's face?" Gerald spoke quietly enough that she didn't hear him. "Because if you do anything to hurt her, I'll end you."

Dylan held up his hands. "I wouldn't dream of it. She's a special woman, your daughter."

"She is." Gerald gave him a good hard look before turning around and heading toward the kitchen. "Show me what's over here."

Dylan chased after him, strangely hoping that his work would impress her dad. Though why it mattered to him, Dylan wasn't sure.

It wasn't as though they were dating.

Right?

* * * *

Simone had raced back into the office after dropping her dad at his apartment. Carl had wanted an update in person regarding both the development and the sugar daddy stories, and she was far from ready for a report. At this stage, she didn't even know if she wanted to do the sugar daddy article, not wanting to risk Dylan's reputation if anyone got as curious as she did and went looking.

And yet that was still her best opportunity to break out of the community stories that she seemed forever obligated to do.

With her mind continuing to spin, she raced to her cubicle and dumped her purse and sweater on her desk. Elena looked over and whistled. "Is that a new purse?"

She'd completely forgotten that the bag she'd been carrying was new. "Yeah. I just got it a few weeks ago."

"That's beautiful. How much did you pay for it?"

Simone turned around, knowing that Elena would realize something was up. "It was a present. I'm not even sure where he bought it."

"He?" Elena was on her feet and in Simone's cubicle. "Who is the mysterious he, and how can I get him to buy me a nice purse like that?"

Oh, you know, join a sugar daddy site and ask. Here's the link! "He's a friend, and I'm not going to tell you anything else because I have to get my ass into Carl's office, like, now."

"You're killing me with the secrecy. You're never around anymore. What the hell am I supposed to do with you having an exciting adventure and not sharing the details?"

"I'm sure you'll survive." Simone flashed her a grin before grabbing her cell phone and her notepad. "I really have to go."

"Good luck."

Carl was waiting for her, sitting in front of his desk as he usually did. He looked up to see that it was her and pointed at the guest chair before returning to what he was reading. Simone sat, using the few moments she knew he'd give her to catch her breath and mentally prepare for what she needed to say. Carl finally turned to face her, crossing his arms and leaning back in his chair.

"Where are you at on the Williams Development piece?"

"I've been on site with Dylan for a few weeks now. They're working on an accelerated time frame for some personal reasons that I won't go into for the story. I have managed to get a person who would be their target demographic to come and look at the place. We were just there before I came to the office. Dylan thought it was great, and they'll now be working together. It will be a great angle for the story. Gives it more of a human touch."

Carl nodded. "I take it you haven't given up on your other project?"

Simone's eyes widened. "I promised that I'd make the Williams Development story my priority. And I have."

"But that's not the story that you want to be working on. I know you, Leblanc. Once you've set your mind on something, there's no stopping you." He shook his head before leaning forward on his desk. "What's the status on that one?"

Well, there wasn't really any sense in denying that she wasn't working on the sugar daddy story, not when it was so painfully evident that she was. "I've uncovered the identity of the owner of the site."

Carl straightened. "You have?"

"I was able to track him down based on some key words and school records." Simone didn't dare say anything else or risk exposing Dylan's identity. "I'm working on securing an interview."

"After you were here in my office talking about all this daddy stuff, I did some digging on my own. It's a good lead and a great opportunity for you. If you've gotten as far as you claim, this might be a big break for you." He cocked his head to the side as he narrowed his gaze at her. "If I like what I read, I'll give you prime placement and online marketing runs for the website. *If* I like what I read. If I don't, the story will go to Mark, and you'll be doing food trucks for the rest of your career here at the *Record*."

No fucking way was she going to let him take her story. "That won't be necessary. It will be the best thing you've read this year." She got to her feet. "In fact, I need to get going. With two stories and all the in-person research I've been doing, I don't really have time to be here."

"That's what I like to see, Leblanc." Carl grinned and waved her away. "Go. Get out there and dig up whatever you need to. There might be hope for you yet."

Simone nodded, not quite sure how she felt about her boss's praise. Not once in all the years that she'd worked for the paper had Carl ever given her encouragement like that. No matter how hard she'd tried. And now that he'd done his own digging and knew that she'd found something good, he wanted her to succeed, or else.

Elena wasn't at her desk when Simone returned, which gave her the opportunity to get out of there without getting pulled into a conversation. That was good because she needed time to think. If she did the sugar daddy story, there was a chance she'd put Dylan's reputation in danger.

If she didn't, she'd lose her chance to move up at the paper.

The last thing she wanted was to screw this up and have the story end up on Mark's desk. While he wasn't the friendliest of men, Mark was far from incompetent. There was no way, given the information she had, that he wouldn't be able to discover Dylan's identity. She was damned if she did and damned if she didn't.

She needed to figure out what the hell she was going to do.

Chapter 20

Jonathan and Sarah had invited Dylan over for dinner a few days ago. He'd accepted, knowing he needed the chance to spend some more time with his soon-to-be sister-in-law before the big day next month. Usually, he'd show up to something like this with a bottle of wine and an escape plan so that he wouldn't have to spend more time than was necessary with the happy couple. This time, he had a different idea.

"Do you mind if I bring someone with me tonight?"

Jonathan sat up straight and stared at him. "You mean a date?"

"A friend." The last thing he wanted to do was give his brother any inkling that there was something serious going on. "The reporter who's been working on our story."

"Simone." Jonathan grinned. "I was wondering if there was something between the two of you."

"Why the hell would you say that?" Dylan had been more than careful to ensure no one knew that they were anything more than two people working together. "I happen to find her articles interesting and figured she and Sarah might get along."

"Sure. If that's what you want to tell people, then I'll play along." He smiled as he pulled out his phone. "I'll let Sarah know that we have one more for dinner."

That was why Dylan was now standing outside of Simone's apartment, doing his best to ignore the neighbor staring at him while he waited for Simone to open her door. He knocked again, the bouquet of flowers he'd bought from the little convenience store next door securely behind his back.

When Simone finally answered, she was dressed in jeans and a black top, her blond hair loose around her shoulders and a grin on her face. "Hey!"

He held out the flowers. "I know these aren't a very fancy bouquet, but when I saw them, I thought of you."

Simone's face morphed into a look that Dylan usually only witnessed when someone was looking at a cute puppy. "They're beautiful. Let me put them in water really quickly, and then we can go."

"I'll wait here."

She ducked back into her apartment, and Dylan was left once more with the nosy neighbor. He gave her a little wave. "Hello."

The small Asian woman looked him up and down, before giving him a little thumbs-up and shutting her apartment door.

Okay then.

Simone was back in a whirlwind of activity, shutting and locking her door in practically the same motion. "I'm all set." She linked her arm in his, and they headed out.

"I know you haven't met Sarah yet, but she's quite lovely and far too good a woman for my brother. She's been a calming influence on him so far. I just hope he doesn't say something that screws up their relationship." He shut her car door before jogging around to get in on his side. "It shouldn't take us too long to get there."

"Why do you think your brother will screw things up?"

"History. This is marriage number three for him, so it's not exactly like he has a good track record. I just hope this one lasts longer than his most recent marriage, which lasted eight months, if you're curious."

"No wonder you have such a negative view of marriage."

"I'm surprised you don't. Your parents are divorced as well."

"Yes, but that's different." She pushed her hair from her face and tucked it behind her ear. "My dad thought he was doing us damage with all of his mental health problems. He walked away from us. If he hadn't, my mom would probably still be with him. She's never even dated anyone else."

Dylan couldn't imagine being that dedicated to someone who'd turned their back on him that way. It just wasn't worth the heartache. "She's a better person than I am."

Simone nodded. "She's better than most. I normally switch between loving him and wanting to throttle him. But I think that's a common father-daughter relationship. Right? I hope so."

They chatted about inconsequential stuff for the remainder of the ride, until he turned down his brother's street. Simone sat up to turn and look out the window. "Wow, some of these houses are crazy."

"Jonathan has expensive tastes, though not as lavish as he used to have. He's got two support payments on top of living expenses." It was one of the reasons Jonathan had asked Sarah to sign a prenuptial agreement. "They're just up here."

Considering the neighborhood, the house wasn't as impressive as some of the others. Still, the two-car garage and large hedge wall around the property set it up quite nicely. Dylan turned the car off but didn't get out right away. "We need a game plan."

Simone leaned close. "Okay. Why?"

"I love my brother, but when I come over, something usually happens. We need a look or a key phrase, something that indicates that one of us is uncomfortable and we need to leave."

"I've never been part of a couple that's had a *look*, and I can't tell you how excited this makes me." She squealed in a way that didn't sound quite natural. "I've arrived!"

"You're crazy." And yet he couldn't stop from grinning. "So, what's our phrase?"

They stared at one another, and Dylan had to fight the urge to close the remaining distance between them and kiss her. Simone's gaze slipped to his mouth before she looked back into his eyes. "How about, 'Oh crap, I forgot I had a call to make'?"

"That's a bit obvious."

"Maybe keep it simple. Say, 'Gee, look at the time.'"

Dylan nodded and, ignoring his inner doubts, kissed her quickly. "Works for me."

Grabbing the wine from the back seat, they got out and met in front of the car. He wanted nothing more than to take her hand, squeeze her fingers, and pull her close. But that would do nothing but confirm Jonathan's suspicion that something was going on between them. Instead, he kept pace with her and let his arm brush against hers as they approached the door.

He rang the doorbell three times before he heard footsteps and Jonathan appeared. Dylan knew there was a problem the moment he opened the door and looked at them both. "Hey."

Dylan held up the wine. "I got the good stuff. As requested."

Rather than immediately invite them in, Jonathan hesitated before stepping aside. "Sarah's in the kitchen."

Shit. Dylan tried to catch Simone's eye to let her know that something was up, but she'd already snatched the bottle from him. "The kitchen's straight ahead? I'll go say hi."

Within a moment, Dylan was left alone with his brother. "What's going on?"

Jonathan looked for a moment as though he might deny there was a problem, only to sigh, his shoulders drooping. "We were getting supper ready and were talking about you and your date. And then that got onto the topic of relationships and expectations, and I finally asked her about the prenup and she kind of lost her shit on me."

"Wait. You haven't talked to her about that before now? Dude, you're getting married in a month."

Jonathan shoved his hands in his pockets. "I know."

"That's a pretty shitty thing to do to someone." No wonder his brother was twice divorced. "What did she say?"

"She's pissed. And thinks that I don't trust her or love her enough to want to make the marriage work. She sees it as me giving up on us before we've really started."

Dylan knew it wasn't intended that way, but he could absolutely see it from Sarah's perspective, especially since Jonathan hadn't talked to her about it before now. "Will she sign it?"

"Don't know."

"Will you marry her if she doesn't?"

"We've opened the wine!" Simone's voice reached them from the kitchen. Jonathan used the distraction to end the conversation. "Coming."

Dylan knew things weren't going to go well. He followed Jonathan into the kitchen, where Sarah and Simone were standing and talking. The animosity rolled off Sarah in waves, nearly palpable to him. Dylan caught Simone's gaze, only to have her widen her eyes slightly.

So it wasn't just him.

"I'm so happy you brought Simone over," Sarah said, before taking a sip of wine. "It's nice not to be the only woman here. Sometimes the male arrogance can be a bit much."

"Dylan took pity on me when I told him I had nothing going on tonight. I've been working day and night on a couple of stories for the paper. It's nice to have a night off."

"It's nice to meet one of Dylan's lady friends." Jonathan stepped behind Sarah and put his arm around her waist, only to have her step away. "Even if you're just friends."

"Why don't we take our drinks to the living room." Sarah moved toward the door. "Supper will be ready soon."

Jonathan trailed after her while Dylan took the opportunity to move beside Simone. "Jonathan just asked for a prenup. Sarah isn't happy."

"Shit." She didn't let her smile drop.

Sarah patted the spot on the couch next to her. "Simone, why don't you join me?"

With a pleading glance to Dylan, she moved to join her. "I hear you're into yoga and meditation."

The tension in her shoulders lessened as Sarah faced Simone. "I am. I just got back from a retreat in Greece a few weeks ago. I spent a lot of time soul-searching, trying to learn more about who I am as a person while increasing my mindfulness about others around me."

"That's awesome." Simone sipped her wine as she leaned in. "I've tried meditation, but I last about five minutes before the silence gets to be too much for me. I can't shut my brain down long enough to relax."

"That's not uncommon. You eventually learn to let the thoughts wash over you, past you. It really can help with focus and stress levels. You should try it again."

"Maybe I'll come by the housing development for one of your sessions once it's up and running. I know it would be a great addition to the story I'm writing."

Sarah frowned as Jonathan stood up. "Right, we should probably get the appetizers out—"

"What housing development?"

Dylan wasn't able to interrupt her in time to save the surprise. Simone straightened and waved her free hand around. "The Buddhist housing development. It's such an amazing idea you had, and I know people with mental health problems will thrive there. I can't wait to get the article out so we can drive as many people your way as possible."

Sarah turned to Jonathan. "What's going on?"

"Oh shit." Simone pressed her hand to her mouth. "You didn't know."

"It was a wedding gift for her." Jonathan scratched his fingers through his hair. "Surprise."

But instead of the joy Dylan had expected from her, Sarah stood up, looking more than a little angry. "You've taken my idea and done it without asking me?"

"I wanted to give you a gift. Help get your dream off the ground, so you could take it and run with it. We had a building that had been mostly finished for another project, then abandoned. I was able to take it and repurpose it for your idea. It was a win for both of us. I thought you'd be thrilled."

"Thrilled? *Thrilled*?" Sarah got to her feet and moved to stand in front of his face. "That building was my dream! Did you think for even a moment that I might want to be involved with its creation? That I might want to plan and organize it? How could you be that selfish?"

Simone's head snapped around to stare at Dylan, her eyes wide. Without saying a word, he knew exactly what she was thinking. *This has gone from bad to worse in no time.* He hated when he was right. "We're not so far along that you still can't make suggestions and changes."

But neither of them heard him. Sarah put her finger in Jonathan's face. "Is that why you wanted me to sign the prenup? You wanted to make sure that the building didn't leave your family if we ever split up?"

"Oh, gee, look at the time."

They stood and looked at one another, even as Sarah and Jonathan continued to fight. Dylan held out his hand, and Simone immediately took it. He pulled her close as they moved toward the front door. "I think maybe we'll leave you two to work things out."

"I can't believe you're that arrogant, that thoughtless that you'd take someone else's dream and stick it in a fucking contract!"

"I can't believe you think that this was all about you!"

And just like that, Dylan pulled Simone away from the fight. He looked down at his watch the moment they were back outside in the fresh air. "That was only ten minutes. Barely."

Simone burst into laughter before racing to the car with both of her hands pressed over her mouth. He unlocked the car, and she jumped in without waiting for him. When he climbed behind the wheel, she was doing her best to keep her laughter in check. "I'm sorry. That was horrible of me. They're fighting, and I'm laughing. I do that when I get overwhelmed and nervous, and that was the most intense thing I've lived through in forever."

It was pretty fucking shitty that she'd had to witness his family drama. He stared at the house, imagining the ensuing fight, remembering the last argument he'd had with Andrea before she'd left him for the last time. The reasons never seemed to matter, only the end results. "Now you know why I'm anti-relationship. They never seem to work out for my family."

Her hand was on his lap, drawing his attention back to her. "Maybe your brother just sucks at them. That doesn't mean they're horrible for everyone."

"Maybe." He'd had enough of that sort of talk. He wanted to get back to enjoying the night and Simone's company, despite what had happened. "Well, Sugar Tart, what should we do now?"

The humor that generally shone in Simone's eyes was gone, replaced by concern. "Why don't we go back to your place?" She slid her hand up his thigh, dangerously close to his groin. "Let me show you the upside to being in a steady relationship with someone."

He knew this was probably a bad idea, but with her fingers that close to his cock, he was willing to risk it. "My place it is."

They'd worry about his brother, the building, and the rest of the world later. Tonight, he'd be selfish and let himself get pulled into a moment that would be just for them. A moment of happiness that he could take with him when everything would eventually fall apart.

Putting the car into reverse, he took her home.

Chapter 21

Simone's heart was racing and her stomach flipping by the time they stepped into his condo. He hadn't said anything about sex, but she knew that's what they were going to do. It was weird, especially after having seen Jonathan and Sarah fight, that that was what they both needed to do—to have that physical connection with another person to ensure that all was okay.

She'd never been with another person long enough to find herself craving their touch on an emotional level. It was a need, deep down in her soul, wanting his hands on her skin. The longer they spent together, the more Simone realized that she not only genuinely wanted his company, but that he filled a void in her life she hadn't realized was there.

Of course, the confirmed happy bachelor was the man she fell for.

Yes, she was that much of an idiot.

"Do you want a drink or something to eat?" He tossed his jacket on the chair as he walked past to the kitchen. "You got shortchanged a meal."

"What do you have?" She watched, fascinated, as he rolled up his shirtsleeves to his elbows before opening the fridge and looking in. "I'm easy."

"I've heard that about you." He winked at her over his shoulder before returning his attention back to the fridge. "I have leftover Chinese. Not a lot, but it was excellent."

Simone made grabby hands and was quickly rewarded with a box of noodles. "Oh, those look great."

"Want me to heat them?"

She growled, stealing a fork from the counter when he set it down. "Mine."

"You really do love your food." He chuckled, but followed suit, eating his own cold noodles from a second box.

"I do. Access to the quality of food we have here in Toronto is a blessing that I promised myself I'd enjoy every day. So many people don't have the opportunity to explore different cultures the way we can here. I love it."

"So why do you want to walk away from doing those types of stories?" He leaned across the counter close enough to her that she could feel his body heat. "You're a talented reporter who can get to the heart of a story in a way I rarely see anymore. Why do you want to leave that?"

A few weeks ago, the answer to that question would have come to her far more easily. But as she'd spent time working on the two stories—the housing development and the sugar daddy story—she found that her effort had slid away from what had initially brought her to him, to focus on the former. "My dad wanted to be an investigative reporter. He'd taken journalism in school, but as his mental health challenges increased, he had to switch to something less stressful. I guess a part of me wanted to give him a glimpse into that world. I wanted him to be proud of me for picking up where he left off."

"Having met your dad, I think he's proud of you no matter what you do." Dylan set the container down on the counter, before gently taking hers from her hands. "You're an incredible woman."

It was quite hard for her to breathe, but somehow Simone managed. "Thanks."

Dylan didn't let go of her hand as he moved around the counter to stand beside her. He didn't say anything as he lowered his mouth to hers and kissed her softly. They stood that way for several minutes, kissing and touching. It was sweet, gentle, the exact opposite of what they'd ever done before. There was nothing hurried or frantic in their caresses, and Simone's mind went blank from the pure joy she got from the contact.

His hands moved into her hair, caressing and scratching her scalp as he pressed his body against hers hard. She became aware of his every muscle, his hard cock against her body. Letting her hands roam, she ran her fingers along his back and down to his ass, where she paused long enough to squeeze him.

Dylan chuckled into her mouth. "We don't have our toys here."

"That's an oversight on our part. We'll have to get another set."

"His and hers." Without any warning, he scooped her up in his arms. "To the bedroom."

"The bedroom."

Simone closed her eyes and laid her head on his shoulder as he carried her. She was a fool to let herself get so attached to him, but she couldn't help it. There was something about Dylan that fit with her, that filled a void she hadn't been aware of. And she could tell from his touch, the way he looked at her, that he was feeling something as well. He might not be willing to admit it yet, but she could tell.

When he stepped into his room, he didn't bother to turn the lights on, instead letting the moonlight from outside illuminate their way. There was no tossing on the mattress, no giggles as he stripped her naked. Dylan instead set her on her feet next to the bed and dropped to his knees in front of her. Using his hands to push her shirt up, he trailed a series of soft kisses along her belly as he undid the front of her pants. Simone pushed her hands into his hair, massaging the scalp and encouraging him until her pants dropped to the floor.

"Step out of them." He helped her, moving them to the side once she'd complied. "Panties next."

The cold air in the room caused goose bumps to rise on her skin, down her legs, and across her ass. Dylan's warm touch countered the chill and pulled a small moan from her as he ran his hands up and down the length of her legs. He pressed his mouth to the joint of her leg, kissing just beside her pubic hair.

"You're so beautiful." He kissed her again, over and over along her mound, down her thigh, before finally kissing her clit. "Amazing."

"Dylan." She sighed before leaning forward and kissing the top of his head. "Make me come."

He hummed and encouraged her to sit down on the edge of the bed, gently pulling her thighs wide, giving him better access to her. "Lean back."

She did, but only so far, so she could watch him. He didn't look her in the eyes, instead focusing his full attention on her pussy. Using his fingers, he brushed aside her pubic hair, exposing her hot clit to the air. The difference in the temperature only lasted a moment as he moved his mouth to suck it into his mouth.

Simone sighed not only at the sensation but at the look of pure bliss on his face. "You like that, don't you?"

"There's nothing better than being able to make a woman come. The taste, the smell. Sweeter than any candy I could ever eat."

"You're amazing." Anything else she was going to say left her as he sucked her clit into his mouth and pressed a finger into her pussy. "Shit."

He hummed again but didn't say anything else as he went to work eating her out. It finally became too difficult for her to keep watching, and she stretched back against the mattress and let the sensations wash over her. She'd never really been on the receiving end of someone who truly enjoyed giving oral sex the way Dylan did, and she knew that she'd have a hard time being with any other lover who didn't have the same enthusiasm.

Maybe she wouldn't have to.

Pushing that thought away, she closed her eyes and tried to ride the wave as much as she could. He was really fucking good, pressing his fingers in just the right spot inside her as he licked and sucked her clit. Her pussy, deeper inside her, began to feel warm, like a trickle of hot water surging inside her that brought pleasure wherever it went. Simone rolled her head from side to side as Dylan pressed a single spot harder than before. The sensations became overwhelming, and before she realized what was happening, her orgasm exploded.

The intensity of her pleasure, combined with the feeling of wetness, were the only things she was aware of as her body seized up in response. Dylan continued to fuck her with his fingers, milking her body for every last bit of her release, until she finally fell in a heap on the bed.

He slowly pulled back, removing his hand carefully from her. "Jesus, are you okay?"

She cracked open an eye as she tried to get her breathing under control. "Yes. Why?"

"Your come is all over my face and throat. I've never had anyone come that hard."

"You've got the magic touch." *You're my Candy King.*

"Let me clean up and find a condom." He placed a kiss on the inside of her thigh, before heading out to the bedroom.

Simone lay there for a moment to catch her breath before she realized that she hadn't even removed her shirt and bra. Wow. She'd never been so overcome with desire, with wanting to be with a man so badly that she'd been oblivious to her state of undress. With effort, she pulled the rest of her clothing off and tossed it onto the floor before climbing onto the bed to make use of the pillows.

Dylan came back into the room, and with her eyes now adjusted to the low light, she was able to see the grin on his face. "You nearly drowned me."

"That would have been a wonderful way to die."

"Death by come. It would have made for an interesting story to tell at my wake."

"May that be many, many years in the future."

The thought of what it would be like to grow old with him flashed across her mind. They could travel, she could write stories about the places they visited, the food she ate. Dylan no doubt would want to scope out potential business locations, buildings he could buy and develop.

She smiled and spread her legs. "I hope you found a condom."

He held it up as he moved to the side of the bed. "I have a whole box."

"That's good." She sat up and took it from him. "I haven't put one on a man in a long time."

With the moonlight shining on him, it was easy to see his eyes grow wide as she gripped his cock in her hand to hold him steady as she ripped open the condom packet with her teeth and roll it down his shaft. "Fun."

"You're going to be the death of me." It didn't sound like he minded much. "Mind if we do this face-to-face?"

"God, that sounds *horrible.* How could you even *suggest* such a position?" She rolled her eyes before holding her arms wide. "Come here."

He climbed between her legs and lined up his cock with her pussy. With a single thrust forward, he filled her as he covered her body with his own. They lay that way for a moment, and Simone let her body adjust to the size and weight of him. She turned her face so her mouth rested against the side of his throat and let her tongue dart over his salty skin.

"I—" She leaned harder against him, cutting off the words that she knew she couldn't say.

Dylan was either so wrapped up in his own pleasure that he hadn't heard her, or else he chose to ignore the potential of what the two other words of that sentence might be. Instead, he began a slow, steady thrust as he pulled her body hard against him.

They fit so perfectly together that she knew that he was the man who could make her life complete. Dylan's bucking hips pressed against her clit, and it didn't take long for her pleasure to begin to crest again. How could he do this to her when no other man could? She wrapped her legs around his waist and tipped her hips at just the right angle to ensure that she'd come again.

Dylan rose up on his forearms so he could look down at her face. They held each other's gaze, the moonlight splashing across their naked bodies as his thrusts increased. Simone lifted her face, kissed him hard on the mouth as a second, less powerful orgasm ripped through her. Dylan sucked in a breath before pounding into her, his body squeezing her so hard that for a moment Simone didn't think she'd be able to breathe.

"Shit." He curled his arms under her and thrust one final time as he cried out.

Simone relaxed against the tension in his body, riding out his release. Finally, he collapsed down, pausing there only for a moment before sliding to the side of her. She wasn't aware of anything for a long time as exhaustion and pleasure pulled her down into a light sleep.

Eventually, Dylan moved to pull a sheet over them. "You were shivering."

"Thanks." She nestled back against his side and settled her head against his shoulder.

This was perfection. A man who wasn't afraid to show her how much he cared for her. Someone who was kind, smart, and secure enough in his own skin to trust her to do things to him that she couldn't imagine many other men asking. Things that it turned out she really enjoyed doing to him. She knew that neither of them had set out to have a relationship, but now Simone couldn't picture her life without him in it.

With her hand over his heart, she began to play with his chest hair. "Dylan?"

"Hmm?"

"I need to tell you something."

He yawned as he pulled her a bit closer. "What's that?"

She was many things—hyper, silly, a lover of food—but a coward wasn't one of them. She knew that, for better or worse, her feelings were important. She owed it to both of them to be honest.

Okay, Candy King. Let's do this.

"I love you."

Chapter 22

Dylan had to force his body to relax as he released his grip on her shoulder. The weight of her head on his chest made it next to impossible for him to breathe. "What?"

Simone pushed herself up on her elbow and looked down at him. "I said, I love you." There was no hesitancy in her statement, no giddiness or hidden meaning. It was said plainly, with sincerity, precisely the way he'd assumed Simone would say something like this.

He rolled away, swung his legs over the side of the bed, and braced his hands on his knees. Shit. He should have known that it was going to come to this, should have known that spending this much time with one person would end up creating an attachment on one of their parts.

It wasn't ever going to be with him. Seeing Jonathan and Sarah's fight had only reinforced how horrible an idea being in a permanent relationship with another person really was. No, he'd been right to shun this intimacy. And there was no way he'd put himself back into harm's way ever again.

"Dylan?" The gentle brush of her fingers along his back had him cringe. "Did I do something wrong?"

She wouldn't know, wouldn't be aware of the heartache that he'd lived through. That was on him. "I've never told you about Andrea."

He felt her shift on the bed, the tug of the sheet behind him as she wrapped herself up. "No, you haven't. Who is she?"

"She was my fiancée." The words nearly got stuck in his throat, forcing him to swallow hard. "We'd been together for five years, since university. If you look at that rugby picture of me from the school, I wouldn't be surprised if she was there in the crowd. Andrea was always around, almost from the first day I was on campus."

God, he'd loved her. She was nothing at all like Simone; Andrea was far more serious about everything in life. Everything had to have a deeper meaning, every person needed to have a purpose to live up to, something to give back to others.

"What was she like?" Simone's voice sounded small.

"She'd studied philosophy and religion, and she'd had the intention of becoming a minister. After we graduated, and she started working toward that goal, something changed. We never fought up until then. Before I realized what was happening, we started having these…disagreements over little things. She started going on trips without me, which wasn't a big deal seeing as I was getting busy with work." He hadn't even realized that she'd been pulling away from him at that point. Everything seemed to be in flux, as though they were both adjusting to the new normal of their lives.

"Was she cheating on you?"

"No. God no. Andrea wasn't like that. But she wasn't happy with her life. It didn't matter that I was rich and could have given her anything she wanted. One day she came home from work, sat down at the kitchen table, and told me that she was leaving me."

Andrea had placed her engagement ring on the table. Dylan hadn't been able to look at her, his gaze locked onto the diamond between them.

Simone placed her hand on his back again. "I'm so sorry."

Now that the dam had broken, there wasn't any way he could stop the words from coming. "It wasn't about me. That was the problem. I couldn't fix what was wrong or change the thing that was bothering her. This was about her and what she needed. She ended up working with Habitat for Humanity building houses in Haiti. The last I heard, she was working with Me to We building schools in Tanzania."

"She sounds like an amazing person. No wonder you're still in love with her."

He turned around to see tear tracks on Simone's face. She hadn't made a noise the entire time he'd spoken, leaving him with no idea that he'd broken her heart. He reached over and wiped some of the tears away. "I'm not. Not anymore. She went and did what she needed to do to make herself happy. I'm not so selfish as to stop someone from doing that. But it also made me realize that love isn't enough for most people. If anything, our love was hurting her, holding her back from accomplishing what she wanted with her life. What kind of person does that make me, for wishing she'd pick me over her life's purpose? Believe me when I say that I *wanted* her to choose me."

He'd been so fucking angry for so long, not just at her but at himself. It had been the driving force behind him setting up the sugar daddy site to begin with. When he took love out of the equation, everyone's lives were the better for it.

Taking her hand in his, he ran his thumb across the tops of her knuckles. "I can't love you. I know you'll think that I'm horrible and stupid; most people do. But I'm never going to put myself in the position where I'm the reason someone isn't happy. Where I'll fall into a sense of security and comfort and then have my heart shattered into a million pieces for something I had no control over. I can control sex. I can control who I give my time and money to. I can't control what other people want, how their lives change. I'm not going to be my brother, who spends his life trying to make women happy, only to have their world fall apart."

Simone gently tugged her hand from his and, taking the bedsheet with her, stood up and walked to the bathroom, shutting the door behind her.

This was the inevitable conclusion to their relationship. From the moment they'd first started talking on the app, he'd told her that he had no intention of ever becoming involved with another person beyond a transactional arrangement. He hadn't lied to her, not once. It wasn't his fault that she'd let her emotions get involved. It wasn't his fault that she'd encouraged him to take things further than he'd typically allow with someone.

It was his fault that he'd gone along with it.

Because there was a not-so-insignificant part of him that was in love with Simone. He'd allowed things to continue because he'd liked being a part of a *we* instead of only being *me*. That part of him that he'd long thought dead and shriveled to dust had burst back to life the first time Simone had looked at him with love in her eyes and smiled. It had been so tempting to fall into her arms and never let go.

But she was ambitious. She wanted more for her life and her career than she had right now. He didn't blame her and wanted her to succeed. The best thing he could do for her was to end things, to let her walk away so she could become the best person she could be.

The bathroom door clicked open, and Simone stood there, now dressed. Her hair was pulled back into a ponytail, giving her a severe look. "I should probably go."

His body was a bit sore from the sex, but he ignored it as best he could, stood up, and walked over to her naked. There was no sense in hiding anything from her now. "Simone, I'm—"

She held up her hand and took a half step away from him. "Stop. I need you to listen to me, and then I'm leaving."

He nodded, ignoring the way his heart pounded hard in his cheek and neck.

She licked her lips, her gaze dropping to the floor for a moment before she straightened up and looked him right in the eye. "You're a coward."

"Simone—"

"Let me finish." She took a breath and let out a little huff before continuing. "You're a coward. I understand that your fiancée hurt you, and I know that was hard for you, but you've reacted by shutting the world out. You don't want to be single. Or, at the very least, when you're faced with the option of having something more with another person, you're too chicken to take a chance. Do you think the world is full of guarantees? Do you think that somehow you're better than the rest of us and don't need to put yourself out there? Do you think that every other person is going to be so selfish that they're not going to take your feelings into account?"

"Andrea wasn't selfish." His throat tightened, and for a moment, he thought he might cry.

Simone's eyes widened. "Yes, she was."

"She's off helping the less fortunate."

"And if she truly loved you, she could have done that and still married you. Can you stand there and honestly tell me that if she'd wanted to go to Haiti or wherever else she's been in her life that you wouldn't have supported her?"

"I would have gone with her." He couldn't stop the tears this time. "I would have gone anywhere with her."

"Like I said, you're still in love with her. That's the real reason you can't have a relationship with anyone else. It has nothing to do with you enjoying being single, or not believing in relationships. You gave her your heart, and she took it away with her. There's nothing left for anyone else." She sucked in a sharp breath. "There's nothing left for me."

God, how the hell was he supposed to respond to that? Andrea had taken a piece of his heart with her, and he wouldn't insult Simone by denying it. And yet...

And yet that void had shrunk in recent years, leaving room for someone else to move in. Someone like Simone.

She wiped the tears away and chuckled. "I don't know what I was expecting. We met through a sugar daddy site. Even if Kayla and others found love there, the odds were never really in our favor."

He wanted to deny her words, but knew he couldn't. "Just because it didn't work out with me doesn't mean you won't find love. Maybe even with someone else from the site."

She shook her head before he was even finished speaking. "God no. I'd never intended to be someone's sugar baby. I don't have issues with it, but that wasn't what I'd wanted for a relationship. If I was going to be with someone, I want it to be because they want me in all parts of their life. But it was fun, and I'd like to thank you for giving me a glimpse of what being with…"—she swallowed as she looked away— "of what being a part of a temporary relationship is like."

Without thinking, he pulled her into his arms, not wanting to see her cry. "I'm so sorry."

"You don't need to be. You were honest about what this was and what it could be when we started. I was the one who tried to make it more." She pressed her nose to the side of his neck and took a breath. "You need to go to her. Reach out to see if there's a chance you can be with her now." She pulled away from him, spun around, and marched out of his bedroom.

Dylan should have chased after her, but his feet might as well have been nailed to the floor. He was unable to do anything but listen as Simone gathered her things and left. The air in the condo changed the moment she was gone. As though he'd been released from a spell, he bolted from the bedroom and ran out into the far-too-empty living room.

She was gone, and he knew that even if they saw one another again, things would never be the same between them. With his face still wet with his tears, Dylan stared at the door for a moment longer, before going to the bathroom to have a shower.

Life would go on. It always did.

Even if he felt as though the remaining piece of his heart had just walked out the door with Simone.

* * * *

Simone didn't say a word to the Uber driver the entire drive back to her apartment. She tipped him well and gave him a perfect rating just because he hadn't tried to engage her in conversation. Ignoring the few people she passed, Simone headed straight into the elevator, then down the hall to her door.

The moment she was safely inside, and not a second sooner, a sob ripped from her chest. It was so loud, so painful, that she pressed both hands to her mouth to try and prevent any others from escaping.

Oh, fuck you, Dylan Williams. Fuck you.

She should have known that telling him that she loved him was going to cause problems. And yet, given how close they'd gotten, what he'd trusted her enough to do to him in bed, Simone had foolishly thought that maybe they had a real chance. She couldn't have known that it wasn't that he couldn't love anyone. He just couldn't love *her*.

It took her a few minutes to pull herself together. Only then did she carefully toe off her shoes and head to the fridge. There was an unopened bottle of wine that had her name on it. She didn't bother with a glass, instead drinking directly from it. What the hell was she going to do with herself now?

This was her fault. She'd been a fool to think that she'd be one of the lucky ones who ended up finding their happily ever after because of the sugar daddy site. That wasn't ever going to be her fate. No, the only way things worked out for her was for her to make her own magic.

Looking over at the table, she saw her laptop sitting there charging.

Yes, that was precisely what she needed. With the wine bottle in one hand, she grabbed her computer and headed over to the couch. Falling onto it, she took another long drink from the bottle and turned the computer on. Despite what had happened between them, Simone was a professional and still had a story to write. While she wouldn't say anything negative about the development, she had no such qualms about taking on the sugar daddy site.

She didn't need to reveal Dylan's name to expose the sham that was his site. All she had to do was tell the truth. Carl would eat this shit up, and she'd get good placement in the paper. Or even better, she'd skip print and angle for a prime place on the website. Dylan's clientele was primarily online—what better way to hit her target market.

Opening a new Word document, she began to type, even as her heart continued to break.

Chapter 23

Dylan had done his best to ignore nearly everyone who reminded him of Simone in the week since their fight. She'd been thankfully unavailable as the final week of work on the development was getting done. He needed to be as focused as he could be on every little detail now that they were getting down to the wire. Jonathan hadn't been around either, but that wasn't surprising. No doubt he was licking his wounds and trying to figure out if he could get any of his money back from the wedding bookings.

Looking over the project schedule, he shook his head as Michael, the foreman, came over. "I know it's busy today, but we really need to make sure the plumber is done by this afternoon. I need to have the electrician come so he can finalize the kitchen and we can be ready for the building inspector to look things over."

"It's going to be tight with the new changes, but I think we'll get there." Michael shook his head. "God, he's back."

Dylan looked up to see Simone's dad standing in the doorway. "Shit. I'll handle him."

"Thanks. His suggestions have turned out well, but if he says anything else, I think I'm going to lose my shit." Michael shook his head. "I'm outta here."

"Coward," Dylan said as Michael bolted in the other direction, giving Dylan the finger as he went.

You're a coward.

Dylan shook his head to clear Simone's voice and headed over to her father. "Mr. Leblanc, it's good to see you again."

"I told you, call me Gerald." He looked around and frowned. "Is Simone here? I thought she was going to be around today."

"No, I don't think there's really anything else she needs from us to do the story." *There's nothing else that I can give her.* "We're in the final phase here, getting a lot of bits finished up today. I don't really have a lot of time to give an updated tour."

Gerald looked at him, his gaze narrowing. "I wasn't looking for a tour. I was looking for my daughter."

Dylan couldn't bear to think about Simone. His heart was still bruised from what had happened between them. "As I said, I don't think she'll be here much anymore. The construction is just about finished, and then we'll have the grand opening. I suspect her story will be out into the world at that point."

Gerald looked confused for a moment before nodding. "Sure, that makes sense. She's probably at home writing."

"Probably." Dylan hoped that was all she was doing. He couldn't quite shake the feeling that she might still be upset at him. That he might have broken her heart when that was the last thing he'd ever intended. "You can look around a bit, though. I think the crew is on a break right now. Just make sure you're careful. This is still an active construction site."

"Thanks. I wanted to see if everything still made sense." Gerald shoved his hands in his pockets as he looked around. "I needed a second opinion."

"About what?"

"Applying to live here." He shrugged as he looked over his shoulder. "I'm not expecting any special treatment or anything. But I wanted to maybe see if I should put my name on the waiting list."

Dylan was about to ask him who he was waiting for when a blond woman walked in. It took him all of three seconds to realize that she was Simone's mom. The family resemblance was beyond striking, to the point where he knew this was what she'd look like when she reached her fifties.

"That's your ex-wife?" It was more than a little weird to see the two of them and realize that they were divorced. His parents wouldn't be caught dead together in the same building, let alone side by side. "You invited her?"

"I always ask Linda to be around when I have to make major decisions." Gerald waved when she looked his way. "She's one of the few people I trust."

"I thought you were divorced."

"We are. I left her because I saw how much she was suffering because of my mental illness. I wasn't going to put her or Simone through any more of that shit. I moved on so she could live her life the way she needed to." He smiled sweetly at her as she came close. "There's my girl."

"Sorry I'm late. You didn't tell me that parking would be such a nightmare. I had to circle the block twice until I saw a spot, and then I cut off some dude in a truck in order to steal it. I'm sure my car will be keyed when I get back." She grinned in an all-too-familiar way and stuck her hand out. "Hi there. Linda Leblanc. Nice to meet you."

Dylan shook her hand instinctively, doing his best to keep his face as impassive as he could. "Dylan Williams. A pleasure to meet you. As I said to your husband, most of the crew is on a break, but this is an active construction site. If you're going to look around, please be careful."

"We will. I'm more than a little curious about your development, given everything Gerry has told me." She crossed her arms, looking more like she was giving herself a hug than that she was upset. "So far I have to say I'm really impressed."

"They actually took my advice about a bigger island for food prep." Gerald smiled, nodding his head in the direction of the kitchen. "Wanna see?"

"Oh my God, you mean you're actually going to get your dream kitchen?" She chuckled. "Okay, let's go. I'm sure I'm going to be jealous by the time we leave."

"Jealous? I hope you'll be able to come over and do some baking for me."

Dylan watched as they wandered in the direction of the kitchen, unable to get Gerald's words from his head. He'd left his family, walked away from his wife and daughter because he didn't want his life to hurt theirs. He couldn't imagine Gerald knew what the impact of leaving Simone was, how she'd felt abandoned and needed to prove herself to him with everything she did in her life.

It was strange, some of the reasons people did what they did, thinking that they knew better than another person what they wanted or needed in their lives. Andrea had done that to him, had taken their collective happiness and, without a thought for him, crushed it. But it was all for the greater good, for some higher purpose. Who the hell was he to stand in the way of someone else's hopes and dreams?

No one, that's who.

Didn't you just do the same thing to Simone?

He pushed that thought away as quickly as it popped into his brain. He was allowed to be selfish here. They hadn't made any arrangements, had any formal commitments beyond what they'd agreed to for their sugar daddy relationship. In that way, he'd done everything exactly as he'd told her he would. His money for her time—and nothing more.

It wasn't his fault that her heart had gotten involved. He hadn't set out to woo her or win her over. They were mutually assisting one another, and that was it.

And sure, maybe he'd had a great time with her. He enjoyed her company, and she was able to make him laugh. Yes, the sex was pretty fucking amazing. She didn't question or hesitate to help him explore some of his kinks, even as she shared some of her own with him. The way she'd made him laugh in bed at his own ridiculousness, even that made him smile.

They were supposed to be sugar baby and sugar daddy.

Or journalist and client.

The entirety of their relationship was supposed to be transactional. He'd been up front and super clear about not letting his heart get involved. She'd been clear in her understanding, yet she still fell in love with him.

Shit.

Dylan squeezed the edge of the table in front of him and let out a shaky breath. Shit, he'd really fucked up here. Simone was wrong when she'd said that he was still in love with Andrea. That wasn't it at all. He honestly hadn't thought about her in ages, not since he'd started talking with Simone online. And that was the rub—he hadn't set out to get involved in a relationship with someone. But he was maybe a tiny bit in love with Simone.

And he'd thrown that away.

Double shit.

Unable to ignore the ache in his chest, Dylan pulled out his phone to see if there was a message from Simone. Of course, there wasn't, and he was a fool to think that something would have changed between now and when he'd last seen her.

Really, he was probably overwhelmed with everything that had been going on. Too many things on his plate and not enough time to adequately process everything. And yes, even if he had feelings for Simone, that didn't mean that a relationship was the best thing for them. That had worked out like crap with Andrea, and his desire to avoid dealing with that level of heartache hadn't changed.

No, he needed to stick to his guns. There was nothing wrong with wanting to remain a bachelor, with wanting to merely drift from woman to woman, leaving when things got to be too close for his comfort. Just because he'd done to Simone what her father had done to her and her mother didn't mean that it wasn't the right choice.

What he needed to do was move on. Find another date on the sugar daddy site, go out, and have a good time.

Closing his active conversation with Simone, he opened the page, scanned through the list of women who'd favorited his profile, picked someone who looked the complete opposite from Simone, and sent her a message.

There. What was the point in being the Candy King if he didn't take advantage of his creation? Slipping his phone into his pocket, he did his best to ignore the laughter coming from the kitchen and focused on next steps.

Because the last thing he needed was to focus on what he couldn't have.

"Try not to peek. Just…careful. Watch your step."

Dylan's stomach bottomed out as Jonathan led a blindfolded Sarah through the door. *What the hell was this? Grand Central?* "Hey."

Jonathan waved, a grin plastered on his face. "I know, I know. I'm supposed to let you know if I'm coming over." He nodded toward Sarah and mouthed, "Surprising her."

It was impossible to take his eyes from them as Jonathan moved her into the heart of the room, his hands firmly on her shoulders. After their fight, Dylan hadn't thought he'd ever see Sarah again, let alone with his brother. She'd been rightfully hurt by what he'd said, and the fact that she was here gave Dylan a glimmer of hope for his brother. A group of workers came in and started to laugh as they moved upstairs. He didn't know what his brother had planned, but if giving him a moment of privacy would be helpful, then he'd do it.

Without a second glance, Dylan rushed over to the crew. "Hey, guys. I know this is a pain in the ass, but can we give them a minute? Coffee's on me." He pulled his Starbucks gift card from his wallet and handed it over.

They all smiled and nodded, heading out the way they had come in. Dylan skirted around the edges, doing his best impression of someone who wasn't hanging on every word that was spoken.

"Jonathan, what's going on?" Sarah stepped out of his grasp, pressing her hands to the side of the blindfold. "Can I take this off?"

"In a minute." Jonathan let out a little sigh, letting his arms fall to his side. "Now, I know things have been bad between us. That's on me. I screwed up, and I want to apologize. You were right when you said I was selfish. That I wasn't thinking about you and your needs. I hope you'll be able to find it in your heart to forgive me."

Sarah bit down on her bottom lip but didn't say anything.

"I needed you to know that you make me a better man by being in my life. What I'm about to show you isn't meant to try and convince you to change your mind about marrying me. This is happening regardless of that. But I needed you to know that you were the reason for this. It's my gift to you, not as my future wife, but for being an amazing woman."

It was then that he reached up and pulled the blindfold from her face, revealing the converted space. Sarah's mouth fell open as she looked around, taking in all the details. "Is this…? What is this?"

"You'd mentioned about wanting to run a housing project that melded meditation and wellness with a safe environment for people with mental illness to live. We had a building we've converted for just that purpose. I'd originally intended to give it to you as a wedding present, but now... it's because you're an amazing person."

Dylan was full-out staring at this point, unable to tear his gaze away from Sarah's face, her tears, or his brother's look of regret. In all the years he'd seen Jonathan in relationships, not once had he seen him this raw or honest about his feelings. This was different. He was different.

This time, maybe he was really in love.

Dylan's stomach twisted as his phone chirped. He immediately fished it out of his pocket as he held up his hand. "Sorry. Sorry."

Without another look, he bolted for outside, checking the message as he went. The moment daylight hit his face and his gaze landed on the message from the sugar daddy app, Dylan realized he'd made a terrible mistake. The words shining up at him did nothing to fire his spirit or even bring a smile to his face.

Hey there, sexy.
I'd love to get together for a date night. I charge $200 for dinner and show. Less if you only want to talk. Let me know when and where and we can have fun.

Dylan read the message twice, before deleting it. He didn't want some random encounter with a woman. He wanted Simone.

Ignoring everything he had to do, he made a beeline for his car. He needed to figure out what to do next. How best to beg forgiveness for being a complete idiot.

He needed to win Simone over. He needed to tell her that he loved her.

Chapter 24

Simone's head ached. Well, everything in her body ached at this point. She'd spent the better part of a week in front of her computer writing, sometimes for hours on end. It had gotten to the point where she'd had to set the alarm on her phone to remind herself to get up and move. To drink water. To eat.

It was hard to force herself to step away from the keyboard as the words were flowing so smoothly. It had been a long time since she'd felt this way, since the phrases and images were this crystal clear in her head, and she wanted to get them down before the inspiration slipped away.

Who knew that a broken heart was perfect for journalistic expression?

Not only had she written enough on the sugar daddy phenomenon in Toronto in general, and the millionairesugardaddy.com site specifically, to fill a full week of features; she'd even tackled the opening of the housing development. That one had been difficult to write, mostly because she struggled to reconcile the positive things Dylan was doing there with the broken heart she was nursing. It had taken her twice as long to ensure she didn't let her personal feelings get in the way of her reporting.

Her emotions would shift from anger to sadness. Her frustration at wanting to call him and tell him what an idiot he'd been would inevitably morph into frustration at him for not wanting to take a chance on her.

Well, screw him.

Pushing up the bridge of her glasses, Simone read over the final paragraph of her sugar daddy article, making sure that she'd hit precisely the right tone with it. She wanted it to be calm and hard-hitting. She didn't want to pull any punches or have anyone think that she had a soft spot for the site or for the infamous Candy King.

It had been tempting to out Dylan as the owner, but no matter how angry and annoyed she was, there was no way in hell she'd give in and compromise her ethics. He wasn't worth that. She'd managed to get through the first third of the story when someone knocked on her door. Squinting at the clock on her computer, she forced herself to stand up, giving her body a little shake as she went. "Coming."

Her dad stood on the other side, his hands in his pockets and a grin on his face. "Okay, so the building is turning out pretty awesome."

It had been an awfully long time since she'd seen a genuine smile on his face, and a bit of her anger melted away. "You went over there today?"

"I asked your mother to come. I know she's been worried about what I've been doing recently, and I wanted to put her mind at ease. Plus, there's a chance that I might be able to be one of the first tenants. I've put my name on the waiting list."

She watched as he went straight to her couch and sat down. "You know, if you ask Dylan, I know he will make sure that you have a room. Given all you've done to help him, I can't see it being an issue."

"I don't want to take advantage." But there was a sparkle in his eyes that told Simone he was simply looking for validation. "If you don't think he would mind, maybe I'll ask."

"He won't care. In fact, it wouldn't surprise me if he's put you down already." That was exactly the sort of thing Dylan would do. He might be many things, but heartless wasn't one of them.

Well, not heartless when it came to people who weren't interested in a romantic relationship with him.

"Whatcha working on?" Before Simone could move to stop him, her dad picked up her laptop and began to read. "Oh, you're a bit snarky with this one. Not your usual…sugar daddy site?" He looked up at her and frowned. "You're doing a story on a sugar daddy site? Why the hell would you waste your time on this shit?"

Simone made a grab for the computer, but he moved it from her. "Dad, I need that back."

"Not until you tell me what you're doing? This isn't your normal type of thing."

"I'm not going to be writing about food trucks and community theater for the rest of my life, Dad. If I want any chance of making a real name for myself, I need to start doing some harder-hitting stories."

"Like trying to determine who the owner of a porn site is?"

"It's not porn. And your attitude is exactly why I chose to do the story. These women need financial aid, and the men are helping them."

"It's prostitution." He sighed and handed her the laptop. "You're better than that."

"It's not. Most of these women don't even have sex with their sugar daddies. Some just go to plays or concerts. Some will have supper and maybe go to a movie. I interviewed one woman who specialized in dates with men who wanted to pretend that she was their daughter, and they wanted nothing more than to pretend that they had some family. Hell, I know one couple where it was a sugar mamma, and she helped him pay for his student loans. Not everything is about sex. And even if it is, what the hell is wrong with two consenting adults wanting to get together to have a good time? Nothing. Our society is full of a bunch of prudes."

Her face had grown heated, and her heart pounded the longer she spoke. She couldn't even look at her dad. Instead, she dropped her laptop on the table with a not-so-gentle thud. It shouldn't surprise her that he didn't get the whole sugar daddy concept; it was partially generational, but also, he didn't exactly see shades of gray. Her dad had always been a black and white kind of guy, and she shouldn't have expected this to be any different.

Dylan no doubt would roll his eyes and say that this only reinforced why he never wanted it to come out that he was the Candy King. Too many people would fault him for his side business, and his development company would suffer as a result. But that didn't mean that the story wasn't an important one to tell.

"Baby?"

She looked over to where her dad stood. "What?"

"I want to ask you a question, but I don't think it's going to come out the way that I intend."

"Just ask."

"Why are you writing a story like that?" He sighed and moved closer. "I don't mean because of the sex stuff. I mean, you're so good at the community stories, why would you want to do something edgy like this?"

Tears welled up in her eyes, and she didn't know where to look. "I needed a challenge. I wanted to write something that would put me on the map."

"You've never said anything about wanting to do that type of journalism before now. I thought you loved going out and eating at restaurants and writing about the marathons and stuff. You always made me laugh when I'd read your stories. I'm glad that you still write for a paper that puts out a weekly print. It's going to kill my printer if they end up switching over to online only."

Sniffing, she finally looked up at him. "What do you mean?"

"I have a copy of every story you've ever published. I have a scrapbook that I keep—well, two, actually. You've written so much over the years, it's been hard to keep track of it all." He reached up and gave her shoulder a squeeze. "I wanted to be a reporter so badly when I was a young man, but here you are living the reality. I couldn't be prouder of you."

There was no way Simone could keep a sob from escaping. though she did manage to hold herself back from throwing herself into her father's arms. "You are?"

"Shit, why wouldn't I be?"

"I knew you wanted to be an investigative journalist. You used to ask when I'd tackle something hard-hitting. Something that would make a real difference."

He squeezed her shoulder again, letting his hand fall to his side. "That was something I had to talk a lot about in therapy. It wasn't that I was exactly jealous. Not really. But I was living vicariously through your successes. My therapist told me that I was putting pressure on you to fulfill my dreams, and that that wasn't fair. In fact, he suggested that I make the scrapbook of your stories. I'd already started, so it wasn't difficult to follow through."

She'd spent much of her professional life trying to live up to an expectation that wasn't there. One that she really shouldn't have focused so much on, instead of doing the things that brought her joy. And she did love the community stories, enjoyed getting out there and making people smile. It was those aspects of the sugar daddy story that had driven her to want to do it in the first place. She wanted to show how special these relationships could be, how much they were needed by both sides of the equation.

The Candy King had been a bit like her Moby Dick.

Dylan had quickly become so much more than a mere obsession. He'd somehow worked his way into her heart and taken root. Nothing she could do was going to get him out of there, which meant she was going to have to find a way to live without that piece of her. He'd made it perfectly clear that he wasn't interested in a relationship. That he didn't want her.

"Baby?" He moved a bit closer. "Are you okay?"

"I'm…not really." She didn't cry, even though her heart had shattered into a thousand pieces. "But I will be."

"Did that man do something to you? I won't live in that place if I think for even a moment that some rich asshole did something to hurt my baby."

"He didn't. It's all on me."

"What do you mean?"

She wasn't about to go into all the details with him about Dylan's aversion to relationships, but she told him enough. "He made it clear how far he was willing to go from the beginning, and I'm not about to throw myself on someone who isn't interested." He pulled her in for a hug, and this time she didn't resist. "I don't know what to do."

"I'm shit at relationships. I somehow figured you and your mom would be better off with me out of the picture than having to constantly put up with my mood swings and anxiety. She still gives me hell about that, but I did what I thought was right. Sometimes, men can be idiots."

She laughed as she wiped her tears on his shirt. "She calls you that all the time."

"Called me that a few hours ago when I showed her the new place. Told me that I wouldn't need to pay rent if I wanted to move back in with her."

Simone looked up, ignoring the flutter of hope in her chest. "She wants you to move back home?"

"Always has, but I can't do that to her. I think living at the complex is a better idea." He shrugged. "But I might see if she wants to come spend some time with me. As friends, if not partners. Did you know she's taking a college course in the evenings? Economics."

"What? No. When did she sign up for that?" Simone couldn't imagine anyone purposely signing up for a course that involved numbers.

"Last month. I promised I'd lend a hand if she needed it. Not that she would. She was always better at numbers than I was. Still, I want to support her any way I can."

She couldn't imagine her parents being more than that, but it was wonderful knowing, despite everything that had happened between them—the tears and yelling, the frustration and heartache—that they were still able to be there for one another. Friendship was something special and absolutely the thing that she knew her father could do for her mom. "That's great."

"I also want to be there for you. I know I can't make up for a lot of the time when I wasn't stable. And I can't promise that I won't go back to being like that. Right now, though, my meds seem to be working, and I'm able to hold down regular jobs. If I can move into the complex and take up this meditation that Sarah was talking about, I think that will also help."

"Sarah?"

"You know, Jonathan's fiancée? She's the one who's going to run the place. She has plans to offer daily meditation and yoga practice. I'm not really into all that religious stuff, but I've been doing some reading, and meditation is good for people with depression and anxiety. It might help."

Simone shook her head. "Back up. When did you meet Sarah?"

"Today. Your man took off when Mom and I were visiting, but Jonathan and Sarah were there. We got to talking about what her dreams are for the place. I think she'll do great."

"I thought they'd broken up?"

"Not the way they were sucking face while I was there. I'm not sure she's going to live there with us, but I know she wants to have a room just in case people want or need her to be around."

If Jonathan and Sarah had worked out their issues, there might be hope for everyone else. Shit, there might be a chance that she'd find a love of her own. Maybe not with Dylan, but with someone, someday.

"That's really good. I'm happy for them." She pulled away from her dad and got herself a glass of water from the fridge. "I should probably get back to work. I need to turn my stories in to Carl by next week or else I'm going to get my ass fired."

She heard her dad move around and wasn't surprised to see him back at her computer, reading. "You know, this would be far better if you were a little less cynical. It's not your style, and I think it detracts from what you're trying to accomplish."

Rather than become defensive, she took a breath and let his words sink in. "I just want it to be taken seriously."

"Then be true to yourself. Your voice. Simone Leblanc doesn't write cynical stories. A Simone Leblanc piece is fun and witty. You focus on the people and their problems, what connects them and makes the reader care about what they're doing. Not…whatever the hell this is. Go back and really think about what you're trying to say. Then write it."

It was funny how having someone on the outside look in at what you were doing could help bring things into focus. It was going to mean a ton more work, but that didn't matter. Getting the story right did. "I will. Thanks, Dad."

"You're welcome, baby." He smiled before clapping his hands. "Right. Let's order a pizza, and then I can read over your other story, which was the real reason I came over. You're buying because I'm helping."

"I am?" She chuckled. "Fine, but that means I get to pick the pizza."

"Just nothing with pineapple." He shuddered. "Fruit doesn't belong."

"The Hawaiian pizza is a Canadian invention. You should show your civic pride and eat it." She wasn't a fan herself, but if push came to shove and someone offered her free food, she'd eat just about anything.

"I'll drink a Keith's beer instead." He waved her away and sat back down.

Simone ordered their food online, even as her mind kept circling back to Jonathan and Sarah. She'd been so confident that after their fight there was no way they'd be able to work things out. They'd both been so adamant, determined to move on without one another that Simone couldn't imagine a scenario where the outcome would be any different.

And yet...

According to her dad, Dylan had been there too. That meant he'd seen that, despite everything, his brother was going to get his happy ending after all. Maybe that would be enough to remind him that he didn't need to go it alone. He might not want Simone, but she hoped that someday he'd find someone to change his mind, someone he'd let into his life for longer than a few weeks.

Someone who would love him the way he deserved.

Even if she wanted that someone to be her.

"Pizza is on its way."

"Great. Baby, you have some sort of message on your computer. I didn't want to open it in case it's a sex thing."

"I don't have any sex things." Well, except for the—"Shit, don't open that!" She raced to take the laptop from him once again. "You didn't look, right?"

"I didn't have time to blink, let alone look."

Sure enough, there was the sugar daddy message icon blinking in the corner. She hadn't uninstalled it from her phone or her computer, as she hadn't finished the article yet and didn't know if she'd need to look something up.

Sure, that's the reason.

There was still only one person in the world who would message her through the app. Only one person who she hoped and prayed might someday see her as something more. She should look at it, but there was no way she could do that with her dad sitting in front of her.

"I have my issues, but I can still tell when your brain is working in overdrive." He got to his feet. "I'm going to go. E-mail me your story on the housing development, and I'll send you any comments I have later."

She blinked at him as she held the computer a bit tighter to her chest. "You don't mind?"

"I'll get some pizza on the way home." He leaned in and kissed your cheek. "I hope that message is good news for you."

"Me too."

Simone held off clicking the icon until her dad was safely out the door. With her body shaking, she sat down on the couch, trying to catch her breath after everything that had happened in the last thirty minutes—way too many emotional twists and turns for her liking.

Taking a deep breath, she double-clicked the icon and read. Then she reread the message.

Shit, what the hell was she going to do now?

* * * *

Sitting in Carl's office, waiting for him to once again read her article, was proving to be more difficult than she'd anticipated. It had taken him ten minutes to finish a call he was on, and then another ten minutes to scroll through the document she'd e-mailed him before she'd come over. As always, he gave little indication as to what he thought about the story.

"Interesting." He leaned back in his seat as he narrowed his gaze at her. "Has Williams seen this yet?"

"Not yet. I was planning on sending over a copy, but I wanted to run it by you first." Carl was many things, but he'd never let her put out a garbage story that would make either herself or the paper look bad.

He nodded, glancing back over at the computer. "It's good. Your normal piece." There was something in the way he said that, not quite dismissive but not exactly impressed. "Have anything else for me?"

She'd thought hard about what she was going to say to him about the sugar daddy piece on the way over here, had even mentally practiced a few lines ad nauseam. Simone got to her feet and stood in front of Carl's desk. She opened her mouth to give her rehearsed speech, but instead let out a small sigh. "I quit."

It was Carl's turn to stand. "You *what*?"

No, that wasn't what she'd been planning to say, but Simone knew that it was the right thing to do. The weight that had been pressing down on her for years lifted, and she felt as though she could finally breathe. "I wanted to make sure you had the Williams story, but I won't be completing the sugar daddy story, and I'm officially giving you my two weeks' notice. I can put it in writing for you when I get back to my desk."

"You couldn't do it, could you?" Carl shook his head and retook his seat. "I knew it was too much for you."

Oh no, we're not playing this game. "Nope, I did it. Found out the owner's identity and even wrote the story. It has since been deleted." The last thing she'd wanted to do was leave any trace of the link between Dylan and the website, so she'd made sure to purge all her research files as well as all her drafts.

"I don't believe you." Carl tapped his finger along the edge of his desk. "Not that it matters. If you were able to uncover the owner of this site, I have no doubt that Mark will be able to do the same, and I'm sure in half the time it took you."

"I had a feeling that you might say that." Simone braced her hands on the side of Carl's desk and leaned over to stare at him. "I took the liberty of warning the owner that you might do that when you found out I was scrapping the story. They're now in the process of removing the traces of the information I discovered. By the time Mark gets around to looking, there will be nothing for him to find."

She hadn't said anything to Dylan yet, but there was no way Mark would be able to catfish Dylan into revealing anything. Just to be sure, she'd give Dylan a heads-up and would make sure that all traces of information that could possibly lead back to him were removed.

For his part, Carl seemed to believe her. "Why? Why would you put all that time into a story and then walk away from it?"

Her conversation with her dad circled in her head. "Because that's not the type of reporter I want to be. I've been trying for years to become someone I'm not, to write articles that would impress you. But you don't care about the local shawarma place, or the food truck festival, or the high school swim meet. You simply needed those stories to fill the back pages; they were filler to give you the word count you wanted."

Carl shoulders visibly dropped. "You're right about our needing those stories, but you're wrong that you never impressed me." He turned to face his computer and began to type. "I'm not going to talk you out of leaving the paper. I think it's the best decision for you. However, I have a friend who is looking for a reporter who knows the local food scene. I'm going to send him your information and let the two of you see if there's something you can work out."

Simone straightened. "Really?"

"It will save him trying to poach Elena from me."

"Wow. Thanks."

Carl hit one final button before sitting back. "I know I'm not the easiest man to work for. I don't agree with you discarding the story, but I won't put Mark on the trail."

"Thank you." That was one less thing she'd have to worry about.

"Get out of here. I'm sure you're going to want to spread the news yourself. And make sure that all of your loose ends are wrapped up before you're done." He waved her away and turned back to his computer.

"Thank you." And without another thought, Simone marched out of Carl's office.

Maybe things were going to work out for her after all. Maybe for the first time in her life, she was on the right path to achieving the happiness she'd always wanted.

And if things with Dylan tomorrow night went the way she hoped, maybe she'd end up with it all.

Chapter 25

Music filled the air as a cool breeze blew off Lake Ontario, ruffling the white tablecloth and making the candlelight flicker. Dylan sat playing with his wineglass, swirling the amber liquid, hoping he'd made the right decision.

More importantly, he hoped Simone would come.

Yes, he'd made the offer, and he knew she'd seen his message. He hadn't groveled like that ever in his life, and he still didn't know if it was enough. If there was a chance that Simone would forgive him and give him a chance to make something work. She owed him nothing, and unlike most other aspects of his life, Dylan knew there was very little he could do to control things. But he was ready to do what needed to be done, to lay things out there and see where they took him.

For the first time in a very long while, he was ready to put his heart on the line.

All he could hope and pray for was that Simone wouldn't crush it.

When another fifteen minutes passed, he started to worry that maybe things weren't going to work out after all. He'd just finished refilling his wineglass when the clicking of high heels coming toward him caught his attention. At the first glance of blond hair, Dylan was on his feet, his heart pounding madly in his chest.

God, she was beautiful.

Simone was wearing a simple black dress that flared out at the waist into a flowing skirt that swished around her knees as she walked. The neckline plunged to the point of revealing enough cleavage to entice even the saintliest of men. She'd left her hair long and loose, the cascade of gold strands bouncing around her shoulders as she finally came to a stop in front of him.

She cocked her head to the side for a moment before giving him a little wave. "Hey."

"Hey yourself."

"I got your message. Sorry I'm a bit late. Traffic was heavier than I'd expected." She bit her lower lip for a moment before looking the place over. "I don't think I've ever seen this place empty before."

"Park owns this restaurant as well. When I told him how I'd screwed up and needed to do something amazing to try and apologize, he offered to rent the whole place to me for a night."

Simone's eyes widened. "Shit, that must have cost you a small fortune."

"It's only money. And besides"—he reached out and took her hands in his—"it will be worth every penny if it has the desired result."

"What's that?" Her voice had gone a bit breathless, and he could feel a tremble in her hands.

"It would make me very happy if you could find it in your heart to forgive me. I…it feels like a cop-out to say that I'm an idiot or a fool for not having known what I had with you. I'm not going to do that to you, and I'm not going to deny what I did or how I felt. Not when my words and actions hurt you. To simply brush them away wouldn't change the fact that I was wrong and what I said wasn't right."

Lifting her hands to his mouth, he kissed her knuckles. "I'm sorry that my words hurt you. I was so mired in my own bruised ego that I'd forgotten to stop and see that the world had moved on. I'd planted myself in the ground and had forgotten to grow, to live my life and realize that not everything in the world is about me. That love for its own sake, no matter where the relationship goes, is worth the effort."

The entire time he spoke, Dylan was terrified to look up at Simone. He knew that with a glance she could shut him down, send him on his way to lick his wounds, and there wasn't a thing he could do about it. Tonight was his one opportunity to make amends, to prove to them both that he was capable of being a good partner.

That he was a good match for Simone.

But when she didn't say anything, Dylan knew he couldn't hold back any longer and looked her in the eye. She wasn't crying, but there was something in her expression that had softened. "That was quite the speech."

"I've been practicing all day." He'd even rehearsed it in front of Jonathan and Sarah, who were both thrilled that he'd finally pulled his head out of his ass and decided to put his heart on the line. "Can I tell them that I nailed it?"

Simone turned his hand in hers and laced their fingers. "Maybe."

"Maybe?" God, he'd somehow fucked everything up. "What can I do to turn that into a yes?"

"It will depend on how you answer this." She took a deep breath before she looked him straight in the eye. "What happens if I say no?"

His stomach bottomed out, and for a moment, he thought he might be ill. Excuses and arguments flooded his mind, ideas to try and convince her to give him a second chance. But when he really looked at her, he realized that she hadn't said no, but was instead asking him what he would do if she did. What would he do if Simone wasn't in his life?

He swallowed, hoping it would ease the sudden dryness of his mouth and throat. "I don't know. I'd be upset, but if that was your decision, I wouldn't chase or harass you."

"No, I mean…would you date someone else?"

"Do you mean, would I go back to being the Candy King? Would I cut off the chance for love because I was rejected by you?"

"Yes. Exactly."

Would he? It wasn't honestly something he'd really thought about, but now that she'd put the possibility before him, he knew he owed her an honest response. "I didn't mind being single, and I still don't think I need to pin my happiness on having a relationship with another person, but I wouldn't actively shun dating the way I did before." He let go of her hand and cupped her cheek. "I'd rather not have to find out if I have any say in the matter."

Simone smiled, chuckling in that low, throaty way that she had. "You don't. But you might be able to convince me to stay with a good meal and some wine."

"Well, I have a chance then." He led her over to the table, pulling out her chair for her and draping a napkin across her lap once she was settled. "Wine?"

"Yes please." Simone smiled up at him, her eyes sparkling the entire time. "I have another question for you."

"Shoot."

"If we were to date—and I'm not saying that we will. But if. Things started for us…differently than most relationships. We were up front, which is great, but you were very clear about how far you were willing to take it." She looked down at her hands and let out a soft huff. "What you said to me back at your apartment hurt. I can't do that again. I need to know that this time would be different."

"Let's fix that right now. Our sugar daddy relationship is over. It was mutually beneficial and came to its natural conclusion." Dylan reached across the table and gave her hand a squeeze. "I'd much rather have a relationship with you where we're on equal footing. Where we're simply two people who care for one another, who spend time together for no other reason than that they enjoy one another's company. This isn't the Candy King and his Sugar Tart. This would be Dylan and Simone, seeing where they can take things."

By the time he'd finished speaking, there was a smile fixed on her face and unshed tears in her eyes. "That sounds perfect."

Dylan sat back then, feeling as though he'd finally done the right thing.

Simone cleared her throat before taking a sip of wine. "So my parents? Dad came by my apartment after he'd shown Mom the development. He wants to be put on the waiting list."

"We already have a room set aside for him. There was no way we were going to not give our consultant a place to live. I'm glad he'll be with us. I know Jonathan and Sarah are as well."

Relief was evident on her face. "I was going to ask if that was an option. Dad would never ask for special treatment, but I have no issues asking for favors."

"And I have no issues granting them." He took his seat beside her, taking her hand the moment he was settled. "I hope you're hungry. We have quite a menu that's been prepared for us."

"I love food." Her grin could power a small country. "I have a bit of news myself."

"You've turned in your stories, and that idiot boss of yours has given you a promotion?"

"Nope. I quit."

Dylan's head snapped up, and he gave her hand a squeeze. "What do you mean you quit?"

"Just that. I quit yesterday." She took a drink of her wine, not giving him any further details until the waitress set their appetizer in front of them. "Oh, I love crab cakes."

It took all his effort not to shake the rest of the story out of her while she bit into the crab cake. Simone moaned as her eyes rolled practically all the way back into her head. Dylan couldn't hold back a smile of his own. "You're going to further inflate Park's ego with reactions like that."

"I'm totally okay with that as long as he keeps feeding me." She wiped her mouth with a sigh. "Right. So I quit. But I'm not unemployed."

"Even if you were, I have no doubt that you'll figure something out."

"But I'm not. I realized that you were right. I was trying to be someone I wasn't, do something that my heart wasn't quite in. I thought being a serious investigative journalist was what I wanted. Until I sat down and starting writing the story. I hated it. Hated how it made me feel. All I really wanted to do was talk about the positive parts of the sugar daddy site, and I knew that Carl would want me to be hard-hitting. I was trying to do this for all the wrong reasons. Not that it wouldn't be good, but it would eventually eat away at me."

Dylan knew every word she said was true as relief washed through him. "What are you going to do then?"

"Be a food critic for a Toronto-focused website. I handed in the Williams development story; don't worry about that. But it will be my last one for the *Toronto Record*. Starting next week, I get to eat my way around the city, including cultural festivals and special events. I even suggested doing a story on food at the baseball game! It's going to be awesome."

"What about the website?"

She shrugged. "The world doesn't need to know about the Candy King. The people who need your services seem to be able to find them on their own. Besides, I'm discovering that I have a bit of a possessive streak. I don't want to share you with anyone else."

It was amazing seeing the spark in her as she talked about something that she was clearly excited about, something that she loved. Dylan's heart pounded as he squeezed her hand again. "I love you."

Simone sucked in a breath, her eyes widening. "Really?"

"Yes. I think I've loved you for a long time now, though I was trying to fight it. Yes, I know I'm an idiot. But I'm a changed man now."

This time a tear did escape the corner of her eye. "I love you too." Simone wiped the tear away with a chuckle. "I hope you're not changed too much. There are a few things that I'd like a repeat performance of. I still have some special equipment back at my place that I'd like to use again."

And just like that, his cock went hard. "I'm sure we can arrange that."

They continued to talk, laugh and drink as the food was brought out. Dylan knew that this was only the first of many nights like this for them. And if, sometime in the future, things between them were no longer working, he wouldn't retreat back into his shell of isolation and loneliness. Simone had broken the carefully constructed shell that had been around him, keeping him safe from emotional harm.

Never again. He was ready, willing, and more than able to open up his heart to love. To take what Simone was offering. To build a life, no matter what that looked like, with her.

She'd just finished taking a bite of sea bass when he realized that he needed to hold her, kiss her. Shoving his chair back with a heavy scrape, he stood and lifted her to her feet as she gave a small squeak of protest.

"What are you doing?" But she didn't pull away as he swept her into his arms.

"Dancing." He bent his head and kissed her hard on the mouth. "And kissing."

"What about eating?" She placed feather-light kisses on his lips. "Did I mention that I love food?"

"It's not going anywhere." Park had been given fair warning that if things went the way Dylan was hoping, they might need to pack up the food to take home with them. "And the night is too beautiful to waste."

With her in his arms, they swayed to the tune of a silent rhythm, bodies pressed together. Dylan knew things were never going to be the same, not with this fantastic, beautiful, and charming woman now in his life.

"I love you," he said again, his mouth pressed to her temple. "I can't wait to show you how much every day for the rest of your life."

Simone pressed her face to his chest, the warmth of her tears reaching his skin. "Thank you."

"For what?"

"Making my fantasy a reality. For talking to me that first day through the app when you had no reason at all to do so. For seeing the real me."

"How could I not see the real you? You're like walking sunshine on a cloudy day. Everyone who comes close to your orbit can't help but smile. I should be the one thanking you. I would still be stuck in the darkness of my own making. You helped me see that there is more to life than work and sex. That being in a relationship isn't just about love, but also friendship and silliness. And I'll always be grateful to you for that."

Tipping her chin back, he kissed her lips softly, breathing in her scent and memorizing everything he could about her. While he didn't need to be in a relationship to have a full and productive life, having someone like Simone with him was going to be amazing.

Life would never be the same.

And that was a good thing.

Epilogue

A bead of sweat rolled between Simone's breasts, making her skin itchy. She had to fight the urge to scratch it, not wanting to draw any attention away from the ongoing nuptials. Sarah looked absolutely breathtaking in her white wedding dress, her hair piled high on her head in an elaborate design of braids and curls, a look that Simone wouldn't be able to attempt without an army of hair stylists at her side.

Dylan looked equally amazing standing beside his brother, a perfectly fitting tux accentuating his body. She'd grown used to seeing him in various states of dress over the past month, but there was something extra sweet about seeing him in formal attire. She couldn't wait to strip the jacket and tie off him to show him her appreciation.

"Do you have the rings?" The minister asked with a smile as Jonathan turned to Dylan, who pulled the rings from his pocket with a flourish. The brothers shared a look before Jonathan turned back to his bride.

Simone was happy for the couple now that they'd finally worked out their differences and made it here. More than that, they'd both been so kind to her father since the housing development had opened, had helped him begin to sort out his life, that she wanted nothing but happiness for them both. She reached for her dad's hand and gave it a squeeze. "They both look happy."

"They do." He patted her hand. "Maybe you'll be next."

While she and Dylan had no immediate plans to get married, she thought that maybe one day there might be a chance. Who knew what the future would hold? "We'll see."

The rest of the ceremony went smoothly, and Simone was one of the first people on her feet clapping and grinning when the happy couple finally walked down the aisle together, hand in hand. Dylan passed by her next, the maid of honor on his arm. He gave her a wink as he went, nodding toward the back of the church.

"Dad, I'm going to go find Dylan. Are you coming to the reception?"

"I think I'm going to head out. I'm done with people for today, and your mom offered to cook me dinner." He gave her a quick kiss on the cheek. "Pass on my regards when you see everyone."

"I will."

The crowd quickly filed out behind the couple, making it hard to work her way through to where the receiving line was. She could see Dylan's head high above everyone else, making it half gratifying and half excruciating that she could see, but not reach him. She waddled along with the rest of the crowd, listening to conversations around her.

"They look so happy."

"Her dress is gorgeous!"

"The brother is hot. I'd like to see what's under that suit."

Simone couldn't help but smile. If luck were on her side, she'd get another private viewing of precisely what was hiding beneath all that fabric in a matter of hours. Maybe sooner if she could convince him to take a little detour to her place.

"Simone!" Sarah pulled her into a hug the moment she got within arm's reach. "Where's your dad?"

"He's peopled out. But he wanted me to pass along his congratulations."

Sarah smiled and gave her another little hug. "Thanks. I'll see him once we're back from the honeymoon."

"Paris, right?" Simone was only a little bit jealous. "You're going to have an amazing time."

"We will. And it helps to know that you're here with Dylan. Jonathan said that he hasn't seen him this happy in a long time. We have you to thank for that."

Simone chanced a look over at Dylan, who was currently talking to an elderly couple. "He's made me pretty happy too."

"Why don't the two of you take off and meet us at the building. We're going to do some of the wedding photos there."

The common area of the housing development had a large fountain and so many tropical trees that it could have been its own rain forest. It was zen—and perfect to help soothe a troubled mind and soul. It wasn't surprising at all that she wanted her wedding pictures taken there. "I'll do that. It will be nice to have him to myself for a few minutes. I've barely seen him this week."

She had to wait another five minutes before she was finally able to throw her arms around Dylan's neck and give him a kiss. "We need to leave."

"But—"

"Sarah told us to go to the house for pictures." She got up on her tiptoes and whispered against his ear. "If we leave now, we'll have time for a quickie in the spare room before anyone else arrives."

Dylan circled her waist with his arm. "Simone and I are heading to the housing complex to make sure everyone is aware that the wedding party is on the way for pictures. We'll see you there."

Ignoring the knowing looks thrown their way by the bride and groom, Dylan pulled Simone toward the parking lot, where the Tesla waited. He opened the door for her and helped her in, pausing long enough to place a series of kisses along her inner wrist. "I'm so hard right now I'm terrified for my suit pants."

Thankfully, the drive wasn't long, and there was a spot for them in the visitor parking section when they arrived. Simone wasn't usually so horny that she'd leave a wedding for a quickie before the photos and reception, but given how much time they'd spent together over the past month, only to be pulled apart for most of this week due to the wedding preparations, she thought she was entitled.

Besides, she damn well wasn't going to let anyone else have sex with the best man.

Dylan took her by the hand and practically pulled her into the building. "I know the best spot."

Only five people were living in the complex, her father being one of them. Most of them worked, and while it was Saturday, she knew it would be quiet around here. Dylan fished his keys out of his pocket and opened up one of the unoccupied rooms, pulling her in and spinning her around so her back was against the wall. He held her gaze as he closed the door behind them.

"That's better." A sly grin slid across his face as he ran a finger down the front of her chest, between her breasts. "You look good enough to eat."

"That sounds like a wonderful idea. I've missed you."

"Me too." Dylan dropped to his knees and lifted her dress up to get a look at the lace panties she'd worn for the special occasion. "Fuck, you're hot."

"You should have heard what the single ladies at the church were saying about you. If I hadn't pulled you out of there when I had, it might have come to blows between a few of them and me."

His response was to pull her panties to the side and lick up across her clit.

Simone moaned as she pressed her head back against the wall. She nearly fell over when Dylan lifted her leg and draped it across his shoulder, exposing her completely to him. It was difficult to keep her balance while he began to lick her, fucking her with his hand and holding up her dress so she could see exactly what he was doing. She would have taken off her shoes if she'd had two seconds to think about what they were doing.

She sucked in a breath and squeezed the fabric in her grasp hard when he increased the suction on her clit. He pulled back with a pop. "I feel like you might be a tad distracted."

"Hard to stand still in heels while you're doing that."

"Well, I don't want you to be uncomfortable." With a few smooth moves, Dylan got to his feet, picked her up, and swung her around to land on the bed behind them. "That's better."

Oh, much better.

She lifted her hips, letting him slide her panties down her legs. Dylan held them up and, with a smile, slipped them into his pocket. "Let's hold on to these for later."

"You better give those back."

"Maybe. After the pictures are done."

God, the mere thought of going out there without her panties was nearly enough to make her come. Thankfully, she wasn't going to have to wait long for that inevitable fate, because Dylan climbed onto the bed and resumed his position—face to her pussy—and began to lick.

Her eyes squeezed closed, and she knew it was going to be challenging, at best, to hold off coming too quickly. But given that the entire wedding party wasn't too far behind them, maybe that wasn't a bad thing. Spreading her thighs as wide as she could, Simone let the sensations wash over her. Dylan was a master at this, knowing exactly how to flick his tongue over the nub, how to curl his fingers just so to press against that hidden spot deep inside her that sent warm waves of pleasure through her pelvis.

Ah, right there. That was the exact spot she needed him to hit. Her back arched as her hips came off the mattress and Dylan doubled his efforts to push her over the edge. She hung there on the precipice for what felt like an eternity but couldn't have been much more than a few seconds, before the first waves of her orgasm rolled through her. She cried out, squeezing the sheets on the bed as pleasure overrode her senses.

She barely caught her breath, falling onto the mattress in a heap when Dylan pulled back and got to his knees. "We don't have time to get undressed. Get on your hands and knees, and we'll do this doggy style."

It took her more effort than she realized to roll over and assume the position, her body still humming from the release. Dylan tossed her dress up, fully exposing her ass to him. "I've never been so thankful to have a condom in my wallet."

"Me too. And I think I'm going to start carrying them in my purse because if we keep doing shit like this, I want to be a good Girl Guide and be prepared."

"Of course, you were a Girl Guide." She heard him tear the condom wrapper open before he took her hips in his hands and slid his cock into her. He sucked in a breath and began to pump his hips. "I'm not going to last long either."

"Hard and fast and dirty. We can do the other stuff tonight. Or tomorrow."

He squeezed her hips hard and fucked her with purpose. It was precisely the sort of sex she'd imagined having with the Candy King back when they'd first started talking online. It was raw and exactly the right thing for her.

A door slamming and a chorus of voices came from somewhere outside the room. Shit, the wedding party was here far sooner than she'd thought they'd be. Dylan didn't say anything, but he flexed his fingers against her hips and increased his rhythm.

"Dylan? Simone? You here?" That was Jonathan's voice.

"Be right there!" Dylan slammed into her one final time, his body shaking behind her as he silently came.

They only took a few seconds to savor the moment, before scrambling to fix their clothing. Simone held out her hand. "Panties."

"Nope."

"I'm going to have come rolling down my legs."

He held up the used condom for a moment before tossing it in the garbage can. "You'll be good. Consider it an extended tease. Because when we get home, I plan to do that all over again. Only slower."

He pulled her in for a kiss, but she was more than a little startled and pulled back. "Home? You mean my place?"

There was something in his eyes, a look that sent her heart pounding. He reached up and cupped her cheek in his hand. "About that. We've been going back and forth between our places for almost a month now. I thought it might make sense, if you were okay with the idea, that we move in together. I assumed you could move in with me because I have the bigger place, but I hate making that assumption. We could always get a new place, one that we both pick out. If you agree. And maybe someday we'll do something more. Maybe not. We can just be together forever if you like."

Simone threw her arms around his neck and held him tight. "That would be amazing. I love you, and I want to be with you every minute that I can be."

"I have something else to tell you." He cocked his head to the side before licking his lips. "I know we talked about selling the sugar daddy site to an investor, but I have another idea."

She pulled back a bit. "What?"

"It didn't feel right to get rid of it. Especially since I have you in my life. I thought rather than someone else running it, you and I can make sure people are finding their matches out there in the world together." He kissed her one more time before pulling her back into a hug. "You were right that the site is special. If there's a chance we can keep it going, can somehow open people up to possibilities beyond why they'd come to the site in the first place, then I think that's what we need to do. I want you to be my business partner for the site. I'll still keep the day-to-day elements going so it doesn't impact your writing, but I couldn't think of anyone else better suited to help me run it. If you want."

"Yes." She burst out laughing before pressing her forehead to his chest. "I would love nothing more than to run the site with you."

They stood there hugging while the voices downstairs grew louder. Simone didn't care, because for the first time in her life she was with a man who not only loved her but wanted to be with her forever. "I love you."

"I love you too. My beautiful Sugar Tart."

She chuckled. "We better get downstairs before they come looking for us."

"Yup." He took her by the hand, gave her a quick once-over. "Let's go."

Hand in hand, they left to join the wedding party, and Simone knew that her life with Dylan would give her the happiness she'd always wanted.

* * * *

Dylan stood on the edge of the party in the hotel banquet room. Jonathan and Sarah were in the middle of the crowd on the dance floor, laughing at how ridiculous Jonathan looked while trying to do the Macarena—because that was still apparently a thing. Simone was out there with them, dancing with his dad, while occasionally stopping to beckon him over.

No fucking way was he going to dance, no matter how much he loved her.

And yet, when she looked over her shoulder at him and batted her eyes, he found himself pushing away from the wall. It was only an inch or two, but enough that she laughed at him. Great, they'd only officially been together a short time, and he was already at her beck and call.

Not that he minded. Things with Simone were so different than they'd been with Andrea. Not better, just different. They had an easy comfort between them that he'd never felt in any other relationship. They were in sync most of the time, and she was constantly challenging him to do more, do better.

The music changed to a slow dance, and the couples around Simone instantly paired off. She cocked her head, put her hands on her hips, and licked her lips.

Yup, time to move.

Without looking away from her, he crossed the dance floor and pulled her close to his chest while immediately stepping to the rhythm of the song. "Hello."

"That was smooth. You've totally practiced that." Her face was flushed from dancing. "I approve."

"I like to pride myself on being able to sweep a woman off her feet." Dylan spun her around when the beat of the music changed before returning to their sway. "Even if I'm not a fan of wedding dances."

Simone snorted. "You don't like to look silly."

"You do." He leaned down and placed a soft kiss to her lips. "Which makes me want to try, Sugar Tart."

Her eyes widened slightly. "Pet names?"

He shrugged. "Might as well own them. They're an important part of who we are." He shifted his hand to cup her cheek. "I love you."

"I love you too." She leaned against his touch. "We should get out of here and go home."

With one final spin and a wave to his brother and sister-in-law, he wrapped his arm around Simone.

Home. With Simone. "That sounds like heaven."

Got a craving?

Don't miss the rest of the Sugar series

SUGAR SWEET

And

SUGAR & SPICE

Available now from

Christine d'Abo

And

Lyrical Caress

Printed in the United States
by Baker & Taylor Publisher Services